SILICON
GALAXY

ERIC R. BALL

The characters and events in this book are fictitious. Any similarity to real persons, living or dead, is coincidental and not intended by the author.

Silicon Galaxy
by Eric R. Ball
Copyright © 2022 Eric R. Ball

Published by Together Editing Press
Editing and design by Together Editing & Design
855 El Camino Real, Suite 13A-190, Palo Alto, CA 94301, United States
www.togetherediting.com

Library of Congress Control Number: 2022906250
ISBN-13: 978-1-939698-09-4
Printed in the United States of America

First Edition: April 2022
9 8 7 6 5 4 3 2

Contents

Foreword

COMMUNICATIONS BETWEEN CULTURES ARE what makes the free market thrive. Eric Ball's sensational book—about aliens taking on celebrity form and trying to build a fit with the venture capital and entrepreneurial culture—is a science fiction metaphor for so many communications issues.

When the Berlin Wall came down and the Eastern Bloc recognized that socialism was a failure, people from the East emerged into the more successful Western capitalistic world like moles seeing the sun for the first time. For three generations, they had believed that government was the best way to distribute goods and services (not the free market), and capitalism had been a crime. When they tried to apply their new technologies to the more successful free marketplace, they had no concept of how to productize their technologies or build their businesses. Their young entrepreneurs had to adapt to an environment that was anathema to their inherited system of belief. Over time, though, the great technologies of the East were productized and distributed, so the people of the world could benefit from the trade across the former Iron Curtain.

Silicon Galaxy is also indicative of when two entrepreneurs come together: one who is immersed in technology, and the other a businessperson trying to exploit that technology in the marketplace. These two cultures are so different, but if they can figure out each other's languages, culture, and thought processes, enormous businesses can blossom, industries can be transformed, and amazing things can happen for the people of the world.

A typical venture capitalist must raise money from investors who are, on the whole, risk averse, careful, deliberate, and stable—and then must invest that money into entrepreneurs who are daring, fearless, erratic, futuristic, and fly by the seat of their pants. If venture capitalists can properly bridge the two cultures, they can bring about positive change around the world.

I highly recommend that you read this book, not just for the beauty of the imagination that all good SF brings us, but for Eric Ball's creative thinking around how different cultures, different ideologies, and even different species communicate, and the power in positive communication.

Tim Draper
Venture Capitalist
Founder, Draper Fisher Jurvetson, Draper
   Associates, Draper University
Early investor in Tesla, SpaceX, Skype, Baidu

To my family, Sheryl, Spencer, and Carter,

who make each day its own adventure.

Prelude

FIRST LIEUTENANT MARGARET NELSON, who went by Peggy when not on duty, sipped her beer in the officers' mess at Peterson Air Force base in Colorado Springs, where she had graduated from the nearby Air Force Academy just two years before. Despite a long shift, she was too wired to sleep.

Two days ago she had tracked a small incoming meteor on a collision course with the western part of North America. It was moving so improbably fast that there had been no time to warn anyone beyond her immediate supervisor. They had prepared themselves for news of the impact—and then the object had instead simply disappeared, only a few seconds after being identified. If there weren't a record of it in her system, she wouldn't have risked her career by speaking of it.

Her surprise was compounded when she learned that there was *a friggin' standing order* covering exactly this scenario, calling for a written report to be sent up the chain of command. She had stayed after her shift ended to brief her CO, and that briefing had included the four-star Brigadier General who had command of the North American Aerospace Defense Command (commonly referred to as NORAD). The Lieutenant was *not* accustomed to spending time with the NORAD CO. He had listened, thanked her, and then instructed her to forget about the incident entirely, an order she was even less accustomed to receiving.

And here I thought that tracking objects in the sky would be a boring posting . . . She wondered if she would ever learn what the real story was—and decided that unless she received several promotions in short order, that was probably not in the cards.

The Beginning

Celebrity is no different from any other energy. It's a force for good or evil. It's no different from money. It's power. (Jerry Seinfeld)

As Zach regained consciousness next to the crumpled mess that had moments before been his car, his first thought was: *This isn't even the worst part of my day.* After that difficult morning meeting with his boss—not to mention the troubling relationship talk with his girlfriend last night—wrecking his car on the shoulder of the Sand Hill Road on-ramp to the northbound 280 just didn't seem quite so bad.

Wait, is my music still playing? From his Spotify playlist of 1980s hits, he could hear Debbie Harry still singing about a man from Mars eating different types of cars.

Oh, thank God for this! The wreck gave him an airtight excuse for missing the deadline on the startup due diligence report due tomorrow morning. He felt a flash of guilt for this relief, before he was distracted by strong arms pulling him onto a stretcher.

Zach was mildly surprised to see that the hood of his midnight-black Tesla Model S Plaid was wrapped around a tree separating the on-ramp from the tennis courts adjoining the 10th hole of the Sharon Heights Country Club (a 536-yard par-5, he oddly remembered). The front passenger seat looked crumpled. Good thing he hadn't given his boss' assistant Amanda a ride home after all. Then he looked at the driver seat, and saw the steering wheel touching the back of the seat. *How in the world did that steering wheel not go through me?* He started taking inventory of his body, and realized that he appeared to be physically unharmed, though quite confused.

He turned to see two paramedics above him and noticed that the first one was ... *Harrison Ford?* Not the grizzled, beat-up Harrison Ford from

2

recent movies like *Blade Runner 2049*, but the young vibrant Harrison Ford from, well, *Blade Runner*.

Zach looked to the other paramedic, and was not thrown quite as much to see that it was Eddie Murphy, circa *Beverly Hills Cop*. At least he wasn't making that obnoxious huh-huh-huh laugh, which was all Zach remembered from the late-night Cinemax showing many years ago.

As Zach's mind drifted away, he saw a bright flash, and it occurred to him that perhaps he was more injured than he realized.

PART I

Down and Out
on Sand Hill Road

CHAPTER 1
Beautiful Loser

Never trust a woman who says she isn't angry.
(Kevin, *St. Elmo's Fire*)

CAITLYN AND ZACH SAT in the living room area of his Atherton studio, located in the backyard of a beautiful estate. Atherton is about halfway between San Jose and San Francisco, one town north of Menlo Park and two towns north of Palo Alto, and requires all homes to sit on at least one full acre, which automatically makes it the most expensive real estate in the Bay Area. Zach had scored his place through nepotism: the owners were Don and Jenna Sams, parents of his best friend Spencer.

"So you don't want to move in with me?" One disadvantage of a small studio was that even the furniture was small, and the couch was really more of a loveseat. Physical proximity to Caitlyn Gordon was usually a thing he valued, but right now he wished he were sitting a little less close, and as he spoke he found himself looking down at the floor. She was the only woman he had dated since moving to the Valley from Austin four years ago. She wasn't the first woman he had loved, but she was the first that he had fully admitted he loved, and so this was the first relationship he hadn't sabotaged from the start.

Caitlyn sighed, and used her left hand to move her long dark hair to the side of her face. "Zach, this is more your doing than mine. You have not been fully engaged in our relationship, and I'm just the one saying that out loud, which will let you tell your friends that you were the victim here."

"Hey, that's not true. At least, I don't think that's true. . . . Is that true?" Zach pushed down his initial instinct to get mad. He found that Caitlyn rarely said anything to deliberately anger anyone, and she seemed

7

to have more interpersonal insight than he did—which was a low bar, he reckoned, but it meant that he had a tendency to trust her view of even his motivations more than his own. Which made arguing with her particularly painful, as it tended to become both of them against him. As it felt now.

Caitlyn looked directly at him. "Zach, you worry that I won't stay with you because your career is not doing better. But it's not your career that's the problem, it's your own reaction to your career. You don't seem to think you're successful, and you mope about it all the time. Which does not make you unsuccessful; it makes you not fun to be around. It's not your fault that the company that you left grad school early for had a CEO who went to jail, but it's not anyone else's fault either. Either accept your career or change it, but when you complain about it all the time you don't do any good for yourself or the people around you. And most people would not consider working for a Silicon Valley venture firm to be a tragedy." Zach was used to the unfiltered Caitlyn. She was sweet and diplomatic to strangers and co-workers, saving her bluntness for people she viewed as important—but at the moment, her candor felt more like a buzz saw than a compliment.

Caitlyn's directness came in part from her experience as a nurse practitioner at Stanford. The first two years of the coronavirus pandemic in 2020-22 had been brutal. Caitlyn kept her cool and helped get the hospital and patients through a no-win situation. She also had been forced to realize that her then-boyfriend (a doctor completing his residency at the campus hospital) did not look better to her under shared quarantine. Spending more time together had just made his narcissistic traits more evident, and that was before she lost her father to Covid while working long shifts herself. After it all subsided, she was drawn to Zach's fundamental decency, though she had later expressed surprise that someone whose life appeared to be on track could at the same time exhibit so much angst about his direction. Both she and Zach came to the slow realization that she had some post-traumatic stress, and she retired from nursing after just four years in an attempt to lead a more normal life. She was recruited quickly into the world of pharmaceutical sales, which left her time for her moonlighting job as a fitness instructor at the Equinox gym in Palo Alto.

The rest of the conversation became a blur for Zach, and he soon found himself alone in his studio. One part he did clearly recall was that Caitlyn said she would be taking a promotion at her pharma employer—which meant an office in San Francisco rather than Palo Alto, and she planned to get an apartment nearby. This did not exactly constitute long-distance, but it meant an hour to see her instead of the five minutes to her old apartment or the zero minutes to his backyard studio that he had been anticipating. She hadn't said that she wanted to break up, but with regard to their relationship, it was clear that her head was not moving in a forward direction. He consumed at least one Scotch more than necessary while binge-rewatching *Game of Thrones*, which appeared to be a documentary about working in Silicon Valley, in that both contained a large number of young motivated people energetically engaged in the violent acquisition of power.

In the morning, despite his blues, he got going early enough to stop at Fitness Power, a small studio his friend Ken had situated well, near the venture capitalists that surrounded the famed Rosewood Hotel and the Stanford Linear Accelerator. When Zach arrived, Ken was busy helping a billionaire 79-year-old tech founder with a grueling workout designed to help him keep up with his 29-year-old girlfriend. Zach suspected there was more to it than good cardio, since this particular executive also funded an anti-aging institute and Zach had long ago decided it had yielded something beyond the typical vitamins and hormones that some senior managers of a certain age used as supplements.

As he huffed up the endless staircase of the Model 12G StairMaster, he thought about what Caitlyn had said, that the problem was his own reaction to events rather than the events themselves. He had dropped out of a doctoral program in economics at UT-Austin to join a startup that used virtual reality to improve medical diagnoses. He had felt a true sense of purpose in the company's mission and pride in his own role. The company was briefly a darling, and then a unicorn. But when it came out that the CEO had exaggerated the results, to investors and to everyone else, the lead investor creatively took his own life through deliberate misuse of the particle accelerator at Stanford. Although Zach was too junior to receive much blame, that stint on his resumé had not done much for his career. He had been unable to find work at either startup companies or venture capital firms in the life sciences. He was fortunate that his Uncle George (an engineer who had been an early employee at Intel) had helped him get a junior position at one of the smaller VC firms on Sand Hill Road that invested in startups applying artificial intelligence to conventional business sectors. The firm did not typically invest in health-oriented start-ups that offered therapeutics, but some of the business models that the firm did support involved digital medicine, and even the investments in non-health startups made use of his economics training and spread-sheet skills. Still, the combination of failing to finish his economics degree and then joining a company that flamed out left him feeling decidedly underemployed.

It was a short walk from Fitness Power to the Trancos Ventures office on Sand Hill Road, on the west side of Menlo Park. He managed to get to the office at 10:00 a.m., up the stairs to the second floor of the modern, beige two-story building, and through the glass doors to his cubicle. A year earlier this would have stressed him out, since his weekly one-on-one with his boss to discuss the portfolio pipeline was scheduled to start at exactly 10:00. Now he had learned that his boss never started this meeting on time, not because Bill Abrams wasn't punctual—but because Zach was low-status enough to leave waiting indefinitely. Zach accepted this. He had taken to wearing a red Star Trek-style shirt that said "Expendable" on his chest, but no one at work appeared to appreciate the reference or the irony. At 10:37, Amanda rang Zach and said only, "He's ready."

Bill was not the head of the firm, but he was senior enough to have one of the corner offices. One wall had shelving to hold the myriad of Lucite deal toys from various financing rounds and exits of the more prominent tech startups the firm had invested in. Missing were mementos of the even more numerous flameouts, but the ratio was favorable enough to keep Bill comfortably ahead on the ledger. Bill was wearing a green golf shirt emblazoned with the firm's "TV" logo, and appeared to be on his second Trenta-sized Starbucks coffee, as there was no way his first was still this full or warm by midmorning. Bill leaned back in his black Herman Miller chair and gestured vaguely in Zach's direction. "What've you got, Zach?"

Zach shifted in the noticeably less comfortable visitor chair on his side of the desk. "As I mentioned in my weekly report on Saturday, I've made recommendations on the three companies we were looking at. I suggest we pass on Future Vision. Even though they've pivoted from the initial idea of showing in 3-D what your date will look like in 20 years to what your kids will look like, I still think it's a limited market." To this, Bill only nodded as if to say, *get on with it.*

"The second company is the VR startup RealTainment. This is backed by one of the guys who started Netflix. They're building through the steps to eventually provide holographic movies that place the viewer in the middle of the scene. Entertainment is a huge market and this might take a while but could be really disruptive."

"Zach, do you know what they said in 2009 would totally disrupt movie box office? It was 3-D. You know, *Avatar.* You know when the first 3-D color film was made? 1935. Do you know what the annual box office total was ten years ago? It was $12 billion in today's dollars. Do you know what it was in 2019, even before the coronavirus? Half that. So this sector has been in decline for decades, even before Covid, and you believe another whiz-bang advance is going to save it? And that's assuming it even happens! Have you researched how many advances in the technology there have to be between now and holographic films? It's just going to take too long to get there and require too much capital for any kind of rate of return. Venture capital has never supported entertainment, and there's a good reason for that, Zach. We will pass on RealTainment. What else you got?"

"Well, there is a third company I have not yet had time to fully dissect, but it looks promising. Indivi-Jet expects to develop a self-flying personal aircraft within a year and a half with better range than some other companies have in that space. That may be optimistic, but it's a big addressable market and I am suggesting we take this to the next level by setting up a meeting with you before they hope to close a new financing round next quarter."

"I need to see a deeper analysis before I commit to meeting with these guys. I'll reserve judgment for now. In the future, please do not suggest I spend time meeting with someone until you've done all the homework. These guys want to create a sense of urgency—that's their job. Not buying into it is yours.

"Look Zach, I hired you after Therapeutix cratered because I knew that you had nothing to do with that fraud. And you've been putting in the hours. But narrowly avoiding scandal is not enough to succeed here—you have to leverage my time, and the other partners' time, and get yourself associated with a home run if you want to make it to the next level. You helped me source the bond markets startup, and that's doing well. You need to demonstrate progress in sourcing and developing your own winners, and I suggest sooner is better than later, as in before the annual reviews next quarter. You should know that we won't be keeping all the current principals."

Great, now my job AND my relationship are on life support. Zach drew in a breath. "Message received and understood, Bill." This was shaping up to be his worst week in a long time, and it was still Monday.

CHAPTER 2
Starman

We're from . . . France. (Coneheads, *Saturday Night Live*)

ZACH CAME TO AND found himself in a brightly lit room with no windows. He assumed it was some kind of upscale urgent care, but it looked more like a conference room than a hospital.

"He's here now." The source of the voice was a woman facing the door. As she turned toward him, he saw that she didn't look like a nurse. She was dressed more like an attorney, complete with a dark navy business suit with shoulder pads that had gone out of fashion in 1990 (and had recently come back).

More disturbing was the fact that she looked *exactly* like the actress Sigourney Weaver. Not the modern Sigourney Weaver, but a dead ringer for the young version: Ripley in the movie *Alien*, who vanquished the alien in her underwear. That thought made Zach unhelpfully and acutely aware that he was still wearing his jeans. Weren't they supposed to put patients in hospital gowns? He doubted she had managed to reverse the aging process *and* execute a career change into nursing (though he didn't doubt she would make an excellent medical professional).

He tried to frame a coherent statement, which came out as a question. "What the hell?"

"What's wrong? Are you in distress?" Nurse 'Sigourney' asked.

Zach looked around. "Where am I? This isn't the Stanford ER! Is this some kind of movie set?"

"I am part of a small team that would like to talk to you, Mr. Randall. Please let me get my colleague so we can explain."

At that point, in walked Michael J. Fox, the actor from the TV show *Family Ties* and the *Back to the Future* movie trilogy. He also looked like he did in 1985. He was wearing a white suit with white pants, a pastel shirt, white shoes, and no socks. "Hello, Mr. Randall. I would like to apologize for startling you," he said. "Please rest assured that you are physically unharmed."

"But you don't have Parkinson's," was all Zach could think of to say in response.

"Excuse me?"

"Parkinson's. You're the most famous sick person in California. I donated to your foundation last year. And you're, like, at least sixty years old."

"Mr. Randall, we have never met before."

"No, but you're famous, or at least you were. Ah, shit!"

"I told you we were too exact," the woman said to 'Michael.'

He sighed. "Perhaps."

Zach was surprised at how calm he remained, despite his rising level of confusion. "So, um, whiskey tango foxtrot. What happened?"

"Mr. Randall, you fell asleep at the wheel of your vehicle. We have been wanting to speak with you, and we chose to intercept you before your vehicle collided with a tree, so that you would not be injured. We initially moved you just a few feet away, and have now brought you here. Please forgive how suddenly we have come together; we had hoped to have longer to plan, and to ease you into an introduction before initiating this conversation. To start with, I am not Michael J. Fox, and she is not Sigourney Weaver. We are, uh, immigrants, and we may have gone a bit far in our desire to fit in around here. That's OK, because we are here to ask for your help."

"Well, if you're not who you are, then who are you?"

"We are visitors."

"Well, most people in the Valley come from somewhere else. I grew up in Detroit."

"We're from farther away."

"So, Europe?"

The two 1980s icons glanced at each other. The man nodded for the woman to respond. "No, we are from what you call the Large Magellanic Cloud, which is the sixth closest galaxy to your own."

"Yeah, of course you are."

"And we created our appearances based on inhabitants who seem to engender the most admiration and trust among your people."

"OK, I'll play. So, are you saying you're celebrities from outer space?"

The two exchanged a look before returning their focus to Zach. "In a manner of speaking, yes," the woman replied.

Zach decided that the only thing more ridiculous than this conversation was to engage in it while still seated with his legs crossed. When he stood up though, he realized he was behaving as though he were having a normal chat, which made him suspect he might be more injured than advertised. That thought sent a wave of vertigo up from his feet through his body and cut through his consciousness like a surge of white noise. As his face hit the floor, he did not feel his nose break.

⌐ ∩ ⁄ ⌐

Professor Spencer Sams looked out at the rows of MBA students in the immersive classroom at the Stanford Graduate School of Business. Situated on Campus Drive opposite the Maples Pavilion basketball arena, on the eastern side of Stanford's sprawling campus, Spencer loved both the physical environment and the academic prestige of teaching at this particular school. "Okay, that wraps up this week's session on effective management in a startup environment. Before we adjourn, I want to remind you that for our next meeting I am asking you to come prepared to talk about Peter Thiel's book, *Zero to One*. I want to know what you agree with and disagree with in Mr. Thiel's prescriptions for success as a venture capitalist."

Spencer was not using the video connection technology, so everyone attending was physically present. Spencer was in his third year as junior faculty at GSB, after completing his doctorate in management at the University of Texas and then returning to live and work where he had grown up. He was wrapping up the first lecture of the semester in his course on entrepreneurship, which had proven to be one of more popular courses in Stanford's business curriculum. It helped that he leaned on his friend Zach Randall to bring in some prominent venture capitalists and successful startup CEOs—their stories of success in the battles of Silicon Valley gave life to the review of academic literature and traditional case studies.

Spencer and Zach had become close friends at UT, spending a large fraction of their time bemoaning the lack of gender balance in their doctoral program. They had come a long way, now bemoaning a lack of gender balance in the startup community. (After Zach's bicycle—briefly—occupying the same space at the same time as a Grubhub driver's Prius on Alameda de las Pulgas resulted in meeting Caitlyn at the Stanford emergency room, Zach's own complaints had become less vocal than Spencer's.) And now Zach had left him an uncharacteristically stressed-sounding voicemail asking to meet for beers at the venerable Rose and Crown pub in downtown Palo Alto. Despite it being a Tuesday, Spencer had the feeling that they would not be playing trivia. Zach sounded like he had reasons beyond his relationship issues to need his friend's ear.

One hour later, he found himself sipping his Magner's Dry Apple Cider and looking sympathetically across the table at his friend. The bar was relatively uncrowded, and conversations were occasionally punctuated by the *thwtt* of darts landing on one of the pub's two dartboards. "So your car is wrecked and you may have a concussion? That's a tough way to start the week, brother."

Zach looked rattled, and took a sip of his pint of Belgian Delirium beer while looking across at Spencer. "It gets weirder." He told Spencer about the exchange with the medical staff and about waking up on his own couch later, feeling better than he should have. And about finding a text on his phone requesting a meeting four days later at Zach's office. "So, what would you do?"

"Um, buddy, have you been listening to yourself? I am certain that you're telling me the truth; you were never good at lying or pranks. But come on, we learned statistics together. What's more likely, that someone is pranking you, or that aliens from the 1980s have decided to make you their special friend?"

"Who, other than maybe you, would care enough to pull off a prank this elaborate and time-consuming? If it's a con, what's the angle? And how do you explain the celebrities?"

"Hey, every time we go to Vegas we see look-alikes that look more like celebrities than the celebrities do themselves. And every movie now shows flashbacks of old celebrities as they were in their twenties. And, hate to say it, but you haven't really been yourself since Caitlyn told you she was celebrating Christmas back east."

"Well, Atherton isn't Vegas, Spence. I was in the room with these people. And my stuff with Caitlyn has made me sad, not batshit crazy. And dude, I can't sort this out on my own; I really could use your help."

"I'm not even a venture capitalist. Or, perhaps more relevantly, a xenobiologist."

"What's relevant is that I trust you and your judgment. Will you join me for this meeting tomorrow?"

"Shit, Zach. Okay, you introduce me to these . . . people. And let me see what I can make of it. Just remember, I don't appreciate pranksters fucking with my friends."

CHAPTER 3
Money for Nothing

I don't believe that there are aliens. I believe there are really different people. (Orson Scott Card)

"**YOU DON'T THINK THAT** looking like movie stars might draw unwanted attention to yourselves?" Zach asked 'Sigourney', who was now seated opposite Spencer in the glass-enclosed conference room closest to the second-floor entrance of Trancos Ventures, looking out at the two-toned brown exterior shared by all of the venture firms in that complex. The whole place looked more like a national park ranger lodge than cutting-edge office architecture. It was both comforting and disorienting to meet in his familiar space, and he was trying hard to treat this as he would any other office meeting. A glance at his friend, however, revealed that Spencer was perhaps earlier in the shock-disbelief stage of the sequence.

"In our species, there is less individuation among specific persons. We did not fully appreciate until we were here that this is less true for humans."

"Are you saying that you all look alike?" Zach responded. *Because it would be racist—no I think the word I am looking for is* speciesist—*if I were the one to say it.*

"We do not look exactly alike, but it requires some familiarity to distinguish us. Rather like identical twins on your world. In addition, we wanted to be sure we looked human. And our research indicates that it is better to look like attractive humans."

Spencer found his voice. "Yeah, that works better for actual humans too." Zach started to wonder just how far the physical similarities went on this speaker. Sure, Sigourney Weaver was an attractive woman at any age. But this 1980 version was positively radiant. He decided that this line of reasoning would only get in the way of clear thinking, and shook himself out of it. He remembered that the female lead character in the old TV show *V* was some kind of lizard underneath. He also resolved to start checking out some old Sigourney Weaver movies just as soon as he could (he had read that *The Year of Living Dangerously* was particularly good). Spencer continued, "Er, you might want to rethink that. Especially if you interact with young guys. Or old guys."

"You know, this is the kind of advice we were hoping to receive from you," interrupted 'Michael'.

Zach reinserted himself into the discussion. "Wait, can you change your appearance at this point?"

"For those of us already here, not fundamentally. Once we assume a human form, it would be somewhat complicated to alter it beyond the steps that you yourself could take to look different."

Zach sighed. "Okay, I guess we're stuck with celebrities, that's good to know. Whoever you are, why would you seek advice from me? More to the point, how would you even be aware of me to evaluate whether to seek my advice? I am in charge of exactly nothing. Hell, I am barely even at the level of principal at work."

"Mr. Randall, we evaluated a large number of individuals and looked at their activities over an extended period of time. We selected you based on optimizing over multiple criteria. There are too many to list concisely, but I can share a few of the more significant ones. First, you have ordered online a large percentage of books in the science fiction genre, and we assessed that you would be more receptive to the idea of engaging with someone who is not . . . local. Second, and importantly, you have a knowledge of venture capital and business formation. Third, for someone with your expertise, you have a relatively low bank account balance. Fourth, we assess that you combine ambition with ethical restraint, and we need to entrust our technology to someone with both of those attributes."

"Wait, you have hacked into my book orders, my job, my finances, and god knows what other personal information? That's just aggressively creepy. And you want business advice? Because I read space opera and I am an unproven investor?" Zach had wanted to be an astronaut when he was young, and had never stopped reading SF. Those stories had long been a form of stress relief; Zach never thought that reading them could turn out to be useful for his career. Crap, not all of those books and magazines he ordered were in that specific genre. Zach hoped the, er, "erotic" magazine titles were not part of the criteria. Better not to even think about that, especially with the visitor version of Sigourney in an outfit straight out of *Galaxy Quest* . . .

"Yes. We want to engage in profitable trade with your planet. We have technology you would find sophisticated. Your profession is about advancing the state of engineering in your society, and your reading habits indicate that you have at least given thought to other societies with superior technology. There is also one other reason we think you might be receptive to assisting us. We know that you recently lost your father to a form of cancer that we have the ability to cure."

Zach was too stunned to answer, and Spencer stepped in. "How would you know that? You guys really do your homework. I'm impressed with your diligence, but I have to say I'm a bit creeped out by your intrusiveness. There is a fine line between finding someone you think will be sympathetic to your stated aims and finding a sucker whose grief you think you can manipulate."

"Gentlemen, we apologize for looking at Mr. Randall's personal information. We have to be extraordinarily careful who we reach out to. We hope that if you allow us to tell you more about what we can do for you, and for your people, that you might forgive the infringement. We do not seek to capitalize on your grief; we merely thought that those who had been closest to an illness might be more motivated to help others with that illness. Just as the celebrity that I resemble seeks to help others with his illness."

Zach got up, slowly this time, and started to pace. "Just for argument's sake, if I were to accept any part of what you say, wouldn't the same technological superiority allow you to just take whatever you want?"

"Yes. But we have an unfortunate history of exploiting primitive natives and have evolved a set of ethical procedures that proscribe anything other than voluntary trading relationships. We would be frowned upon by our peers if we resorted to coercive arrangements."

"So, your own version of the Prime Directive? Well, in this country we do have some experience with colonialism. How long have you had this newfound concern for not running roughshod over the natives, beyond invading their privacy?"

'Michael' and 'Sigourney' exchanged a look. 'Michael' replied, "These ethical guidelines are still somewhat recent and we are still refining them. But we are committed to voluntary trade. We have advanced technology that we are confident your citizens will pay for, which will allow us to buy what we want on this planet."

"And what is it you wish to buy?"

"We would rather not say, as we do not wish to affect its price."

"Sounds like you have some grasp on economics. And you're looking for a venture capitalist?"

"Yes. If we are going to sell our technology, we need local help in setting up the proper organization and going about this in the correct manner. We were led to believe that this location, Menlo Park, is an appropriate place on this world to launch a new business."

"If you're so good at research, why do you need a local venture capitalist? I presume you've already read all the textbooks on venture."

"We considered doing that. But we found that your internet and other resources are better at transmitting data than knowledge. We found much contradictory information, and decided that your record-keeping tools are insufficient to teach by themselves."

"That makes a lot of sense. I've always told Spencer's MBA students that venture investing involves as much art as science; you can't just apply formulaic multiples to each startup you evaluate, despite what some VCs think.

"I'm not sure I buy your story, and even if I did, I am not the guy to manage First Contact on behalf of everyone else on Earth. But I will grant that this is more interesting than the typical first meeting at the Rosewood for drinks. So I guess you can show me your pitch deck."

MJF looked confused. "Why does it matter what our ship's deck looks like?"

"No, a pitch deck is a presentation that entrepreneurs make when they want to convince a venture firm to invest in their business. And I'm wondering if yours might be more interesting than the dog-treadmill company I'm scheduled to meet with this afternoon. Spencer and I need to discuss this. I'll reach out to you on the same cell number you used on Monday."

·· ⊥ ∴ ⅃

"Are all your first meetings with entrepreneurs like that?" Spencer was pale, even for his usual complexion.

"Do you believe them?"

"I well and truly don't know what to believe, Zach. They seem sincere. But their story still seems less probable than it being some kind of con, even if I can't figure out how they benefit from it. It kind of pissed me off that they brought up your father; that just seems like dirty pool."

"I just took that to mean they did their homework, regardless of who they are."

"Alright, let's just work through this. First, assume their story is bullshit. You can still check out their startup businesses and evaluate those; their business models probably won't hold water either. So all you lose is time."

"Right. But what if they are telling the truth?"

"Yeah, some non-trivial implications there, starting with you and me managing a first-contact situation. Despite not being military, or scientists."

"Let's put ourselves in their shoes. If we were visiting a primitive tribe, who would we approach?"

"It would depend on our motives. If we wanted to conquer or annex them, we would approach their political leadership. But if we wanted to trade with them, it could make sense to approach their tradesmen."

"Yes, but we would approach their chief tradespeople. Not some kind of junior apprentice like you and me."

Spencer laughed. "Who you calling junior? But I'm not sure you're right there. Successful businessmen have the biggest investment in the status quo. You'd want someone who understands business and trade but whose livelihood doesn't already depend on the current state of affairs. Like a young venture investor who understands how to commercialize new technologies but hasn't yet been successful enough to be afraid of changing the rules. The billionaire VCs like to talk about disrupting industries but only when they're controlling the disruption a single industry at a time. I cannot even imagine which, or how many, industries may cease to exist if a civilization that has faster-than-light travel wants to start selling its technology to consumers."

Zach sat up. "So are you saying they need someone junior enough to not be invested in the current state, but knowledgeable enough to parse out the implications of new technologies?"

"Yeah, that's right. A young Henry Ford might have realized his cars could solve the horse manure problem in Manhattan but it may have taken him awhile to realize it would reshape the global economy."

"Is the world even ready for their technologies?"

"That's a good question, Zach. We'd have to learn a lot more about what they are before we could even hazard a guess."

"So it sounds like you're saying our next step is to take a meeting to evaluate whether their claims about technologies are just hot air. If the technology holds up, then we can reconvene to decide if we should be part of this."

"That's about the size of it. Let me know when that meeting is. This is certainly more interesting than most of my faculty seminars."

¦ ⅃ ⅀ ⅂

"Okay, what am I looking at?" Zach eyed 'Michael' and took a sip of his lime-flavored soda water. They were again in the Trancos conference room. When the visitors had signed in at the front lobby this time, he noticed that MJF had signed in as Andrew Fox, and the young version of Sharon Stone had signed in as Vonne Stone. Zach decided to adopt these names for them, to help remind himself that these individuals were not actually the movie stars that he thought of as familiar.

"You said you wanted a technical demonstration, is that not correct?" Andrew had the same earnest look that his counterpart brought to all his roles; it tended to make him appear trustworthy. Andrew and Vonne sat across from Zach and Spencer at the end of the long, polished wood table that was closest to the large television screen and the door.

Before Zach could answer, Spencer leaned in and spoke first. "Well, what we *want* is a full overview, including a description of the management team, total addressable market, evolution of penetration of that market, financial projections, and reassurance that the intellectual property cannot be appropriated by others, based on some combination of patents or challenges in reverse engineering or at least first-mover advantage. All in a beautiful Prezi deck with bright graphics. But sure, why don't we start with a technical demonstration?"

Andrew was taking notes. Zach heard another voice ask, "Zach, what are your physical imperfections?" It was Vonne. A little before *Basic Instinct*, more like *Total Recall*. He guessed he wasn't the first guy to find her distracting.

Zach glanced at Spencer, then back to Vonne. "Well, that's a little bit of a personal question, don't you think?"

"Please, Mr. Randall. It is part of the demonstration."

"Well, for starters, I have an appendectomy scar and receding hairline, I'm about 10 pounds heavier than I want to be, and I need glasses to read. Also, I seem to be one of the few people you hang out with that doesn't literally look like a movie star. Why, are you going to make me better looking?"

"Actually, we already have, by local standards."

"Oookay. You're freaking me out a little."

"Please check your abdomen."

He had not yet heard the visitors try to be humorous, and thus concluded that she was serious. After squelching the thought *I'd rather check yours*, Zach lifted his shirt, and noticed three things in rapid succession. First, he had no scar where his appendix had resided until the day after his 14th birthday. (And it had not been a short scar like Spencer's; the doctors had some trouble locating his "errant appendix," and so the scar meandered like a Wyoming river. His dad had told him at the time that "chicks dig scars," a statement that made him feel better until personal experience led him to doubt its veracity.) Second, his abdomen was noticeably flatter. Not quite six-pack, but certainly had a couple of indentations he had not seen since he'd started graduate school. Third, he definitely had improved blood flow. Weren't there any unattractive females in this group?

"Damn. How did you do this?"

Andrew interjected for Vonne. "We placed a small liquid additive into your glass of water. It identifies minor deviations from the body's optimal configuration and makes corrections."

Spencer stood up, and literally placed himself between the visitor and Zach. "What happened to those damned ethics that you emphasized to Zach after you destroyed his car? You can't just slip people drugs in their drinks. Don't you have the concept of informed consent in your society?"

"There are no risks from this additive. And Zach asked for a technical demonstration, so his consent was implicit in the request." Sharon Stone—damnit—*Vonne*, smiled. It was, of course, a gloriously perfect smile. "So Zach, what would *you* say is the total addressable market for this product?"

Zach stood up. "Holy crap."

CHAPTER 4
The Living Years

Life ain't about how hard you hit, it's about how hard you can get hit and keep moving forward. (Rocky Balboa, to his son, in *Rocky Balboa*)

AFTER ANDREW AND VONNE left, Spencer and Zach remained in the conference room. "Okay, Zach, for argument's sake, let's say I believe they're who they say they are."

"Yeah, for argument's sake, let's say I believe them too, Spence. But that still doesn't mean I should be their venture capitalist. Or their liaison to humanity."

"Why the hell not? Seems to me that the hard part is believing their story. Once you do that, well, finding startups to invest in is kind of your gig, isn't it?"

"Yeah, but I cannot even wrap my head around the implications of the kinds of technology we're talking about. They need an experienced VC with more capital and a stronger network, not a rookie like me. And someone better able to evaluate whether their intentions are as benign as they would have us believe."

"But Zach, this changes everything. And like we said, revolutionary change rarely comes from people who made their living in the old status quo. More successful VCs aren't going to risk decades-long careers to tell the world they're investing in extraterrestrials. They have too much to lose."

"And I don't?"

"No. Sorry man, but you don't. You've only been at this for a couple of years. You know how the game works but—and I say this with love— you're not well-known, and are not constrained by a reputation. And I

26

remember you telling me you would've done anything to help your dad avoid his last six months before the cancer took him. Think of how many people could avoid that kind of pain."

"But this is way above my pay grade, Spencer. Not just as a venture investor, but as . . . " Zach just waved his hands in a vague, broad gesture.

"Everyone who has made a difference started as someone who hadn't, Zach. As far as being a liaison to the world, well, I don't think there is anyone who's trained for that, so you're just as good a candidate as anyone. And you at least have experience with technological innovation."

"All right, Spence, let me think about it."

$$\lambda \quad \dddot{} \quad \| \quad \dot{\imath}$$

Zach went home, and got the celebrity rock star greeting that his golden retriever always gave him, even when she was tired out from the long walks that Spencer's mom took her on in the middle of each day past the Menlo Circus Club. He stared at the photo of him and his dad from a trip they had taken to Joshua Tree two years ago, while absent-mindedly scratching Cookie's ears. He and his dad were standing under Arch Rock, looking triumphant despite the fact that it was only about a third of a mile walk from a parking lot, which was itself only an hour's drive from Palm Springs. It was the last time they had traveled together before his dad had been diagnosed with stage four lymphoma the following year. The doctors had given him weeks; he had lasted eight months. But he had lost weight precipitously as the tumors started taking all his caloric intake. Dad never complained, but Zach never again saw the broad smile he showed in that hiking picture. Zach thought of his mom, now living alone in the big house in suburban Detroit.

In his dad's last months, Zach tried to talk to his dad about his life, but Dad usually just wanted to hear about Zach's triumphs and challenges, or remind Zach about things that Dad was used to doing for Mom so that Zach could make sure they were handled going forward. Zach regretted not talking more to his dad about growing up. His parents had been intellectuals of modest financial means, and had sacrificed a lot to ensure an education and better opportunity for Zach. Zach had felt an obligation to provide them with a return on their investment. He initially had thought that would take the form of teaching at college, and had felt embarrassed to leave the doctoral program at Texas. He thought that if he were part of a Silicon Valley success story, that would do the trick, but the company he joined had cratered just before his dad's diagnosis. His dad never indicated any problem at all with Zach's move to junior VC. In fact, his dad had more than once made a point of quoting a PBS political commentator who distinguished between the *resumé virtues* that make for a successful career, and the far more important *eulogy virtues* that determine what kind of a person you are and what your loved ones say about you after you die.

Zach knew his dad would think that too many venture capitalists failed to distinguish between the two types of virtue. Zach's own view was that you could find people chasing material success for its own sake in many endeavors. He also knew plenty of VCs who really valued the mentoring and support of entrepreneurs, and many who were not wealthy (at least by Silicon Valley standards). It nevertheless still bothered Zach that he had not been able to take home any real career success before his father's passing, nor pay back his father in any meaningful way. And he had lost the chance to even express his appreciation. He had thought that one way to honor his father would be to invest in life sciences companies, but he found his economics background better suited to hard tech investing like software companies, given that the more successful life science investors often had degrees in biology or medicine. He did speak almost daily to his mom, and had tried to convince her to relocate to northern California. But she found the pace of Silicon Valley a bit fast for her taste, and didn't want to leave her friends in Michigan. Zach's dad had told him to not be surprised if that changed when there were grandkids in California, but Zach couldn't see that kind of radical change to his existence anytime in the near future. Particularly when his relationship with Caitlyn did not appear to be moving in his desired direction.

As Zach climbed into the shower, he thought about the statistics he had looked up the night his mom called him to share his dad's diagnosis: there were over 800,000 people with lymphoma in the U.S. alone at any one point in time, and 20,000 of them died each year. He thought about the chance to do something for those people. If he was being honest with himself, he also thought about the chance to improve his reputation, and getting his boss Bill—and more importantly Caitlyn—to look at him with more respect. He wondered how much of his motivation was improving the world versus vanity, and decided there was plenty of both to go around. Perhaps he could save lives with the technology that the visitors were promising. And if he got paid for it, that would be just fine too. As he climbed out of the shower, he noticed that his vision had improved just enough that he didn't have to put on his glasses to see himself clearly in the mirror. *What a day.*

Zach dialed Spencer's cell phone. When Spencer mumbled a greeting, Zach got straight to it. "Okay, I thought about it."

"I thought you might. What did you conclude?"

"I can't do this on my own, Spence. This has huge implications for business and for whole economies. The ethical considerations alone are hard to contemplate. I really need someone I trust to help work out the right thing to do each step of the way. And these visitors want to learn how to do business here; when it comes to our form of management they seem like your MBA students—bright but inexperienced. You can teach them. Basically, I can only do it if you do it with me."

"Yeah, I figured. I'm in."

CHAPTER 5
Future's So Bright

Back off, man. I'm a scientist. (Dr. Peter Venkman, *Ghostbusters*)

"**OKAY, EVERYONE, PLEASE LISTEN** up." Spencer addressed the Stanford GSB immersive classroom that now looked to him like a casting call for an '80s movie marathon on one of the more obscure satellite channels. In the front row, Andrew McCarthy (circa *St. Elmo's Fire*) was sitting next to Elizabeth Shue (circa *Cocktail*). At least they were dressed in modern fashion; it would have been too much for Spencer if the Andrew visitor had been wearing a skinny tie or Elizabeth had that wavy blonde '80s hair.

"First, we're going to cover the basics of launching a startup company. You have some neat products—well, okay, some mind-blowing products—which is a necessary prerequisite. But that's not a sufficient reason to form a company. Normally, you could license a product to an existing company. That probably won't work here, because you don't want to show other companies how your products are made, and you want to really engage in human commerce."

"So we need to form new startup companies?" 'Beth' was taking notes. Spencer had decided to refer to each visitor by the middle name of the celebrity they resembled, making Andrew McCarthy 'Thomas'—but he made an exception for the visitor resembling one of his own favorite actresses.

"Yes you do. But you need to understand a few things if you're going to build startups from the ground up. First, investors do not invest in products, they invest in companies. More specifically, investors put their money into teams that can build an effective company to generate a series of innovative products that would be difficult for another company to replicate. People buy their products from companies. If you want to build a company of value, you need to combine your products with a first-class team. And you're going to need more than one investor. That's going to be hard, since none of you have actual experience as senior managers, or as junior managers, or as . . . humans." Spencer felt a bit of disorientation, leaned on the podium and closed his eyes for a minute, and took a large gulp of his "lavender chill" Bubly.

'Beth' paused with her note-taking. "So, how do we start?"

Spencer continued. "The first thing we need to do is make you credible to a very distinct subculture of humans, which is Silicon Valley venture capitalists. To do this, we'll start by manufacturing educational backgrounds for all of you. I am justifying this to myself by saying that, based on my own interactions with undergraduates at this country's top institutions, and your unbelievable skills in science and engineering, that you probably know at least as much as those undergraduates. Fortunately, Mr. McCarthy here tells me that you have the ability to hack into university record systems and create transcripts for yourselves. We need to make sure that the ones who will be CEOs attended good schools, particularly Harvard and Stanford, but they don't need to have finished."

"Why not?" Thomas was attentive. "And what about other members of the team besides the CEOs?"

"Some of the founders of our most successful tech companies dropped out of college rather than wait to start those companies, and a mythology has developed where some investors actually encourage young people not to finish school before launching their business ideas. This dispensation is rarely applied to folks below the level of CEO, however. So everyone else should have records of degrees, and also of having some work experience. We're going to hire locals for these companies as well, and we need the visitors to blend in. We're going to seed some of you into larger local firms so that you can serve as references for the others. This is important, because my own willingness to fabricate experience ends at education; I am not also going to support faking job experience. We already have supervisory roles filled at Oracle, Apple, and Google. And we'll ensure that the first startups we form provide work experience for subsequent startups.

"Okay, second, we're going to need to change your looks. My understanding is that those of you already here have bodies that are as set in stone as my own, but you can still take action to look less like the celebrities you resemble, and more like their attractive siblings. You can change your skin tone, dye your hair, wear glasses, use braces to change your teeth, and perhaps try eating some carbohydrates. And can you suggest to any future visitors that they please just look like normal people. You can start with my college yearbook and go from there—though there are at least two girls in there I would just as soon you not replicate, as that would mess with my head even more than you're already doing."

"Why does it matter if we resemble these famous humans?" Alex (for Alexandra Weaver) wondered.

"Because it draws attention to you. Which is never a good idea if you are trying to maintain a secret, or if we have fabricated your background. It's fine to be attractive and healthy looking, just not so much so that it becomes distracting." Spencer paused for a breath, looked around the room, and plunged back in. "Third, let's review the initial products you have for the companies we're starting. Some of these products have overlap. For example, do you want self-flying, ultrafast drone helicopters, or do you want to focus on your transporter that beams and reassembles your atoms anywhere on the planet in seconds? Because I don't see anyone buying both. Once we avoid overlap, we need to assess the opportunities and the challenges for each.

"You have your elixir, which helps improve overall health, complexion, and body fat. But it will alarm people. And if you advertise health benefits, you need approval of the Food & Drug Administration—and to get past some bad history we had about a century ago with people peddling health drinks that actually contained things like turpentine and arsenic. A larger example is your pill that cures cancer. This will undoubtedly save lives. But even this will not be simple. The world spent well over $110 billion last year on cancer drugs alone. How will you price this—maximize profits by pricing high, or maximize lives saved by pricing low? How will we get this approved by the Food & Drug Administration, when each step of the process will involve medical professionals whose livelihoods will be disrupted by your technology? You'll need to convince and hire doctors with good credentials and reputations as advisors. You'll need to craft a series of medical trials: Phase 0 and 1 using very low doses that test more for safety and side effects than for efficacy, Phase 2 with a more useful number of participants with and without the treatment, and then Phase 3 with a larger number of patients. You'll need to prepare for lawsuits for people who take the pill and later experience something bad, who may or may not be correct when they blame your pill as the cause. Please read the article I passed out on vaccinations, which had some resistance from a subset of the types of celebrities that you resemble. I am not the right person to guide you here, but I can help you identify the right people to hire, how to compensate them, and how to package your story for potential investors."

Thomas returned to the discussion. "This is a lot to keep track of. What do we focus on when recruiting investors and employees?"

Spencer nodded. "This is a good time to address our last topic for today, which is the pitch deck. Potential investors in your startup companies are going to be looking for several ingredients in your brief presentations. First, you need a credible team led by a persuasive CEO who can recruit the rest of the team, motivate engineers to ongoing innovation, recruit capital from other investors, and sell the products to customers.

"Second, you need to show a large total addressable market. In venture, the power law governs returns, meaning that in a portfolio of 50 companies, the top one is going to return more than the others combined, and the second one will return more than the 3rd through 50th companies combined, et cetera. The result of this dynamic is that the investor is looking for a company with a real shot of becoming worth at least $1 billion. In fact, most would prefer low odds of a high-valuation outcome over high odds of a medium-valuation exit, because it's the best exits that will drive the overall return for the fund. Remember, a VC can have different objectives than the entrepreneur. Employees of a single company are making an all-or-nothing bet, so they care about both the probability of success and how much money a successful outcome generates. Investors get the added benefit of diversification, so they're trying to maximize the odds that at least one company in their portfolio is outrageously successful."

Beth piped up. "So investors will focus more on the best-case scenario than on the odds of achieving that scenario."

"Well, yes, basically. If a venture investor has 30 companies, and one returns 1,000-to-1, he or she will come out better than if every company returned 10-to-1.

"Next up in your pitch deck is to demonstrate what percentage of that addressable market you can optimistically but reasonably expect to capture. The answer to this question should be based on how well you can protect your technology from being copied by others. This can take the form of what we call 'intellectual property.' Do you have solid patents so that others cannot use the technology without your permission? Is it technologically challenging to find an alternative path to the same solution? Is the product difficult to reverse engineer? Do you have such a strong first-mover advantage that a well-funded competitor could not catch up to you? For your amazing technologies, I am guessing that competitors would be hard-pressed to out-innovate you—but you're still going to need solid local legal assistance to ensure rock-solid patents on your innovations, or perfect security so that no one finds out how the products actually function.

"In addition, you should show a realistic set of financial projections. Based on reasonable assumptions about how quickly you can get customers to learn about and buy your product or service, how much it costs to make, how many employees you need for each aspect of the business, and how long it takes to collect cash that is owed you, what amount of cash outflow and inflow you expect each month in the next year, and each year in the next five. What's important is not that your financial projections turn out to be accurate, but rather that the projections are logical and internally consistent. The investor is not looking for accuracy so much as a signal of financial literacy."

"How long should this overview be?" Andrew asked.

"Your presentation should be concise. Investors look at a lot of business ideas. Your goal should be to convey yours in as few words as possible.

"Lastly for now, use graphics. Make the presentation visually appealing. Make it easy to understand whether someone is hearing the presentation verbally or simply reading it on their own. We have marketing consultants who can help with this part.

"For our next session, please come with draft pitch decks for at least one of the startups inspired by visitor technologies that we can share and evaluate together. Okay, what other questions do you have?"

CHAPTER 6
Smells Like Teen Spirit

The world is changed. I feel it in the water. I feel it in the earth.
I smell it in the air. (Galadriel, *Fellowship of the Ring*)

"**NO, WE CANNOT FUND** ten businesses out of the gate." Zach wiped his brow in frustration as he looked across his second-floor conference room at Andrew, who was now wearing a Patagonia vest, a pair of grey Allbird shoes, a mustache, and ten extra pounds. Now he looked more like the twin brother of Michael J. Fox who went into accounting instead of acting. "Look, I don't think we want to explain the source of this technology to a lot of other VCs. And before any VC funds your business, they have to have capital, from their own wealth or from limited partner investors. I don't yet have an extensive track record or the credibility to immediately raise $100 million, so I am going to have to build it."

"How will you do that?" Andrew was, as always, taking notes on his notepad. Zach found it curious that Andrew's notes were in English. When did he learn English? If they were in Paris, would the notes be in French? And why not in whatever language the visitors used on their home planet? Or did they even use written language? He realized how little he knew about them, and how dangerous it was to think of them as having human motivations simply because they looked like, say, Michael J. Fox. The visitors lived together in a large rented house in the Willows section of Menlo Park, and Zach had not been there but made a note to go visit soon.

"Well, first, I need to convince my existing firm to fund one of your businesses, make sure the deal is attributed to me, make it successful quickly, and then use its quick exit to spin out into my own venture firm and raise new capital. Only then can we turn to funding multiple new businesses."

Andrew looked up from his notepad, and switched his crossed legs. "So which one do we start with?"

"Well, the flying car is out. That's going to require FAA approval, which is hard to expedite. Similarly with the cancer cure, since the FDA's mission is not to save lives from good medicine, but rather to avoid losing people from bad medicine. I think your pheromone-perfume company might be the ticket."

"Excuse me, Mr. Randall, of all our innovative technologies, isn't that one the most frivolous?"

"It isn't about seriousness. It's about maximizing our rate of return for our first business. Return is a function of maximizing profit and minimizing the time it takes to get acquired or go public—what we call an 'exit.' Many of your innovations can save time for the users and even save lives, but those are going to get the most regulatory scrutiny, and the government does not operate at startup speed.

"Regarding the pheromone startup, about twenty-five years ago, the drug company Pfizer experimented with a compound called sildenafil to treat chest pain from reduced blood flow to the heart. The drug didn't help with the chest pain, but it turned out to promote blood flow elsewhere in the body, causing sustained erections. Within ten years of its approval in 1998, Pfizer had over $2 billion in annual sales from Viagra. People spend more on the opposite sex than they spend on their own health. You say that you have a pheromone-based scent that will make any wearer more attractive—I say that's the fastest path to an internal rate of return that can enable me to raise my own venture fund, and then get your other businesses funded."

"Okay, Zach, we can start with that one."

¡! ḋ :: ٦

"Christ, Zach, we invest in tech, not in perfume!" Bill threw down the printout of slides and glared across his Parnian glass desk at Zach. They sat in Bill's corner second-floor office, on the side of the building with a view of trees rather than of the semicircular parking lot.

"Bill, this is biotech. It's based on adaptive pheromones. The scent actually changes for each person smelling it, into whatever chemicals that person finds the most attractive. This will revolutionize cologne and perfume. I am not saying it will make every man Brad Pitt and every woman Emilia Clarke, but even if it helps an average person a little bit, how much do you think that will be worth?"

"Zach, I've invested in software, and even in chips. Our best performing fund is in artificial intelligence. We don't have experience, or expertise, in business-to-consumer, in particular in any part of retail, much less fucking beauty products. Do I look like I know how to sell perfume? This isn't who we are. More importantly, it isn't who our investors perceive us to be."

"Boss, you're the one who told me that investors will forgive any deviation from our investment thesis so long as it makes money."

"Yes, but if an AI application startup fails, they accept that's what they signed up for. When your gigolo perfume company fails, they won't forgive a loser company that was not part of the thesis they gave us money to pursue."

Zach handed Bill a small vial of a rust-colored liquid. "Bill, this is not biotech that requires clinical trials and government approval. Perfume and cologne are only lightly regulated. We are using science to make people more attractive. That's the definition of innovation. I tell you what—all I ask, before I leave this pitch alone, is that you take this sample home, put a little on, and ask your husband what he thinks."

⸱⸱ ¡! ⁓ ⅃

The following morning Zach found himself back in his office overlooking the parking lot, which represented a step up from the cubicle he had occupied until just a couple of months earlier. "He approved how much?" asked Spencer. Spencer was a frequent visitor, and in fact had brought a couple of fintech (finance technology) startup investment opportunities to Zach and Bill the prior year, which had helped Zach convince Bill to name Spencer as a venture advisor. Spencer had a badge and access but no office space of his own at Trancos Ventures, so on days he was not teaching he was found in Zach's space or in the adjoining conference room.

Zach lifted his coffee from Restaurant 3000, the tiny little café in the middle of the parking lot at 3000 Sand Hill. It wasn't Starbucks but it was the closest source of protein and caffeine, and the food was surprisingly tasty given the minimalist look. "Five million from the firm, and he is reaching out to some of our co-investors."

"But Zach, you only asked for $2 million."

"His husband *really* liked it. When he showed up at work yesterday, I have never seen him looking that relaxed."

"Well Zach, you wanted to source some home runs to jump start your venture career, and you're already getting your management's attention. I have to ask, though, what exactly is driving you in all this?"

"What do you mean?"

"I mean, are you working to make a lot of money, or to bring these life-altering technologies to the world?"

"Well, Spence, I don't see the two as mutually exclusive."

"Yeah, buddy, sometimes making money and doing right by the world go hand-in-hand. Until they don't. I am trying to understand why you're starting with perfume."

"That's going to provide the return and the capital to get the more important products going."

"Okay, Zach, just trying to get where you're coming from. About this pheromone scent, do you know if it works on our visitor friends?"

"For god's sake, Spence, how would I know? *Why* would I know? Why would *you* want to know?"

"It's no big deal. It's just that Beth asked for some extra explanation of local norms, and I'm kind of taking her to Reposado for drinks."

"You're having cocktails with an alien?"

"Well, you know, she doesn't *seem* very alien. I mean, you saw *Adventures in Babysitting*?"

"Spencer, your new friend 'Beth' is NOT Elizabeth friggin' Shue. Elizabeth Shue is at least 60 years old by now, she is married, she has kids—adult kids—and she lives in LA. And, you know, I am ten times closer to being the girl in that movie than our visitor is!"

"Dude, can you please just get me a sample of that cologne?"

"No, I'm having dinner with Caitlyn Friday, and saved the last sample for then."

"Let me just say, Zach, for two people who have decided not to move in with each other, you're spending an awful lot of time together."

"Well, not as much as we need to, apparently."

"People who are taking time apart typically don't have dinner together at all. With pheromone-laced cologne, no less. Not that you need her to wear any for you to be interested."

"Yeah, well, I wasn't intending that she would be the one wearing it."

L̵ ┤ ╤ ┊

"You're asking my permission to use a new cologne?" Caitlyn looked up from her Maker's 46 Old Fashioned. They were sitting just inside the entrance to Sundance The Steakhouse in Palo Alto, two tables over from where former 49ers wide receiver Jerry Rice was, as usual, holding court. On the site of the old Stanford View Restaurant, Sundance had been a Palo Alto institution since its opening in 1974, and had changed its name from Sundance Mine Company in 1999.

"It's an unusual cologne, Cat. Each person who smells it smells a different aroma, one that they themselves find the most alluring. So the cologne adapts to each person it reaches to make the wearer more attractive."

"So if you think it requires informed consent, is every person who uses it going to also ask others for consent? If so, doesn't that make it a little unworkable? If not, doesn't that make you a little hypocritical?" Caitlyn's words struck home, though he noted that they had more curiosity than heat in them. Perhaps the cocktail was a good idea.

She continued. "Well, making the wearer more attractive is a bit of an optimistic assessment. Okay, Romeo, I suppose I will be your beta tester over dinner, but don't get your hopes up. You should know by now that it takes more than a wee bit of rye and some cologne for me to stretch a date to breakfast."

Over the next two hours, Zach shared everything that was going on with the visitors. Zach had already told Caitlyn about his initial interactions with the visitors, and she had partially gotten over the fact that they had started their relationship with Zach by invading his privacy, failing to prevent injury to Zach or his car, and making him think he had traveled to the 1980s. As well as the larger fact of their claimed origin. She was, however, inherently more cautious than Zach, and less willing to take their statements at face value.

When the waiter brought the bill and ran off without a word, Zach realized that the waiter had concluded that Zach was in fact batshit crazy, and decided he probably needed to be more circumspect in the future. He seemed to be clicking much better with Caitlyn than he had in some time. He wasn't sure how much of that was his genuine thrill to be near her or his interest in hearing about her own travails in pharmaceutical sales, or if it was possible that the cologne might be playing a role. She seemed to find his listening a little more evident, and his jokes a little more funny. When it came to the visitors, she mostly let him talk and asked occasional questions he hadn't thought to ask himself.

As they drove the four miles north on El Camino Real toward Atherton, Zach realized that he had hit the car's default button for "home" as his destination, and the car had passed the turnoff for the Palo Alto rental home Caitlyn still had for another month, and that she had in fact not objected. He felt a rush of adrenaline and hormones as he tapped the button that automatically offered the car in front of them a micropayment to move to the right lane (one of the more practical applications of blockchain, enabled by a startup called Geeq out of Waterloo in Canada, and it worked for both self-driving and driver-piloted cars). He didn't know what was creating this interlude, and decided that on this night it just didn't matter. As his father had told him in a very different context, sometimes you just need to take "yes" for an answer.

II ⅃ : ⅂

The next morning, Zach climbed out of the sofa in the small in-law unit he lived in. As intoxicating as he found being alone with Caitlyn, and really connecting, he had reluctantly removed himself from his bed after tucking in a mildly tipsy and tired Caitlyn the prior evening, and had slept fitfully by himself on the sofa. He had the sense that she would have been okay if he had stayed in the bed with her, but he didn't want to take undue advantage of the pheromone-based perfume. It seemed to him that she was (as always) emitting more pheromones than he could hope to ever generate or purchase, and his mind went to a song lyric from 1996, *I can taste you on my lips and smell you in my clothes.* He found Caitlyn wearing one of his oversized Texas sweatshirts and rubbing the belly of Cookie, who was clearly in the golden retriever version of delight to see Caitlyn again. She smiled, and he asked, "Um, so Cat, can I ask you something personal?"

"You mean more personal than you lending me your bed and sweatshirt?"

Despite himself, Zach blushed. "Seriously, I would like to know if . . ."

"Zach, yes, you seemed a bit more, I don't know, polished last night than usual. But I don't think it would lead me to do anything I wasn't inclined to anyway. Besides, the real reason I came home with you is so I could see Cookie. I think I would put your cologne in the same category as alcohol—it won't make a creepy person alluring but it might accentuate the positive a bit. But, hey Zach . . . "

"Yes?"

"For now at least, that doesn't mean I plan to make this a regular thing, okay?"

"I understand, Cat. I guess." Zach chose that moment to turn away for his coat, not trusting his face to avoid revealing what had in fact been the resurgence of his desire to return to regular stayovers from Caitlyn. "At least let me drive you home."

"Okay. But only if we grab a breakfast burrito from Lulu's, and if Cookie rides with us."

ㄱ ∷ � ·|·

"Where do we stand with our fragrance company?" Zach sat across from Leslie Gould, the recently named human CEO of Irresistible Fragrances, who had visitors rounding out the chief technology officer position and other management roles. Leslie was a former classmate of Caitlyn's who had left the New York office of the French luxury company LVMH for the chance to live in Silicon Valley. She had not expected her background to land her at a venture-backed startup, nor to be working with such unusual colleagues. She was short and bubbly and hyperactive, and good at her job. She was not yet aware of the precise provenance of the company's breakthrough in pheromones, though Zach was slowly getting comfortable bringing her into the circle of those who were.

"We have built out our business plan in three parts, Zach. First we'll make a small batch of perfume and cologne ourselves with our phero-mone additive, *Phragrance for Him* and *Phragrance for Her*. If we can sus-tain the categorization of the fragrances as cosmetic, we will not need FDA approval to market."

Zach paused his leafing through the status report. "Doesn't that require that the pheromone is not classified as a drug?"

"Yes, Zach, but as written, the rules are about the impact of the fra-grances on the wearer. To the extent that the idiosyncratic pheromone works, it is on the person smelling the fragrance, and it works in the same natural way as genuine physical attraction. We think we're on safe ground to avoid the FDA. But the manufacture of the fragrances is another matter. Since that involves chemicals, it does fall under Environmental Protection Agency rules for the industrial classification 2844. Rather than get a new manufacturing plant certified by the EPA, we found an existing plant in Riverside where we can mix our initial batches."

"What do you see as the next step, Leslie?"

"Based on our testing, we are very confident that the initial small batch will be highly sought after and command a high premium. This may quickly become the most expensive perfume made. After we establish the price point, we can simply license the active pheromone additive to other high-end perfume manufacturers. We'll be able to command a high percentage of their revenue, and enable them to raise their own prices. Ultimately, we can become a supplier to the rest of the industry, and then make a decision about whether to keep this independent or sell to one of the existing larger players. Nothing sells like sexiness."

"Okay, please remember that your investors, including me, place a value not just on how valuable this business can get, but how quickly it can get there."

"Got it, Zach. This is already moving quickly. This is the biggest thing to ever happen in a market that was already over $40 billion in annual revenue. This company is going to be huge."

CHAPTER 7
One Vision (Lessons in Strategy)

A vision without a strategy remains an illusion. (Lee Bolman
& Terrence Deal, *Reframing Organizations*, 2017)

SPENCER AND ZACH WERE proud of their new firm, Regio Li Ventures, and the prime offices they had managed to lease on short notice. Spencer had explained to Zach that the Latin *Regio* has a dual meaning for "regal" or "king" and was also used in astronomy to refer to boundaries, and *Li* for "tie"; the firm's name loosely translated as "tied to the royal other side." Zach decided that Spencer belonged in academia, as Zach had forgotten essentially everything from the one course in Latin from high school, but he still thought everything in Latin sounded classier. And, more importantly, it sounded professional, and consistent with the shocking lease rate of this office complex next to the Rosewood Hotel on Sand Hill Road. Situated at the apex of the Main Street of venture capital, with a view of I-280 up close and the Portola Valley hills behind, the languid setting belied the power contained within. Of course, despite paying for the prime location, Zach had asked Spencer to handle furnishing the new office, and Spencer had simply gone to one of the used furniture stores in San Jose. Spencer explained to Zach that, despite the budget, it still seemed extravagant to buy new office furnishings, and it was faster to just go for high-end furniture from a recently defunct startup.

They had to vacate Stanford on relatively short notice when the Graduate School of Business asked why so many people who were not paying tuition were showing up for Friday lectures. No startup in the Valley had as keen a sense of how to monetize their intellectual property than the academics at Stanford GSB, as evidenced by the amount of money the GSB took in from one-week executive education courses that enabled managers who had otherwise never set foot in Palo Alto to use the word "Stanford" in their LinkedIn profiles. Also, several real MBA students had noticed some of the visitor attendees at Spencer's extracurricular lectures: although they had no reason to even consider that these guests were extraterrestrial, they did realize that there were participants who looked like younger versions of good-looking famous people. So now they found themselves holding their once-a-week lecture for the visitors in this new location. Although the location was expensive, in the interest of both time and expense management, Zach's assistant EJ had found a furniture surplus store with recent furniture from a software startup that had recently failed (the failure had been accelerated by a public sexual harassment suit against the founder, complete with allegations from both the founder's time at the startup and his prior role as a senior executive in one of the Valley's most prominent tech companies).

Spencer looked out at the attendees. "Okay, what have you learned from building Irresistible Fragrances?"

"That people on this planet make decisions based on their hormones. And their pheromones," piped up ' Charlie Sheen' (going by the name Irwin), unaware of any irony in him being the one to make that particular observation—though he was aware enough of his human counterpart that he almost always wore duotoned short-sleeved bowling shirts. Spencer made a note to remind Charlie/Irwin later to take a page from Andrew's playbook and diminish the association with his famous human counterpart. Spencer made a note to order some Patagonia vests to be made with the Regio Li logo to hand out.

"Well, yes, pheromones and alcohol are a powerful combination. But what have you learned besides that?"

"That the price people pay for a product has very little to do with its cost," said Nicoletta, the visitor version of Greta Scacchi.

"Yes. Adding pheromones to existing fragrances was trivially inexpensive, simple to scale, and highly profitable. People place a tremendous value on being and feeling attractive, and one charges based on that value, not on what it cost to make the product."

"That you can make extra money with products that interfere with your first product," stated 'Rob Lowe.'

Zach was attending this particular session, and weighed in. "That's a good point. Airlines make it deliberately hard to change a ticket, so they can charge you more to take away the obstacle they created themselves. Television shows bombard you with commercials, then providers charge you to remove that obstacle to enjoying their product. Makers of drones now sell anti-drones to fight the original drones. And Irresistible Fragrances could later make as much money on fragrance-blockers as they did on the original colognes and perfumes."

"Right you are. Another point no one has mentioned," Spencer added, "is the critical importance of speed. Of all the products you visitors have offered, many can have a bigger impact on improving the quality of life for people than your pheromone perfume. But none could have been grown from launch to more than a $2 billion valuation in just months. The return is great, but the speed means that the *rate* of return is phenomenal. And that enables our venture firm here to raise more new capital and sooner, and fund several new businesses faster than any of your other contributions could have.

"I want to spend the last few minutes today summarizing academic research on strategy in businesses. *Corporate* strategy addresses which lines of business a corporation will participate in, and *business* strategy focuses on how a particular business competes within its industry.[1]

"In the 1980s, the Harvard scholar Michael Porter described five competitive forces whose collective strength determines the ultimate profit potential in an industry: threat of new entrants, bargaining power of suppliers, bargaining power of buyers, threat of substitutes, and rivalry among existing firms."

"Which of these five is most dominant?" asked Alex.

"That's a good question, and one criticism of Porter's model has been that it does not address the relative importance of factors if one is strong and another is weak. But I think the framework is useful in ensuring that a strategist consider all the players and their potential influence on the value chain.

"The institutional economic approach also came to the fore in the 1970s and '80s, and focuses on transaction costs, which are costs of

---

[1]   All references to academic work are available in the appendix, and serve as a reading list for those who wish to dive deeper into actionable insights for entrepreneurs and executives from management research.

coordination incurred in making an economic exchange, including search and information costs, bargaining costs, and enforcement costs. Costs associated with market transactions sometimes favor in-house production (that is, hierarchies) and sometimes favor contracts (that is, markets).

"Some researchers in the 1980s observed that strategies not based on resources are unlikely to succeed. Firms have different initial pools of resources, and it takes time and money to change these endowments. In addition, competitive market dynamics ensure that a firm will always be up against the best in whatever market it chooses to compete. This school of thought argues that the key indicators of the value of resources are monetary value, rareness, imitability, and substitutability. Resources can also include capabilities, and more capable managers can create economic advantage separate from technology."

Thomas looked puzzled. "So a company could be thought of as a collection of resources?"

Spencer responded, "Yes, but other models expanded how we can think of companies. The 1990s then brought us the strategic capabilities framework. Executives are judged by their ability to exploit the core competencies that make growth possible. It's not resources but rather resourcefulness that drives success, and the resourcefulness of a company can be stimulated by choosing ambitious goals that are clearly beyond a firm's existing capabilities.

"We also saw the introduction of game theory into strategy in the mid-'90s. It turns out to be more profitable to shape the game you play rather than play the game you find. Look for win-win as well as win-lose opportunities in your marketplace. This approach to strategy is based on thinking through how other providers in the marketplace will respond to your own product offerings. Business is not just competitive; it involves a mix of cooperative and competitive elements."

Beth leaned forward. "So the key for a strategy executive is to be resourceful and to create the market dynamics?"

"Yes, Beth, those are both ingredients, but not the whole story. When your company is young, simply having an initial product with a strong technological advantage may be enough to get the company growing. I have stressed the importance of developing and communicating a sound strategic plan. However, much of the empirical evidence has found that competitive advantage is not simply arrived at through a carefully developed plan, but rather through an often-disjointed series of reactions to external events. We call such reactions *learning*, and it's better for a company to be good at learning than planning."

"Because you cannot predict the environment in advance?" Beth continued.

"Exactly. And the younger the company, the less predictable its competitors and environment." Spencer was enjoying the engagement on the various elements of strategy.

"Let's turn to mergers. Small companies get an investment return from being acquired by larger ones, and large companies gain access to innovation by acquiring smaller ones. This dynamic can be hard to explain, however, when academic studies show that 50 to 80% of acquisitions fail, and acquirers take a hit to their stock price. Acquisitions remain popular despite the high failure rate. There are patterns among the companies that beat these odds. It helps if the technology has more fixed costs than marginal costs so that the economics improve with size. Successful acquisitive companies also move fast, communicate clearly, make integration of the two firms part of everyone's job, and measure every metric they can to develop a skill in absorbing smaller companies."

Andrew raised his hand. "Once a company goes from small to large, either through growth or by being acquired, should its strategy change?"

Spencer paused. "That's a good question. A lot of big companies focus on efficiency and making incremental gains, and lose the agility that comes with being small. The best companies try to capture the best of both worlds, which requires applying different skill sets in different parts of the business. Here at Stanford, O'Reilly and Tushman use the term 'ambidextrous leadership' to refer to maintaining new exploratory business units that behave more like startups at the same time as traditional units that leverage size and pursue efficiency. Moving executives between the two helps manage the tension of different emphasis that these two objectives entail.

"Moving on, there is a separate strand of research findings that documents the value to be derived in identifying how projects can create choices that can be decided on later when more information is available about the payoff of differing paths. We call these future choices real options. Recognizing these options leads to strategies that can improve decisions about the sequence and timing of strategic investments."

"Is this a way of saying there's value to staying flexible?" Thomas asked.

Spencer nodded. "Yes, that's a good way to express it. Let me close by making an important point about strategy. It also turns out that execution matters more than getting your strategy perfect. At the end of the day, it's action that matters, and not simply the quality of your thinking. The keys to execution are making it clear who owns decisions and ensuring that information flows to where it's needed. Here we can learn more from consultants who help execute than from academics like me who emphasize strategy formulation.

"I see we're out of time for today. Please read Edgar Schein's classic book *Organizational Culture and Leadership* before our next session."

CHAPTER 8
Eye of the Tiger

A nickel ain't worth a dime anymore. (Yogi Berra)

"WE CAN'T BE SUED for people getting divorced, can we?" Zach looked at his oversized computer monitor. He was having his weekly legal teleconference, which included the general counsels of each portfolio company and the senior partner at Wilson Sonsini, Scott Crawford. These were the types of meetings that they used to hold in person, but after Covid, virtual meetings had stuck for non-sales objectives, and Zach found that the advantages in managing his time usually outweighed the disadvantages from losing face-to-face connection—even when all the participants, as in this case, had offices within a five-mile radius (the distance from Zach's office on Sand Hill to the law office on Page Mill Road). As always, the set of squares of the video teleconference participants reminded Zach of the opening to *The Brady Bunch*, though he doubted very many others under the age of 50 had the geeky retro parents that would enable them to make that association.

The law partner pushed up the glasses on his face. "Well, you can be sued for anything, Zach. But I am confident that you won't be held responsible for the infidelity of someone who bought your cologne."

"What about the publicity? *Wired* says I'm the VC who brought innovation to the hookup culture, and I don't think they meant that in a good way. And they say we gave the walk of shame new meaning when people wake up after the pheromones wear off." Zach didn't want to admit how much the article bothered him. Not just from a tactical perspective, but rather that people might see him as a money-grubbing enabler of shallow hookups. Which, he realized with a start, was not very different from his own assessment of his recent actions.

"But that is itself an opportunity, Zach," interjected the CEO, Leslie Gould. "That chemist who looks like Mel Gibson tells me that we will soon be in a position to launch our counter-pheromone that will neutralize the effect of our first product."

"Do you mean like the drone companies that sell tech to defeat drones?"

"Exactly!" Leslie gushed. "I spoke to the product team and they think this can double sales next year. People who don't want to find other folks too attractive can take precautionary measures."

"Unbelievable. I have turned bars into war zones, and fragrances into an arms race. This is not what I aspired to when I was a kid . . . or even last January. I just wanted to get use started in generating cash flow to support the life-saving businesses. Damn."

"Zach, you may be forgetting an important thing," interjected Scott from Wilson Sonsini. "You have a meeting Thursday with the head of business development at IFF, and I think they're going to make a bid for the company. I think the intellectual property alone contained in those pheromone-laced fragrances will command a unicorn valuation."

"Yeah, that's great. I just hope I can describe our next business to my mom without getting the stink-eye. She says that Silicon Valley is amoral. And her brother runs a car dealership."

∴ ⌐ ┤ ╤

"How much money are we going to make from this sale of Irresistible Fragrances?" asked Andrew. They were in Zach's corner office at Regio Li, which faced away from Sand Hill Road toward the courtyard fountain, and beyond that the Rosewood Hotel pool. It was a beautiful smmer day and the pool was in uncharacteristically heavy use by tourists of various nationalities. Zach noticed that Andrew had taken to drinking alkaline water. He wondered, not for the first time, if the visitors, for all their sophistication, might be gullible when it came to marketing messages. It was hard to tell when they had superior knowledge of what was good for the human body versus when they simply forgot that human commercials tend to overstate benefits. The visitors seemed to be unfamiliar with the concept of exaggeration.

"The acquirer agreed to pay a purchase price of $2.5 billion. Your founder's shares represent about 25% of the company, so you and your team will receive $600 million. My former venture firm also owns 25% of the company, so it receives $625 million with a cost basis of $25 million, and gets 20% of that $600 million gain as carry. I personally receive about 2% of the carry, so my own share works out to be about $12 million."

Andrew squinted. "How is it that you made the investment happen but get such a trivial fraction of the return?"

"Because it wasn't my personal money making the investment, and most carry goes to the partners in the venture firm, so we made my bosses way richer than we made me. But a multiple of over 20x is still a good outcome, especially because of how quickly it happened. What is absolutely amazing is that we achieved that multiple in only months—so quickly that the internal rate of return is, as the late Steve Jobs would have put it, insanely great."

"Okay, Zach, so do we have the money to make new investments?"

"Not really—at least *I* don't. My personal $12 million will not go very far. But what I now have is an incredible reputation as a boy-wonder VC. Now that I've started my own venture firm, limited partner investors will line up to provide capital to our first fund. And my old bosses, even though they're pissed at me for leaving, may co-invest in our new portfolio companies, though it will take some finesse to talk them out of their usual level of due diligence on the source of the technology. And, since you made a lot more money than I did, as a founder, you can take some of your own new capital and become a limited partner investor in my next fund—which you will also provide technology for to give it equally good outcomes. So between other people's money and your own, we should be able to raise a fund to invest in your other technologies."

"Do I need to put all my money into your fund?"

"No. You have a lot, in fact probably more than the fund can use. Why do you ask? Is there something else you wanted to buy?"

"I was thinking of buying a professional football team."

Zach snapped his head around to look directly at Andrew. "Why in the world would you want to do that?"

"I find the sport exciting. One of my team members has received an invitation to try for a walk-on position with the 49ers."

"Andrew, that is a bad idea. Eventually, if people find out that you visitors are here, they will think that anyone playing professional sports had an unfair genetic engineering advantage. And they would not want you messing around with a national pastime. It is not a good public relations move."

"But I enjoy the game. And I am confident my compatriots would as well."

"Fine, I will buy you season tickets on the 50-yard line. Wait a minute, are any of your other team members planning careers outside of startups?"

"Vonne has been studying politics and is planning to run for Congress. She assesses high probability that she can win."

"For crying out loud, Andrew, of course a smart woman who resembles a young Sharon Stone can win! But that's worse than playing for the 49ers. Are you kidding me?!? You're friggin' aliens from outer space, and now you plan to infiltrate our government? We have a real problem here. Wait a minute—was joining our government on the agenda all along?"

"No, Zach. Vonne only recently shared the idea with me. She thought it would be a way to better understand your culture."

"Andrew, the fact that you would even consider this worries me on two levels. First, if you succeed, then I am complicit in seeding our government with the most foreign power possible. Which would be completely unethical on your and my part. Second, with fraudulent backgrounds as humans, and no one who can talk about growing up with her, the fact that Vonne is an imposter is guaranteed to be revealed. Short of killing people outright, this would provoke the absolute worst response possible.

Zach continued. "Andrew, this is not just a matter of bad public relations. I cannot represent you if any member of your team spends their time trying to set policy for humans, even at the local level. The moment I doubt that helping you is good for my world and my nation, I will stop, regardless of my financial incentive. You have got to keep a lid on your team. You need to run every single job that a visitor takes by me, or there will be a mistake. A big one that cannot be walked back."

"Okay, Zach, we will. Please understand, in our society, government work is simply a matter of determining and executing policy consensus. Our intent is not to infiltrate your government, but rather to understand your society better. We find your people fascinating. And members of the team want to engage as much as they can. I understand that we need you to help us filter how best to engage. We will drop this idea from consideration."

Zach decided not to pursue the conversation any further, and to keep a closer eye on non-business-related interests of the visitors going forward. "Okay. Can we please focus on the venture fund now?"

"How long will it take to raise this fund?"

"Normally, a year. Based on this acquisition, we can do it in three months. And we can start identifying the next businesses to invest in now."

⌐ ¡! ⁻⁻ ث

"You need to pace yourself, my friend." Spencer was sitting across from Zach in the part of the Rosewood dubbed "The Library," though neither of them had ever seen a book in that particular room.

Zach sighed. "The visitors are so intelligent and so childlike at the same time. They like football, so they want to buy the 49ers."

"That just makes them like every other rich person, Zach. And you should be enjoying all of this. Earlier this year, all you wanted was to find one good company to gain your boss's attention and make a little money. You can't say a week in which Bill acknowledges you hit a home run, and now is going to pay you $12 million, is all bad."

"Honestly, I hadn't even stopped to think about the money. All I could focus on is whether it would be enough for the next stage of the plan. And I was pissed off that I only get 2%."

"You know, psych research shows that people are more motivated by relative than by absolute compensation. So if you get paid $12 million, and your coworkers get more, you end up angry. And you forget that you just pocketed $12 million. You're going to have a lot of setbacks, Zach; you have to let yourself enjoy good milestones when they happen."

"Okay, but at this point the money is just a tool. One that I don't have enough of to accomplish what we need to do."

"Yeah, I think it feels that way for all rich people, Zach. Which is why there are so many unhappy billionaires around here. It sounds like your goals have shifted."

"This is about more than me not finishing the doctorate or getting a promotion at Trancos. It's taken me a while to wrap my head around how many lives we can improve and save with the visitor tech. Alzheimer's afflicts more than six million people in this country alone, and every year two million Americans get a cancer diagnosis, and a lot more people globally. You know that these are not just statistics for me; the doctors didn't catch my dad's lymphoma until it was stage four and he only lasted a few months after that. We can get this life-saving tech out to people, and the money we are making now on these other businesses is an important means toward making that happen. That all said, I do have to admit, it felt good to watch Bill have to compliment me. It made him so uncomfortable to acknowledge I put points on the board, it almost made me uncomfortable too. But not quite."

"Wow, Zach, I didn't realize how motivated you are. But you should still allow yourself to enjoy the moment. You could even act respectable, buy a house, join the Menlo Circus Club. What's the point of making money if you don't use any of it to buy stuff?"

"Who has time for that? Besides, your parents' cottage is all that I need. And since when have you become so philosophical?"

"I am happy, man. The visitors are really rewarding to educate. And Beth is something else. I've never felt this way about anyone."

"Spence, have you lost your mind?" Zach threw out his hands in frustration, and ended up using them to grab the Salty Chihuahua cocktail in front of him and drain half of it in one gulp. It was a little too convenient to have a high-end bar less than one hundred yards from the office.

"No, man, this is the best relationship I have ever been in." Spencer managed to look sheepish and defiant at the same time. Zach briefly contemplated whether he could pull off that same expression, and concluded that he could not.

"Look, I recognize that I may not be a role model in how to conduct a relationship. I don't want to spend time with anyone other than Cat, yet at the same time I'm not doing much to try to fix things and move forward with her. But I think I need to point out—with love, brother—that your girlfriend is neither a girl nor a human. You have more in common, genetically and culturally, with my golden retriever. Who I now feel obligated to tell you has been fixed and is neither available nor remotely romantically interested in you."

"You're wrong."

"What the hell do you mean, I'm wrong? About Cookie?"

"I mean the genetic part. If you examine Beth's DNA and body structure, she is absolutely human, except for some minor differences in brain structure that only a trained neurologist could spot."

"That's because they made the DNA to match. They could make my body into a zebra, but that doesn't mean I should go to Kenya to find the most attractive girl zebra I can to make zebra babies with. Although on some days, it doesn't seem like such a terrible idea."

CHAPTER 9
Roll Me Away

Success is walking from failure to failure with no loss of enthusiasm. (Winston Churchill, 1945 concession speech)

SPENCER WAS STANDING AT the front of the small auditorium at the offices of Regio Li Ventures. He turned toward Zach. "Okay, let's look at the portfolio prospects."

Zach obliged. He liked to join these business lectures of Spencer's when he could, and sometimes turned them into real-time investment strategy sessions. He learned from both Spencer and from the visitors. "Right. First up is the flying car. What do we like about it?"

Alexandra Weaver raised her hand. Most of the aliens had followed Andrew's lead of taking the middle names of the actual celebrity they resembled. He knew that the visitors often got questions about their looks. At least they looked a different age than their local counterparts, so they were more likely to get "hey, you know you look exactly like a young Sigourney Weaver" instead of "hey, it's Sigourney Weaver!" For the time being, the visitors usually adhered to Zach's suggestion to respond with "yeah, I get that a lot" or "she's my aunt." He wondered what would happen if one of the visitors stumbled into their older human celebrity doppelgangers.

"Yes, Alex?" Zach returned to the topic at hand.

"Your ground-based vehicles are crowded and inefficient. In Palo Alto, it takes me an average of 15 minutes to get 1.4 miles from the 101 intersection to downtown each morning. It would be far more efficient to take a direct path through the air."

"Also, we can make the vehicles self-driving, and significantly less expensive than traditional cars," added Regan (who'd adopted Eddie

Murphy's middle name).

"I suppose it would be more time-efficient," Zach responded. "And I will take your word for it that you could have all these flying cars moving in a direct path toward their destination without running into each other, or falling out of the sky onto pedestrians if they run out of fuel or have a mechanical difficulty. But it's not me you have to convince. We have a regulatory agency called the Federal Aviation Administration, and they do not let anybody in the air without approving both the aircraft and the pilot. The FAA has not even arrived at a regulatory framework on drones yet, much less self-flying personal vehicles."

"So, Zach, are you saying we should not fund this company?" Spencer interjected.

"No, I think the upside is pretty strong. But this is a long-term play, and even with a high multiple it probably will have a lower rate of return than our pheromone company. But if we can get the FAA looking at it, and if we can get it bought by a car company getting disrupted or an existing player in aerospace, we can certainly justify an investment now. Our return won't come when the product is actually used by people in the world, it will come when a large company buys this startup and then they can wait for their own return later. It would also make sense to run this by the corporate venture arms of the aerospace players—Boeing's HorizonX Ventures and Lockheed Martin Ventures—and try to get at least one of them early on as an investor."

"What about the cancer cure pill?" asked Andrew.

"I think that's a similar story," responded Spencer. "It has a massive return, can save a huge number of lives, and has no measurable side effects that we have been able to determine. But, if you think the FAA is an obstacle, they're nothing compared to the Food and Drug Administration. The FDA requires Phase 1, 2, and 3 trials, over a period of years, and we have to prove to their satisfaction first that the drug is safe and second that it is effective. It will all be worth it in the end, but it's going to take years."

"This would have been easier if you had arrived in time to provide a cure or earlier vaccine for the coronavirus. That really knocked all of us off our feet until we developed the vaccine ourselves, and people would have paid a lot to a company that could have provided it faster. With all the tumult, I think the FDA would have put those trials on a fast track."

Zach looked out at the assembled team. It had grown since the first meeting. The newest arrivals didn't look like celebrities, though they all had perfect skin tone and figures. He guessed they all looked better than their inspirations from Spencer's yearbook. And none of them looked overweight, or underweight, or over 30. "I also think it will help our process for the cancer cure if we first establish credibility for the life sciences company with another drug that isn't quite as big. You described a cure for Alzheimer's. In this country alone, there are more than six million people with this disease, and it is one of the top three causes of death for older people. Eliminating the disease will save the insurance companies money on care for these patients, so they should be willing to spend for the drug. It will also keep these people productive much longer. We should be able to make a great return and set the table for the cancer pill as our next big drug."

"Okay," Spencer summed up. "We start with the flying car company and the Alzheimer's cure. Now we head to the Dutch Goose to brainstorm names for these companies, which requires a pitcher of Stella and some deviled eggs."

‖ ⅃ ⋮ �

"What do you mean, rejected?" Zach shouted into his office line at Regio Li. He did not typically yell at people, but he found that lawyers, more than other people, seemed both more used to it and sometimes also responded better because of it.

"The FAA says this technology is unproven, they don't believe the self-flying mechanism is failsafe, they don't believe these are so reliable that some won't fall on people. And that drones have been around longer and need resolution first." Nick Yakoboski was the general counsel to the flying car company, Hermes Air, which had taken up hangar space at the nearby San Carlos airport, not far from the Surf Air hangar that represented the only departure point between San Jose and San Francisco for commercial flights.

Some jobs required humans, particularly those that did not always involve logic. Legal, despite its claims to the contrary, was one of those roles.

"I thought the FAA allowed aircraft manufacturers to self-certify safety," Zach responded. "And in any event, we only just reached out to them, they couldn't have conducted a review this quickly.

"In some circumstances they do allow self-certification. But typically only for aircraft designs that are arguably tweaks on proven designs from known manufacturers like Boeing. And they got a lot of heat in 2019 over the 737 MAX, so even there they're more conservative. The Hermes self-flying miniplane is not like anything they have seen before. And this was a blanket 'no'; they do not even consider this to be in a category that warrants review at this time."

"But Nick, this self-flying technology has never once failed. And it will make current drone technology obsolete!" Zach sputtered.

"Doesn't matter. The FAA guys said they're impressed with the demonstration of the self-flying personal aircraft. One of them said he wanted to buy one himself eventually. But they have limited resources and drones are first in line."

╤　⋮　·⊩·　⊐

One hour later, Zach was standing at the whiteboard in his office, facing Spencer and several boxes of takeout from the Old Port Lobster Shack. Although it was in neighboring Portola Valley on the other side of the 280 freeway, the Shack was still a closer source of takeout than any of the choices in Menlo Park.

"Okay, we *were* going to spend a decade making profits from the autonomous flying car before introducing transporter technology. With the delay in getting FAA approval for the car, we may want to consider moving straight to Star Trek even while we are still going with the Jetsons approach."

Spencer had to wait until he swallowed his last bite of lobster roll. "Won't we need approval to disintegrate and reintegrate people?"

Zach had already finished his own clam strips. "Actually, no. The transporter beam goes through other matter until it reaches its destination, so there is no danger to others. More importantly, there are no laws that foresee the possibility of this form of transportation. With one important caveat."

"Come on, Zach, don't leave me hanging."

"Yeah, if we are unable to reintegrate the people at the other end, then we will have killed them. And apparently there are laws already on the books that address killing your customers. So there's that."

Spencer gave Zach a pained look. "Right, don't cross the streams. There is another issue. When I asked Andrew what percentage of transporter trips are successful, he said essentially 100%. But when pressed, he said there had been a handful of fatalities due to deliberate sabotage, which were treated as murders."

Zach stopped pacing. "Wait a minute, there, Bucko. You just told me that our technologically superior and supposedly highly ethical alien visitors are capable of murder. *And* that the transporter technology is not perfect. That one-two punch may take a moment to sink in."

"Well, yes. But I think all sentient species are probably capable of killing. Here on Earth, many species kill their own kind: spiders, wolves, lions, primates, meerkats. But most of them only kill newborns, either to convince the females to mate with them instead or to conserve resources. Humans are somewhat unusual in killing other adults of their own species."

"Okay, Professor, I am now learning more about species here on Earth and away from it. I think it is really critical to note that our alien species has murder in its history. And that they chose to admit that to us. That's going to be a separate and long conversation. But back to transporters: how are we going to proceed if it is not foolproof?"

"Nothing is foolproof, Zach. But your chances of surviving the trip are orders-of-magnitude better than driving, walking, flying, or any other form of transportation. This is no different than self-driving cars that can choose to kill one pedestrian to save four people in a car. That technology saves lives in the long run, and so do transporters. We just need to follow the example of self-driving car manufacturers who run a strong public relations campaign. And learn from their example that even one death early on can paralyze an industry."

"I don't think that the lives saved will make the family of the occasional disintegrated person feel better. And it won't make me feel better either if I fund the company that killed him. Or her." Zach sat down.

"I am more worried about false positives. I mean, remember how some people get the flu or Covid after getting vaccinated?"

"Right, and in most cases that's because they got vaccinated after they were already exposed, so they were going to get it anyway."

"Yes, Zach, but that's not how people think. They get vaccinated, and then get sick, and then they conclude that the vaccine gave them the disease. In this case, someone could start having a heart attack, then transport somewhere, and arrive having a heart attack, or dead, and people will mistakenly think that the transporter caused the problem. There's a whole literature around cognitive bias that basically just demonstrates that people's ability to establish cause-and-effect is crap."

"Yeah, I read a media summary of bias research last year, and it said that judges and juries fall prey to those same biases. So you're telling me we could be held liable for injuries, regardless of whether the technology actually causes the injury. I don't want to hold up this advance, but I do think we need a pretty good injury release. I want to collect the data and hire really good data scientists so that *we* can establish cause-and-effect for anyone who comes out of a transporter worse than they went in. And let's keep a running tally of lives saved—for instance, by getting people to emergency rooms faster than an ambulance can. If this becomes a public relations war, I want to get a head start on the Luddites."

"Okay, Zach, we can do all that. But I have an additional concern. We will also need to control the technology to avoid moral hazard. If people could have a wrist control to activate an emergency transporter in order to get out of a risky situation, they might get into *more* risky situations."

"I give you credit, Spencer. It is really hard to stay one step ahead of the capacity for human stupidity with all of these products, and my head hurts from trying. So let me see if I am tracking you. Are you saying you could have thrill-seekers jump out of a plane without a parachute and transport away just before they hit the ground?"

"I don't think that would work, because Beth told me that you come out of a transport at the same speed you go in. But you could go somewhere where someone is more likely to shoot or punch you, and count on a transport to get you out. And then not quite trigger the transport on time."

"Right. How do we get around that? Since we can't conduct an IQ test on our users ahead of time, suppose we set up transporters so you can only initiate transit in locations that we control access to, like in old-fashioned phone booths in safe neighborhoods. We make traveling by transport like traveling by air or train, where first you have to go to the station."

"That could work."

"Okay. I am sure there is some angle for stupidity that even you haven't predicted. Good work, though."

CHAPTER 10
Leader of the Pack

The day I am afraid to risk my future as a leader is the day I am no longer fit to lead. (Nelson Mandela, *Invictus*)

SPENCER'S LECTURES ABOUT MANAGEMENT research had evolved into a Friday brown-bag lunch series, where visitors from their various businesses combined their dining with a survey of literature. Zach had suggested that these lunches might have value to humans beyond their worth as crash courses in management for the visitors, and had started live-streaming the sessions (with the camera only showing Spencer, so the unusually-attractive in-person audience was off-screen). These sessions were well-received; Spencer had achieved a small amount of credibility with the Silicon Valley in-crowd. Spencer stepped to the front of the Regio Li amphitheater and looked across the gathering.

"Alright, today we're going to talk about leadership, which conveniently is a topic of equal interest across all stages of the business lifespan. Students of business follow Peter Northouse's definition of leadership as a process whereby an individual influences a group to achieve a common goal. This aspect of human organizations has the longest history of analysis. Over 500 years ago, an Italian diplomat named Niccolo Machiavelli provided a description of how leaders often achieve their own ends by manipulating their followers. One hundred years ago, a telephone executive named Chester Barnard asserted that the primary responsibility of an executive is to define the organization's purpose and convince managers to subordinate their personal interests to cooperate, which itself requires executives to pay attention to the needs of those managers."

"Spencer, this history is great, but can you tell us how leaders actually allocate their time?" Zach had heard some of this before, and was eager to get to the more interesting parts. Zach and Spencer had established some ground rules about questions on livestream lectures, so Zach made sure to ask about "leaders" instead of "human leaders."

"Sure. Starting in the 1970s, researchers began moving beyond telling stories of great decisions to look at how leaders spend their time on a day-to-day basis. Henry Mintzberg found 50 years ago that managers get an uninterrupted half hour only once every two days, and it has certainly gotten worse since then. Warren Bennis told us that it turns out that most leaders do not systematically organize their activities, but rather take on too many projects, allow or encourage constant interruption, and respond almost immediately to any stimulus. They rarely have time to engage in abstract thinking and make their decisions incrementally. Most engage in utterly routine work. John Kotter concluded that the key distinction of leaders is that management is about coping with complexity, while leadership is about coping with change."

Andrew looked up from his notes. "How would a leader help a team through change?"

"Primarily by establishing a culture of adaptation. Culture is to an organization what personality is to an individual. Edgar Schein identified the inextricable link between leadership and the culture of any group or organization: leaders define the personality of a startup company, which tends to persist as the company matures. Culture is the deeper level of assumptions shared by members of the organization, and it is critical to the organization's success. We describe culture as 'the things that go without saying.' The first task of a leader is to create and sustain the organization's culture. The role of the initial leader is crucial, for it will be challenging for any subsequent leaders to significantly change the culture of the business even as it grows in size."

Beth asked, "Is it well-understood by leaders how to achieve this?"

"Well, no, Beth. There is a wide range of understanding by those in leadership roles; some understand their role as a symbol of the company and setter of standards. Others take a narrower view. Recent research provides many examples in human history of constructive and destructive leadership. English researchers Tourish and Vatcha examined tech companies from an anthropological perspective and found that they resemble cults, with a lot of young people who have a strong attachment to their leader and organization, aren't getting enough sleep, and who are taking as okay norms that are far outside of what is considered acceptable elsewhere. Other studies have looked at the prevalence of leaders with negative tendencies like narcissism, and found both bad outcomes, like lower stock returns, but—surprisingly—also good outcomes, like better governance metrics and higher compensation for other C-suite executives.

"Leadership has been found to be isolating, and followers have high expectations. Organizations and tenures have shorter timeframes than in the past. There are real differences in leadership according to the context. Research by Jean Lipman-Blumen shows differences between how upper- and mid-level managers lead, and between how men and women lead. In any event, effective leadership is a long-term developmental process. All of this is explored in depth in your reading assignments. Before our next session, I would like each of you to think about an issue in your work life currently, and relate it to the various theories and observations about leaders that we're covering."

CHAPTER 11
The Warmth of the Sun

I have neither the time nor the inclination to explain myself to a man who rises and sleeps under the blanket of the very freedom that I provide, and then questions the manner in which I provide it. (Colonel Jessup, *A Few Good Men*)

IT HAD BEEN A long day for Zach and Spencer. They had stayed at the office late reviewing the progress of Beam Technologies and continued the discussion over a late dinner at Broma, one of the two highly rated restaurants in the Shashi Hotel across the street from Alphabet's headquarters. Although the visitors had the technology to apply a transporter beam from almost anywhere to almost anywhere else on the planet, Zach had made a deliberate decision to start small. One of the early challenges had been to convince people to be the first to use it. It's one thing to be an early adopter of the newest smartphone, another to allow one's molecules to be disassembled, beamed along waves of light, and then reassembled less than a second later somewhere else. People think it's cool, but they're happy to let their neighbor or ex-boyfriend try it first.

So the visitors and human employees of Regio Li, and its portfolio companies had made a big production of using the beam to transport inanimate objects at first, then farm animals, then pets, then themselves, and inviting journalists to cover it. It didn't take long for a journalist to volunteer, as Spencer had predicted after mentioning to several that it would represent a scoop on the competition. Caitlyn warned them that they would get more protests about transporting animals than they would with people, which turned out to be accurate but faded away when there were no mishaps. Ultimately the wow-factor outweighed the public's worries.

Although the technology worked on both inanimate matter and living tissue, the energy required went up exponentially with the mass of the object being transported. Zach and Andrew, then, determined that it would only be used initially for people. This decision had the additional advantage of allowing them to defer, for the time being, questions like whether they were prepared to wipe out the automobile, trucking, cargo, and delivery industries with one technology. Zach had seen the impact of the coronavirus on whole industries, and had doubts about his ability to think through and forecast all of the visitor technology's implications for the global economy. He was certain that instantaneous transportation of people over long distances would be exciting enough.

The transporter could start anywhere and end anywhere, and came with built-in visitor safeguards to keep anyone from materializing inside other matter or above ground level. The team had set up a test network for the transporters. The company CEO had agreed with Zach's insistence on an incremental overlay; all trips would begin at one of 14 discrete locations worldwide, and the software was coded to only accept as a valid destination one of the same 14 locations. This was not unlike the first several airports in the world that stretched between Maryland, Chicago, and Texas. Although the energy cost to transmit a person didn't vary much by distance, the price charged was based on distance—following the insight Spencer had shared with Andrew that pricing for new technologies was typically based on value rather than on cost. The anticipated pricing varied by the departure point, so that users in poorer economies like Africa or India would pay less than those who left from higher priced areas like Tokyo or New York.

Zach and Spencer had just finished observing the first three days of testing the transporter network with volunteers, and people seemed to be getting used to the idea more quickly than they had hoped. They kept talking while driving back to Spencer's parents' estate; Spencer slept over at his parents' house while Zach headed to his backyard cottage. Zach barely got his shoes off before he fell asleep.

Zach woke up at the sound of banging on his door; by the time he opened his eyes he was surprised to find Spencer inside, standing over him in boxers and a red Stanford t-shirt. "Zach, holy shit, wake up, wake up! The FBI's here!"

"Huh? It's 3:00 a.m., and I've only been in bed for an hour. Can't they make an appointment?"

"No, they seem really pissed off."

With only two rooms in the cottage, it didn't take long for Zach to get to the door—behind which he saw three white guys in rumpled suits and a better-dressed Asian woman. For a second, he wondered if it was a new batch of visitors mimicking the Blues Brothers. But on closer inspection, he decided that each of them would have given off a "cop" vibe even if they hadn't been armed. Also, there was Spencer's mom, Jenna, who was wearing a long and not terribly flattering green night shirt. She did not seem as flustered as Zach would have expected from a suburban middle-aged woman who had armed and agitated federal agents looming over her. His already high opinion of her inched up a half notch, even before she was the only one with the presence of mind to comfort Zach's confused golden retriever.

Zach felt bad that his own life was disrupting Mrs. Sams' sleep. For once, he was not sorry that Caitlyn wasn't here, as he was pretty sure that being rustled out of bed by armed federal agents would not have counted as a point in his favor. "Um, hey guys, you didn't need to wake up everybody else up, did you?"

"Mr. Randall, we need you to come with us." The woman seemed to be the spokesperson. And the only unrumpled one, in an Italian stretch wool suit that looked more appropriate for a board meeting than for a police raid at this unusual hour. He could not imagine this person wearing sweats.

"Wait. Why? Are you arresting me or something?"

She just pointed toward the driveway. "We just need you to come with us. Now. Not optional."

As Zach climbed into the back seat of an immaculate black Chevy Suburban, he found that his hosts managed to combine being polite and contemptuous at the same time. It reminded him of his former bosses at Trancos Ventures, and he wondered if this was a skill he could (or should) integrate into his own leadership style at work. He had once listened to a TED talk (while jogging on the Stanford Dish trail) by a former FBI kidnapping expert on negotiation, and he bet they had other lessons to teach his startup companies.

The bald agent sitting next to Zach had a neck so thick that Zach wondered where he could possibly get dress shirts that fit. As they pulled out of the driveway and onto Selby Lane with Spencer and his mom standing slack-jawed in the driveway in their bedclothes, Zach turned to him while asking, "So are you folks going to fill me in on why I am here, or is this a simple abduction?"

The woman in the front passenger seat didn't give her colleague a chance to answer. "When law enforcement takes you on a ride, it's not an abduction. And we're all going to agree this is voluntary on your part anyway. You're here because three hours ago there was an assassination attempt on the President."

"Holy shit, that's unbelievable. Is she alright?"

"She is physically unhurt. Her husband and a Secret Service agent were not so lucky. They're dead."

"Oh my god, that's terrible. But what does this have to do with me? I've been nowhere near DC."

"As board chair of Beam Technologies, it has everything to do with you, Mr. Randall. This guy entered one of your transporters at the Dubai station, exited directly into the Executive Residence, and shot the First Gentleman and the agent before he was taken down. He damn near killed the President too. All of this as a direct result of technology that you created and provided to the world, including to people who would very much like to see our President—your President—dead. We need you to shut down the transporter network right now."

Zach felt like he had been gut-punched, and struggled to catch up. "Crap. First, the system is designed to only accept 14 destinations, none of which are the White House. Second, you can't just stop the network." Zach looked at her as she turned around from the front passenger seat. He wondered if she was going to shoot him then and there.

"Someone figured out a way around the constraint on destinations and set 38.8977 degrees north and 77.0365 degrees west. Which happens to be the coordinates for 1600 Pennsylvania Avenue. And, in case it isn't clear, shutting down the network was not a polite request. You can and will turn it off immediately."

"No, I mean people would *die*. Transporters are not actually instantaneous. Even at their hyper-fast speed, at any instant several are mid-transit."

"Then stop initiating transits, and within seconds no one will be traveling, right?"

"Yes, that's technically correct."

"So do it. Then we will decide whether to arrest you as an accessory."

"Wait a minute. I simply invested in a company that provided this bad guy transportation. If he had driven to the White House, would you be arresting investors in General Motors?"

"You put out some fancy technology that put this guy in the President's bedroom, Mr. Randall. As a weapons system, that's worse than selling F-35 fighter jets to the Chinese. And you can save your defense for your trial."

⊥ ∴ ⁊ ᵛ

Deputy Special Agent in Charge (DSAC) Leah Perera allowed herself a small sigh. It had been a very long night, with no indication that she would get a break any time soon. First, she had been awakened at a very early hour. She had not been alone, and had been prepared to take out her anger on the unfortunate soul who had called her. Except that this particular soul had been the Director of the FBI, who, despite the three-hour time difference between San Jose and DC, was also operating at oh-dark-hundred. Leah had met the director only twice, as part of larger groups, and knew immediately that a late-night call directly from the Director, bypassing several layers of management, could not mean anything good in the short term. The fact that he had called her could mean something very good in the long run for her career, but only if she fixed the problem.

She had to say goodbye to her date. Her coworkers might have been surprised if they had known that her taste in men ran not to the type of guy that might command a SWAT team, but rather to this genial general counsel to a cybersecurity-based venture fund. This particular lawyer also shared her fondness for firearms and fitness, though, which she had been actively appreciating just a little earlier that same evening.

The Director had filled her in on the assassination of the First Gentleman and attempt made on the President, and the key role that this new transporter technology had played in allowing the assassin to get inside the White House. Her marching orders were clear on evaluating the investor and board chair who had brought this technology to the world. If it was unusual for her to get a call from the Director, the identity of her next caller was even more out of the ordinary. It was from a government official outside the Bureau. It was unusual for the Bureau to interact with other federal agencies or advisors; policy advisors typically did not interact with law enforcement. Even the National Security Agency consisted of analysts who examined communications traffic. It was separate from the FBI, which has a charter to investigate crimes. Since the NSA employs primarily analysts rather than investigators, it relied on the FBI to collect information from foreign intelligence activities that occur within the borders of the United States. But in Leah's career, that was much more the exception than the norm. And this particular caller was not with any other intelligence agency, but instead was considered part of the executive office of the President. But the caller needed boots on the ground in Silicon Valley, with a skill set that differed from the usual security analyst brief of sifting through intelligence. He had called in a favor from the head of the FBI. *The shit always rolls downhill*, thought Leah. And everywhere was downhill from DC, regardless of which three-letter federal agency one happened to work for.

Leah had asked to work in Silicon Valley. She had roots there, as she had been briefly married after college to an ambitious tech engineer who had gone on to found a software company that had become a unicorn and made her ex-husband a billionaire. He had made the transition from a geeky, confident, and decent human being to an insufferable jerk rather quickly. He had also discovered that being rich made him more attractive to women, and he started to assume this attraction even when it wasn't there, which resulted in expensive and embarrassingly public legal actions.

Now, after their divorce, he ran a company that provided "free" services to over a billion users. Leah was constantly baffled by how suspicious many people were of government motives, and how concerned they were about even the remote possibility of government intrusions into their privacy, while remaining far less concerned about how private companies were intruding into their privacy every day. As the saying went, *if you're not paying for the product, you are the product*. Watching entrepreneurs and VCs cash in on the technology, she had concluded the problem was that the profits were insanely high to a small group of people (who were motivated to spend some of those billions to ensure favorable legislation and legislators) and the loss in privacy was too dispersed for any one person to allocate time to fighting it. Her Princeton economics professor would have said that this externality reflected a tragedy of the commons.

She was dedicated to being a constraint on the excesses of Silicon Valley. And if providing guardrails necessitated some violations of privacy by her own agency, she figured that turnabout is fair play. Most targets of FBI investigation are completely outmatched by the resources of the government. With tech companies and their superior capital, this situation was reversed, but she actually enjoyed the role reversal. She had become an adherent of asymmetric warfare, thinking like a guerrilla fighter, and freeing herself from the constraints of the rules that her colleagues followed. With her G-15 pay scale at the FBI earning her nearly $130K, she lived more comfortably than the average person but less so than the majority of even junior players in the tech world. Even if the settlement from her ex allowed her to dress a lot better than her peers and live in the Willow Glen neighborhood among the tech cognoscenti.

After interviewing Zach Randall for several hours, she had concluded that he probably was exactly what he seemed to be, a naïve tech bro. He claimed to have combined luck with a keen eye, having quickly discovered and monetized two large and completely unrelated technologies in personal colognes and futuristic transportation. And it seemed that he had several other revolutionary technologies in the pipeline. None of which was unheard of in the Valley, but it was unusual that this particular investor did not have the engineering chops in any field—and yet, he was finding pathbreaking technologies that were not at all related to each other. She still had not identified a specific law that had been broken, but that might just be a matter of time. Nor had she received explicit instructions to arrest Zach Randall, and had elected not to for now. But she reserved the option to do so later; of course, this guy and his associates bore monitoring. She picked up the phone to return the call from Washington DC that had sent her out to Atherton in the middle of the night in the first place.

CHAPTER 12
Rumour Has It

Actually, he [Captain America] is the boss. I just pay for
everything, design everything, make everyone look cooler.
(Tony Stark, *Avengers: Age of Ultron*)

EVEN THOUGH SPENCER WAS initially unaware of the death of the First
Gentleman, he had still been tempted to cancel his regular Friday afternoon brown-bag lecture session. He had wanted to follow Zach and the
Suburbans, but the FBI hadn't told him where they were taking him, and
he wanted to be ready to help if Zach called. He also wanted to reassure
his parents that his best friend had not suddenly become a domestic ter-
rorist operating out of their backyard. He had not gotten back to sleep. In
the end, he decided that there was no real reason to cancel items on his
schedule and kept the Friday lecture, with just a bit more caffeine than was
his norm. Besides, today's lecture was on one of his favorite management
topics.

"Okay, team. Today I want to cover organizational behavior. Success
in businesses, whether in early-stage or mature companies, depends on
understanding how people in organizational teams behave." Spencer got
into his rhythm quickly. He liked the brown-bag lunches. The sessions
were shorter than the classes at Stanford, but his audience was more attentive, and he was able to cruise faster and still get through most of the
material. And his favorite visitor tended to sit up front.

"Academics like me define organizational design as the alignment
of structure, process, rewards, metrics, and talent with the strategy of the
business."

Beth leaned forward. "That sounds somewhat abstract. Can you give
some examples of what you mean by alignment?"

"Well, one example is around the basic but important issue of under-standing how to best motivate and retain workers. It's a young field; not that much has been established, and much of what is known by academics is not widely understood or practiced in organizations."

Andrew got involved with the conversation. "But isn't knowing how to motivate employees central to an organization's success?"

Spencer smiled. He enjoyed surprising students with how little most executives and students understand about the important elements of organizational success. "Yes, it is important. But there is a tendency for people to oversimplify and even to believe things that are demonstrably incomplete at best and flat wrong at worst. For example, many managers think money is a primary motivator for an employee, when it's not.

"But let's start by examining organizational culture, which is the pattern of shared basic assumptions within a group. The importance of establishing these norms around 'what goes without saying' is one of the most important elements in the launch of a company, and in maintaining the company's distinct identity as it matures. It's how junior managers can assess how the senior executives would approach a problem, and lets the organization act cohesively without each minor decision having to go to the CEO before being acted upon."

As was often the case, Andrew remained more talkative than most of the other visitors. "So you're saying that culture enables a middle manager to have good idea of what decision the CEO would make without having to consult the CEO. What happens if the CEO changes his or her mind, or if there's a new CEO?"

"Then it's incumbent on the CEO to make it clear what elements of the culture have changed, and to do so quickly, so that others in the orga-nization understand a new filter coming out of the C-suite. Otherwise, the resulting ambiguity is going to either result in decisions different than what the CEO wants, or the CEO is going to get an avalanche of ambigu-ous decisions being kicked up the chain of command. So when the CEO establishes new decision criteria, overcommunication is essential."

Andrew weighed back in. "Doesn't this slow down the ability of an organization to adapt?"

Spencer brightened up. "Yes, that's exactly right! And the larger the organization, the harder it is to remain agile as the outside forces and competitive environment shift. The CEO may decide that a riskier approach makes sense, but can't implement it unless the troops adjust their own decision-making accordingly. And there are additional barriers to changing a culture. A large barrier is convincing middle and lower managers that the possible gains, which are still hypothetical, outweigh the losses, which are certain and visible. And culture change can shift who in an organization has more influence, and those losing influence will have an incentive for the organization to go slowly in implementing change."

Beth raised her hand. "Could you go back to what causes the behavior of team members? That seems central to managing an organization."

Spencer started pacing. "It is central. When we want to understand the behavior of individuals in groups"—he caught himself before saying "human individuals" on livestream—"most people believe that personality and character are the primary drivers of behavior. But psychologists have done research that shows that situations are a better predictor of behavior than are personalities. Poor organizational structure can predetermine destructive outcomes. This is the lesson of the Stanford Prison Experiment, where volunteers randomly assigned to be guards acted sadistically, and those randomly assigned to be prisoners acted like passive victims. The roles individuals were assigned drove their behavior more than their underlying personality or character. Please read the article by Philip Zimbardo, who ran this experiment back in 1972.

"As I touched on during the session on leadership, it turns out that many startups and even mature companies have characteristics that are more like religious cults than typical corporations—bringing together young people with a shared purpose and sense of unique identity, isolating them from the outside world with long hours and insufficient sleep, and giving them a charismatic leader. A strong culture can replace, for better or worse, the values that participants say they had going in."

Andrew raised his hand. "Are you saying that leaders create situations that change people's personalities and values?"

Spencer stopped pacing. "What I am saying is that leaders create environments where the structure of the role assigned to a person has the most influence on their behavior, and that these leaders can get people to rationalize a more aggressive set of behaviors than their personalities would have suggested. And I am also saying that the company's culture can overlay or replace values that the employee had. These are lessons from the Prison Experiment and from anthropology research on startup culture.

"Let's move past culture to how organizations learn. The ability to tolerate failure turns out to be essential for learning. It helps if people can fail when the stakes are smaller and then not make similar mistakes when the stakes become larger."

"Are you saying that failure is good?" Alex looked skeptical.

Spencer smiled at her. "It depends on what you are seeking from your organization. There may be a tension between competing positive objectives. The research shows that success fosters reliability, but failure is what fosters resilience. If you need to have both reliability and resilience, it can be hard for a company to stay on top. It may be that large industrial companies, or power plants, should emphasize reliability. But tech companies need to prioritize resilience."

"Another challenge is that there's often a difference between what leaders and followers alike say is the behavior that they want, and the actual behavior that's rewarded in a company or in a society. One of the most illuminating articles in organizational psychology was written by Steve Kerr in 1975 and expanded in 1995. He showed this disconnect between desired and rewarded behaviors in many spheres of human organizations: whether it be politicians, who are supported when they give vague goals but not elected when they're specific about what their policies will cost and how they will be paid for, or soldiers who turn out to be more effective when they're told they can't return home until after the war is won rather than serving a fixed period of time, or doctors who get punished for declaring a sick person healthy but not for declaring a healthy person sick, or universities that base tenure on research and wonder why teaching is not better, or companies that give similar salary increases to average and top performers and wonder why employees don't put in more effort.

"Coming back to an earlier point, another important set of research in organizational behavior is around what motivates employees. Most people believe, erroneously, that job satisfaction drives job performance—despite the fact that there is little in research to show that is the case. People also believe that the level of pay drives performance, when research shows that the level of pay has very little effect on motivation."

Alex again interrupted Spencer's flow. "Are you saying that it doesn't matter what you pay employees?"

"Not exactly. The *absolute* level of pay has little effect on motivation. But the level of *relative* pay—of one person compared to his or her peers—has a substantial impact. People don't mind if Wall Streeters or other people they don't know get overpaid, but they get upset if the person who sits next to them at work gets a larger raise. So a company may be able to get away with underpaying everyone, but it must be deliberate about the differences in compensation among its own employees. Research shows that factors that do correlate more strongly with job performance include setting specific and challenging goals, getting paid more than peers for better performance, and having a good fit between the employee and the job.

"One interesting avenue of research in organizations centers around the composition of teams. As part of establishing culture, many organizations hire employees with similar demographic characteristics, and some research shows that people are less stressed when they're around others who are most like themselves. However, more recent research shows that diverse teams are more productive. This last point has been made by a University of Michigan economist named Scott Page, and he would probably suggest we construct our work forces with a variety of people from different backgrounds." *And in our case, from different planets*, he thought to himself.

"The last topic I want to raise in the organizational behavior research is that of power. Rosabeth Moss Kanter once said that sex and power are two of the topics that humans find challenging to openly discuss. She concluded that power accrues most to those who cope with the organization's problems and is actually the secret of career success. It's not power that causes people to act bossy as much as it is powerlessness. And power in an organization is expanded by sharing it. Jeff Pfeffer at Stanford tells us that the way to get ahead in an organization is to get very comfortable with conflict, seize your power, and build your own brand. He also says that once a person has power, most others will forgive or forget the rude things done to get there."

Beth spoke up. "That seems like a fairly pessimistic view."

Spencer agreed. "It is. But Pfeffer is describing what empirically works, not what we would wish to be true. He observes that a majority of people who work their way into powerful positions engage in deliberate conflict, break rules, interrupt others, and emphasize showing themselves in control. He's suggesting we may have to make a choice between behavior consistent with our view of ourselves and what's needed to get to the top of the management pyramid. Sometimes these same people find that powerful positions don't make them satisfied, and also that they need to alter their approach after they achieve power. But he's describing what seems to work rather than offering a guide to harmony in the workplace.

"There are more positive theories of behavior in organizations that are not necessarily contradictory. Marty Seligman helped bring about the field of positive psychology, with examination of what contributes to a life that can be described as happy and fulfilled. Work is a large part of that. One element of a happy life is a meaningful life. Before his death in late 2021, Mihaly Csikszentmihalyi built a career out of identifying the state of *flow*, a state of deep effortless involvement and intensity that productive work can often bring about. For our next lunch, I would ask you to complete the readings in power and in positive psychology, and come back ready to discuss how we can reconcile the hard-nosed view of how to achieve more influence with the positive psychology view of how to find more meaning at work."

PART II

Unintended Consequences

CHAPTER 13
Dirty Laundry

If you have a bad day in baseball, and start thinking about it, you will have ten more. (Sammy Sosa)

AFTER A VERY LONG morning in the Secret Service field station in San Jose, Zach finally found himself back at work. The television in the background was repeating in a loop the news of the death of the First Gentleman, which the White House had released sometime in the afternoon. The White House was sparse with the details, though at least one network had already connected the tragedy to the sudden closure of the transporter network. Zach had to rely on a spare set of clothes he kept at the office, as he'd not had time to stop back at home. Fortunately, his office had an arrangement with the Rosewood for access to the showers in their fitness center. He was sitting in his office across from Charlie Mendelevitch, the CEO for the transporter business. Charlie was a trusted member of the inner circle, having been unflappable about and among the visitors from the beginning. "We should have seen this coming," Zach said.

"How could we have done that?" responded Charlie.

"Because it is friggin' obvious that a new transportation technology would have military applications! We're lucky that this was one guy with a political axe to grind, and not the Chinese landing an entire platoon in the West Wing."

"It's only obvious in hindsight. The destination constraint was one that the human coders added, so maybe we should have guessed that could be hacked by someone motivated enough. But the transporters came with built-in limits hard-coded by the visitors regarding how many people can arrive anywhere in close proximity to each other."

"The transporter network has to remain closed until further notice,

81

maybe permanently. We cannot even discuss reopening it until we can control with 100% certainty where people can land."

"That will ruin our valuation!" Mendelevitch looked like the vein in his forehead might explode.

"Not as much as enabling war. We already implemented stations to start a journey, and the exits were supposed to be limited to the same places. We should probably also make it so that they cannot transport with any weapons on their person. We're doing everything too damn fast. We got two people killed and nearly also got a President killed, who I voted for, and I nearly ended up in jail myself."

⊢ ∩ ⼂ ⌐

"Zach, you're the one who taught me that having a product with new technology is only one small part of a successful business. Why am I having to remind you?" Spencer was sprawled on the too-short couch in Zach's studio, with a laptop propped up on his lap. Cookie was atypically unsuccessful in her attempts to distract Spencer into playing tug of war with her over a chew toy.

"Probably because these technologies are a thousand times more disruptive than anything you or I have experience with."

"That doesn't mean that the business is a thousand times better, or faster. You still need a team, they need to execute, you need to worry about regulatory approvals, customer adoption, incumbent response. Remember that Betamax was superior video technology to VHS in the '80s, and VHS won that product war anyway."

"Yeah, it's bad enough that I have to deal with honest-to-god aliens from outer space and technologies I cannot hope to fully understand. It's worse to have to relearn lessons that I'm supposed to already know. Spence, I wanted to bring this technology to people to save lives and to save money. And instead, it cost the President's husband—and an agent doing his job—their lives. That's on me."

"Zach, there are always unintended consequences to progress. You can't let it paralyze you. Is it Henry Ford's fault that 40,000 people a year die in auto accidents in this country alone? Cars and trucks fuel commerce that saves lives. Since the invention of the car, fewer people die from all causes. And now the next step in transportation, the transporters, are going to save a lot of the people that would die in the future from auto accidents. Even if a few people die instead from the transporter technology."

"Spence, none of that changes the fact that we made a mistake and two people died."

"So, we'll try harder not to make mistakes. You wanted to be a player, to have an impact on the world."

"I just wanted to get my career going, Spence. I am not ready for this kind of responsibility."

"No one is until they have it, Zach. How do you think army officers feel when they make a mistake and some of their soldiers die? Or how big-pharma CEOs feel when they decide which drugs to pursue and which to abandon? There are a lot of people out there facing these kinds of tradeoffs every day."

"We're going to have to do better, Spencer. *I* am going to have to do better. At least it can't get worse."

⠒ ⟟ ∴ ⅃

"It's worse." Zach spoke into his Bluetooth as he navigated the stop sign on Alameda de las Pulgas that marked the transition from Atherton to the west end of Menlo Park. He was driving his new, dark-blue Dream edition Lucid Air. After colliding with an extraplanetary vehicle, he had declined the chance to replace the Tesla Model S Plaid. He loved the Model S, but had grown weary of the company and the time and expense needed to service it. And that car had become the Ford Taurus of Menlo Park, requiring a hipster to try something newer to stand out. With Lucid Motors being newer and based in Arizona, it was not yet ubiquitous in Silicon Valley— and its CEO was not a household name, nor engaged in side businesses like space exploration or crypto currency.

"Worse how?" From the sounds in the background, Spencer was frying eggs on this Monday morning. Zach believed the only reason for Spencer's career choice as business faculty was because no one expected him to be at the office before mid-morning or to wear colored socks.

"You know how real estate skyrocketed in remote tropical islands after we introduced the transporter?"

"Yes. I am still kicking myself. We could have made more money buying land in Hawaii before we released the transporter than we've made with the transporter itself. I mean, it was totally predictable that people would want to commute from the beach to their jobs in the snow belt, once commute time fell to a couple of seconds from anywhere on the planet."

"That's just the point. People don't seem to believe that our suspension of service is temporary, and beach property values are falling back to their previous levels. We have a couple of lawsuits already from property owners who bought at the peak after the transporter technology went big."

"Okay, so we need to beef up the budget for legal?"

"Yeah, a lot."

"Okay, do it. Hey—wait a minute. So, we know we're getting back into business as soon as we reprogram the transporters to guarantee they only work in stations, right? And beach property is cheap again. So let's not make the same mistake again. Let's open an office in Bora Bora and buy as much acreage in the tropics as we possibly can."

"That makes sense. Though we will have a hard time justifying a station in French Polynesia when most of the world's largest cities do not have one, so we are going to have to expand the number of stations. But before we do that, perhaps we should short all the major hotel chains. People can visit Hawaii for dinner without having to spend the night, or they can just buy their house there. Either way, they don't need to stay in a luxury hotel just to sleep. Hell, they never need to stay in a hotel again."

"Unless they're trying to spend quality time with someone that they can't take home . . . I think hotels are about to become a lot less respectable. Man, between coronavirus and the transporter technology, I feel kind of bad about the impact of the last few years on the hospitality sector."

: ⅃ ḃ ⅂

Zach backed the Lucid Air into his parking space at Regio Li offices. Caitlyn had mocked him for always backing in, accusing him of trying to be Batman. Zach always just felt more comfortable leaving the car in a position for a faster exit, especially since he tended to leave five minutes late for every midday meeting he might have offsite. Caitlyn also teased him for always facing the door in a restaurant or bar. She thought he was worried about being shot, but he just wanted to be able to see who else was in the room.

Before he got to the stairs, he ran into his assistant, EJ, who was carrying two tall Starbucks for herself and for Zach. Zach grabbed one. "Thanks."

"Don't thank me until you see today's issue of *Fast Company*." EJ was never one to mince words. Or to be particularly deferential. Zach may have been her boss, but he was also approximately half her age. And she lived in a nicer place than he did, on a horse farm in Woodside. Zach had met EJ when she had dated his Uncle George. George had been there for Zach when Zach's dad died, but was a bit less reliable when it came to romantic relationships, and Zach was disappointed that his Uncle George had let EJ slip away. When Zach hired EJ, Zach had thought he was doing her a favor. He had later revised this view, having realized her willingness to take the job was doing him the favor.

"Ah crap. Now what?"

"Um, I am going to go now. And just want you to know that I did not vote for you."

"Vote for me for what?" EJ had already disappeared ahead.

Zach's phone rang and identified the caller as Spencer.

"Ah Zach, you're still answering your phone, which means you haven't seen the news."

"No, but I have a feeling I'm not going to like it. What are we facing now?"

"Not we, you, kemo sabe. You have the distinction of being labeled 'the most hated person in Silicon Valley.'"

"Seriously? My mother is going to be take this hard. She was really happy when my freshman dorm voted me 'most likable.' I mean, we live in a country that created Harvey Weinstein, Kanye, and Roseanne Barr. And now *I'm* considered the biggest asshole?"

"Look on the bright side, they didn't say 'in the country,' just in the Valley. Though that probably makes you a national contender. It says here that you're responsible for amping up one-night-stands, creating a record divorce rate, unemploying drivers and pilots, wrecking the hotel industry, and getting the husband of a popular president killed. You're a legit candidate for *Time*'s Man of the Year, but not in a Nobel peace prize kind of way. More of Hitler circa 1939 kind of way."

"Oh man, I hate you."

"You can't hate me. I'm your best human friend. Of which you have fewer and fewer, it seems. But, buddy, you might want to turn off your ringer for the rest of the day. And block calls from any numbers your phone does not recognize."

"Let's increase the budget for security, okay?"

"Already done."

"Um, you don't know if Caitlyn has seen this article yet, do you?"

"No idea, brother, no idea."

⌟ ⁓ ‖ ⡂

Zach called Caitlyn. Whether or not she'd seen the article, he wanted to get to her before it sunk in, and hopefully have her learn about it from him. He didn't want the media perception of him to affect how he looked to Caitlyn's eyes. Her opinion was roughly on an equal weight to him as all other opinions combined. Given the ambiguous state of their relationship, that felt like a precarious position.

She picked up on the first ring. "Hi Cat, it's me."

"Hi Zach, I've got to tell you, I'm having a crap day."

"You mean the article?"

"What are you talking about? What article? Zach, I was assaulted."

"Oh, damn, Cat. What happened?"

"I had a sales call this morning with a doctor at a free clinic in San Jose. You know, they let me give discounts to some of these neighborhood clinics." Cat's job as a pharmaceutical sales rep let her use her extensive medical knowledge, but she also knew that the pharma companies tended to hire attractive female sales reps to call on mostly male doctors, and she counterbalanced the cynicism that this engendered by allocating time to urban neighborhood clinics. "Just before my appointment time, I came out of a coffee shop, and this weird guy tried to grab my purse. I started punching him, and he got a couple of weak punches in on me before he went down."

"Oh my god! Are you okay?" A part of Zach, one that he was not terribly proud of, thought it was pretty hot that Cat was such a badass. He wisely kept that to himself.

"That's not even the weird part. Before I could even process what had happened, out of nowhere, these guys in suits appeared and grabbed the guy. They held him until the police came."

"Wow. Sounds like a good thing they were there."

"No, Zach, it wasn't. I had already put the guy on the ground. These new guys were the problem."

"Did they do anything bad?"

"No, that's just it. They just instantly had me surrounded. Sure, they helped me, but they didn't tell me who they were; they had radios and sunglasses. I think they had been following me."

"Geez, Cat, that's worse than the purse snatcher."

"Exactly. I can deal with a random creep. He figured out pretty quickly he wasn't going to get my purse. But these so-called good Samaritans, they really creeped me out. Do you think I'm being followed?"

"I don't know, but I am damn well going to find out, and get you some security. I am so sorry."

"Zach, I don't want to live a life where I need a friggin' bodyguard, okay?"

"Let's talk about this. Can we have lunch? I promise I won't grab your purse or beat anyone up."

"Yeah, I wasn't worried about either of those things happening. But okay. Something weird is going on, Zach."

By the time Zach met Caitlyn for lunch, he decided that his public relations issues were not going to be the worst part of her day. She took the magazine cover in stride. "Zach, I never figured you for being the bad-boy type."

"I'm not."

"I don't know. I have met some bad boys in my life, but none made it to the cover of a fancy publication."

"Okay, now you're just messing with me."

"Maybe a little. Don't worry, I won't tell anyone that you're actually kind to dogs and old ladies. Wouldn't want to ruin your rep. But look Zach, seriously, I need your strange career to remain yours. I don't care about what a magazine says about you, I know you. I know you're doing something huge here, and I respect that. Even though I left nursing, I still took an oath to practice the profession faithfully, and I want to support you in your own mission. Before all this, you obsessed about your lack of career progress, and now you are understandably preoccupied with this huge opportunity. But please remember that I didn't sign up to be a player. I guess I'm saying that I'm looking for some boundaries here, okay?"

Zach was relieved that Caitlyn was able to joke about the magazine article, though he still wondered if it affected her view of him that the public at large appeared to consider him another rich and egotistical man-child from Silicon Valley. It was definitely affecting his own view of himself. More importantly, he felt terrible that his choice to be interplanetary liaison was clearly disrupting her life. "I understand, Cat. I never thought that my decision to partner with the visitors would blow back on to you like this. I'm sorry."

"I know you are, Zach. And I am not asking you to stop—just to do your best to keep me from being front and center."

As he drove back to his office, Zach's thoughts eventually drifted from Caitlyn to the magazine article and the other challenges associated with the rollout of visitor technology. Despite the backlash, Zach found the nature of his predicament to be oddly liberating. It wasn't a problem because some boss subjectively evaluated it to be a problem, whether fairly or unfairly. It was a problem because he had actually screwed up and the world was providing consequences. If he had enough agency to produce this negative impact, it was still a form of enablement, and perhaps it meant he could produce a positive outcome as well. So he found even this terrible press to be strangely empowering: at least he didn't have a boss any longer, and at least his mistakes unambiguously belonged to him.

i! ȧ :: ꓶ

DSAC Leah Perera was unhappy. Despite being in her own office, she chose to stand behind her desk, and uncrossed her arms to lean forward across the desk toward the tall agent in the visitor chair. "You blew your cover over a goddamn purse snatching?"

"Look, it was a routine surveillance, and the subject was being assaulted." The agent was deferential, but just barely. He did not like being second-guessed by this much younger woman, even if she did outrank him. "We detained the perpetrator and left, though the woman arguably didn't need the help. She may be a person of interest but is not a suspect. We are still law enforcement."

"You don't get to decide when you're law-fucking-enforcement—I decide that. I suppose her being a looker had nothing to do with triggering your white knight complex? Do I have to assign you to fat middle-aged men going forward?"

"Assign us to whomever you want, we will do our jobs." He did not add *which I've been doing since you were in grade school, girlie*, but she was pretty sure it was implied.

"Moving on," Leah said. *I guess I need to work with what I have, even if it is this knuckle-dragging Neanderthal*, she did not say, but she was pretty sure it was implied. "What did you learn about the movie-star house?"

"On the surface, nothing out of the ordinary."

"Okay, Mr. Law Enforcement, what about under the surface."

He ignored the dig. They were working now. "We checked the bills for the house, to see if they were current."

"Were they?"

"That's just it. There were no bills. Rent was prepaid by Mr. Randall, who does not live there. There is no landline, and there isn't even an electrical bill."

"There is no electricity?"

"No, there is electricity, just no utility account. And no evidence of a generator. But that's not the only strange part."

This time she just stared.

He continued. "We ran background checks on all the occupants. They all have jobs. But their backgrounds don't check out—not prior employers, not colleges, not old friends, nothing. They did not exist until a year ago. At least not in this country. At a minimum, we have them for criminal impersonation and probably immigration fraud."

"Let's not settle for that. We need to figure out who these people are. Are these hackers, or worse? Is this a state-sponsored fifth column preparing for some kind of tech invasion, now or later? I need you to get the information on how far this goes. We need way more active surveillance; you are going to tell me everything about these people, and soon."

CHAPTER 14
Another Brick in the Wall

Clear thinking requires courage rather than intelligence.
(Thomas Szasz, *The Second Sin*)

IT WAS FRIDAY AGAIN, and Spencer had elected for the "Larry Ellison" sandwich (salami-bacon-avocado) from the Palo Alto location of Ike's over his usual "Madison Bumgarner" steak sandwich. He loved the steak, but it hadn't been the same since the sandwich's namesake had been traded in 2020 to the Diamondbacks. Spencer had been in Kansas City on that night in late October 2014 when Bumgarner had gotten the last out with the tying run on third base to clinch Game 7 for the Giants, and even now it was tough to see his favorite pitcher and rodeo contestant in another uniform.

Of course, as the lecturer Spencer had to eat his sandwich quickly before turning to the room full of earnest-looking visitors and organizing his thoughts. Since today's lecture was more focused on human behavior, he decided it best not to livestream this one. There was just no way that the visitor questions would not come across as somehow "off" to the human online audience, plus it would allow Spencer to speak to the visitors' specific . . . gaps in understanding.

"Okay folks, today I want to offer a very brief introduction to the fields of decision-making and cognitive bias, which have a lot of relevance to investors and managers here in the Valley. It turns out that people in general are bounded in the time they take to make decisions, their rationality, their awareness, and their ethicality. Individuals tend to take cognitive shortcuts that result in misestimating risk and probability, and so making suboptimal or inconsistent decisions, even when the stakes are high. Understanding these tendencies can enable us to make better decisions, and to better evaluate the decisions made by others."

Andrew looked stunned. "How has humanity accomplished so much, if people think irrationally? How does your society even function?"

Spencer paused, wondering if there was a downside in being so candid about the shortcomings of people and how they think. It was too easy to forget how alien these visitors actually were, and how strange human behavior must be to them, even if they were fast learners. "It's not that humans are always wrong. There are limits to how broadly or deeply people can think about each decision they have to make. They take short-cuts, which work fine in simple situations, and so worked well in our simpler past. But they work less well with the more abstract thinking that is increasingly required of the average person. To ease into this topic, there's a meaningful amount of research on bias in decision-making that has centered on behavioral economics and finance. It turns out that people are not, in fact, rational utility-maximizing agents like economists have assumed for two centuries. People make economic and financial decisions irrationally, and not in a way that cancels out with large numbers of people. To take just one example, when evaluating whether to hold or sell an asset at the current price with current information, rationally it should not matter what price was paid for the asset. But people tend to hold on to an asset if it remains below their purchase price, and are more likely to sell if the price is above what they initially paid. Overall, as you should have read already in the summary from Barberis and Thaler, agents are not rational, markets are not always efficient, and people exhibit biases in how they process information and assess risk. Further, these risks are consistent enough across people to be predictable."

Beth asked, "Can you give some examples of these biases?"

"One bias with specific relevance to your interactions here is the representativeness bias, whereby two things that are similar on one dimension are perceived to be correlated on other dimensions. As an example, a well-known venture investor said in 2008 that his ideal entrepreneur is a white male nerd who has recently dropped out of a top school. This description fit a couple of successful entrepreneurs, including Gates, Jobs, Ellison, and Zuckerberg. This type of thinking has resulted in women receiving less than 8% of venture funding, despite making up 36% of small-business entrepreneurs and having outcomes at least as good as their male counterparts. Similarly, another famous venture investor said in 2012 that 'people over 45 basically die in terms of new ideas,' which can help explain why 75% of venture funding goes to entrepreneurs under the age of 30 even though the median age of founders of successful businesses is 39. The percentage of funding going to entrepreneurs of color represents so small a sample size that it is hard to study. Many in the Valley are aware of these biases; unfortunately, looking for those particular demographics of young-white-male-dropout is considered by many to represent 'pattern recognition,' which an alarming fraction of investors describe as some kind of personal virtue."

Beth followed up on her earlier question. "So, if one entrepreneur is successful, then people think the next successful entrepreneur will share something as meaningless as gender or age?"

"Yes, and it can become a self-fulfilling cycle. If one young white male is successful, and then you invest in another one and he is successful, you may perceive cause-and-effect where there is none. That's called the 'representativeness bias.' It was handy a million years ago: if a lion ate your friend, and then you met another large cat like a leopard, you might have benefited from this kind of generalization.

"Some of these findings from finance generalize to other types of decisions. The Israeli psychologists Kahneman and Tversky found that people avoid risks with respect to gains, preferring a small sure gain to uncertain larger gain—but take risks with respect to losses, preferring a larger uncertain loss to a certain small loss. This has the disconcerting implication that how you frame a problem can determine the response. If you ask people if they would take a medical treatment with a 90% chance of survival, they're likely to say yes. But if you ask them if they would take a treatment with a 10% chance of death, they're likely to say no."

Andrew spoke up. "But it's the same question!"

Spencer loved how engaged the visitors were with the literature about management. "Yes, it is. Simply how you ask a question can predetermine the result, even when the stakes are literally life-and-death. Which puts a lot of pressure on doctors, people who construct surveys, and politicians. Though politicians have always seemed to have an intuitive grasp on how to reframe a decision after the fact to make whatever decision they made look better.

"Let me generalize some of these finding about how people process decisions. In 2008 Bazerman and Moore described decades of research, popularized later by Daniel Kahneman in his 2012 book *Thinking, Fast and Slow*. Individuals make decisions in two ways. For many decisions, they think fast, and make decisions based on intuition: automatically, implicitly, and based on emotion. People are not able or willing to dedicate a lot of time and energy thinking through even important decisions in a disciplined and systematic way. Most decisions are made this way, even when the stakes are high, despite the fact that judgment errors are more likely to occur.

"The second way decisions are made is slower, effortful, and more logical. It's more worthwhile to take the time to make decisions this way when the stakes are high. Unfortunately, busier people are more likely to engage in fast thinking, and in business high-stakes decisions are usually escalated to the most senior and busy person on a team or in an organization. Kahneman co-authored a great study with Gary Klein that intuition works only when someone is in a domain where they get immediate feedback on whether their decision was correct, like a quarterback or firefighter or emergency room nurse. People can develop good intuition if they spend over 10,000 hours of training in a rapid-feedback environment. However, people in domains with longer feedback loops (which includes economists, venture capitalists, policy makers, and presidents) tend to have their confidence increase faster than their skill, and this is reinforced by the fact that people tend to pick leaders who project confidence. These are the most dangerous people to be allowed to make important decisions. Kahneman gives a prescription for people to do the work of consciously applying the effort of slow thinking, especially if they are in a slow-feedback context."

Andrew raised his hand. "Spencer, we have met many intelligent people here, yourself included. Why would they not take the time to think carefully about their decisions?"

Spencer smiled. "Thanks for the compliment. The answer is that our technology has progressed faster than our brains have evolved. We are still built for the savanna, to quickly identify a threat and run or fight. That is, we're built more to make decisions quickly than to parse nuance to arrive at a correct decision in a more complicated environment. And it takes practice and discipline to do otherwise. Amazingly, many if not most senior decision-makers continue to prize their intuition and shortcuts even when the stakes are high.

"Kahneman published another book, *Noise,* in 2021 showing that inconsistency in how different individuals apply judgment also creates a massive variance in outcomes in many fields. For both bias and noise, a lot of progress has been made in generating better and more consistent decisions in a variety of domains through the use of checklists. Pilots and emergency responders are trained to use a checklist rather than their intuition, and that has been extended with success to physicians, equity analysts, and CEOs. The more that a person thinks they're an expert who doesn't need a checklist, the more likely that they've fallen prey to the overconfidence bias and would benefit from that very checklist."

Beth asked, "So, if you're aware of these tendencies, how do you guard against them at your venture firm?"

Spencer responded, "It's likely we don't guard against all of them, because being aware of these biases is insufficient to avoid them when you're making many decisions sequentially. But you can mitigate this somewhat. We work with a checklist at Regio Li for making decisions about which startups to invest in, even when we think we might already have an unfair advantage in the technology that we have access to. And I know of other venture firms that have created frameworks to try to build a quantitative market mapping of each step in a startup's successful access to a market, to de-bias their decisions as much as they can. There are now companies, such as CrowdSmart, which help organizations mitigate some forms of bias by integrating the views of multiple people from within the organization.

"There has been a lot of research in decision-making over the past two decades. Thaler and Sunstein showed how we can use biases to nudge people into better behavior through appropriate framing, by designing choices so that the default option for certain decisions (like 401k participation or health insurance) is one with better average outcomes, even if people still have the freedom to select a different option. Phil Tetlock identified specific behaviors and clear thinking that allow even untrained people to provide better forecasts of outcomes of complex systems than experts. Research in the wisdom of the crowds has demonstrated that groups of forecasters or decision-makers can provide a group forecast that is better than that of even the best individual in the group. One professor I mentioned earlier, Scott Page at the University of Michigan, wrote a second book in 2018 that showed that the best way to make decisions is to create not one but several models to organize data. For any given decision, applying multiple models squeezes more out of the data at hand and yields better decisions. There are now startups that sell decision software to larger companies and organizations, to help them more efficiently synthesize the judgment of groups of employees to arrive at decisions that are both faster and have less forecast error. Those organizations can then also keep a report card of which employees have provided recommendations that turned out to be more (or less) accurate than those of other employees."

Andrew spoke again. "This is very interesting! It's amazing that a species with hard-wired irrationality and inconsistency in its thought processes has nevertheless achieved a high level of technological advancement. There appears to be more variety between individuals than we could have ever imagined."

Spencer smiled. "That is right. For humans, making decisions is as much a creative process as an analytical one. And in organizations, it can matter significantly who is making the decision, regardless of the underlying merits of different courses of action." Spencer looked out at the number of raised hands and smiled once more. Teaching had its downsides, but moments like this reminded him why he made a career of it.

CHAPTER 15

Jammin' Me

Do not hire a man who does your work for money, but him who does it for the love of it. (Henry David Thoreau, *Life Without Principle*)

"CAT, OUR PHARMACEUTICAL COMPANY could really use you." Zach was standing with Caitlyn in the parking lot of the Equinox gym in Palo Alto. She had moonlighted there as a fitness instructor when she lived nearby, which had helped Zach's own fitness level. Even with her relocation 35 miles north to San Francisco, she still occasionally came out to exercise and teach, so it was a convenient place for her to chat.

"Zach, we've talked about this. I do not want to take a job because of my connection to . . ."

"Some guy?"

"Well, yes. You didn't take any of your jobs because of your connection to me or any other woman. I know too many women who take a job with a boyfriend or another guy in their life. I prefer to carve out my own career. I certainly don't want to be famous, and I prefer to get rich on my own power."

"But Cat, the company objectively needs people with your skill set, in both nursing and pharmaceutical sales. Plus you're someone that's already in on the secret about where the R&D actually took place. You are, in fact, the right person for the job."

"Fine Zach. When you step off the board, divest yourself of your stake, and become totally independent of Magellanic Pharma, then I will consider joining. Until then, I am fine with my current job selling medicine for a pharmaceutical company run by, you know, actual humans. However, I have a couple of annoying coworkers and wouldn't mind if you would please recruit them."

"I will hold out for you." Zach winced, as he recognized that the statement may have contained more global truth than he had intended.

She pretended not to notice. "How's your portfolio of businesses going?"

"It's falling together really well. We're working to put guardrails on the transport business to make it unworkable for criminals or terrorists. We have the pharma company up and running, and have to keep the rate of new drug introduction slow if we don't want to trigger the FDA's curiosity about how one small new drug company could be in development on Alzheimer's drugs and cancer and some other conditions, all at the same time. It's frustrating. We could save lives a lot faster by introducing more drugs—but both the visitors and the FDA are wanting to take a gradual approach. Which I have to go along with until we're ready to admit the source of the drugs. I thought about combining the two transportation technologies into one company, but a self-piloting miniplane is a lot different than a transporter beam. We had wanted to introduce the plane first, but that looks like it will involve years of lag with the Federal Aviation Administration."

"I would think the FAA would be more worried about transporter beams."

"They might be, but the lawyers say it doesn't qualify as 'aviation.' It isn't regulated because no one in the government had ever foreseen the possibility. But having introduced that, it's hard to go back to other methods of long-range transportation."

"It will take some significant marketing to get some people to agree to get atomized just to get from point A to point B a little faster. Will probably go over well with your friends in the venture crowd, though, they count seconds saved like Scrooge McDuck counts his gold."

"Some of us do like to spend our time on productivity and play, Cat, and minimize the other categories."

"Is that why you don't do dishes?"

"Yes, as a matter of fact. And neither did Steve Jobs. And it's also why I don't mow the lawn. I divide my time into working, having fun, and sleeping—and minimize all the other categories."

"You know, Zach, some of us think that life happens in other categories too."

⠒ ⠭ ⠶ ⏄

Leah Perera was debriefing the growing number of agents assigned to monitor this strange group of young celebrity look-alikes. "So, what else have we learned?"

Rail-thin, middle-aged Agent Kyle McGee spoke for the team. "Candidly, not much. We were able to get bugs into their house through food delivery. But the bugs simply don't work."

"So, replace them."

"We did. All of the bugs placed in the house stop working as soon as they enter the house."

"So they're being jammed?"

"Not in any way we can identify. We don't get static or interference, just silence."

"Kyle, the fact that they have advanced jamming is information in itself. What about the offices of the startups and their venture capitalist?"

"We got bugs in there, and they started off working. But whenever one of the residents of that movie-star house is in an office, the bugs go silent and stay silent. It appears to be some sort of portable jammer, with no energy source that we can identify."

"What about visual surveillance?"

"That's even stranger. We have eyes on the house, and a camera. We can't see in. Even when the curtains are open, or the door is open, the view of inside just seems . . . fuzzy."

That got Leah's attention. "Fuzzy? You mean to the actual eyes of the observer?"

"Yes. Everything up to the outside of the house is clear, but the inside is not. I've never seen anything like it. I don't even know how it is possible."

"Is anyone there during the workday?"

"No, they all have jobs at different tech firms."

Three hours later Leah found herself at the front door of the visitors' Menlo Park house with two other agents. She had obtained an expedited search warrant by showing a judge, on a hastily arranged Zoom conference, the truncated histories of the identities of the residents and arguing that the house was, at a minimum, some kind of nexus for illegal immigration, and that the house also used sophisticated technology that could represent a threat to national security. When Leah requested a warrant of the "sneak and peek" variety that didn't require the occupants to know of the search, the duty magistrate asked a lot of additional questions, but ultimately granted the warrant.

Leah sent one agent around the back and knocked on the front door. When there was no answer, she nodded to Agent McGee, who was able to unlock the door without breaching it. He opened the door, stepped to go inside . . . and bounced backward as though he had been shoved. He approached slowly and reached out with his hand; at the doorway his hand stopped in midair as though it was touching a wall. Leah looked through the open doorway and found the air opaque, like looking through gauze.

"What could do this?"

"I don't know, ma'am, but this does not look like a case of undocumented immigration. This acts like some kind of sci-fi force field."

The other agent came from around the house. "Ma'am, I was able to open the back window, but couldn't go through it. I tried the same thing on the second story sliding door, no joy there either. I've never seen anything like it."

"Okay, so these people are clearly going to a lot of sophisticated effort to hide their activity. This doesn't seem like any kind of jamming technology in use by the Chinese or the Russians, but I'm going to ask around about that. In the meantime, I need you and your team to get some DNA samples. Tap into their sewer if you need to; I'm gonna go out on a limb and guess that the force field does not extend around those pipes leaving the house."

Pretty sure that wasn't in the Bureau recruiting brochure, McGee thought with some revulsion. "Yeah, we'll get it done."

Ḻ ˧ ₸ ⁝

"What am I looking at?" Spencer passed the sheets of paper back to their Wilson Sonsini lawyer, Scott Crawford. They were seated in Spencer's office at Regio Li, where Spencer had become an unofficial combination of business instructor, chief operating officer, and chief of staff. Basically, Spencer's job was to lower the number of issues to be decided by Zach, based on his knowledge of all the pieces and players. Like all good lawyers,

Scott had also made himself essential enough to have been let in on the details; Spencer still remembered that meeting. Scott hadn't batted an eyelash, but had calmly walked over to the small wet bar in the office and drained a short glass of Whistle Pig rye whiskey, then calmly walked back and started discussing legal implications. He charged $1,400 per hour but Spencer rarely argued his bill.

"It's a demand from the Committee on Foreign Investment in the U.S., commonly known as CFIUS."

Spencer started thumbing through the pages of the document. "Aren't they just worried about investments in U.S. tech companies by the Chinese government?"

"That has historically been their focus. But the law is written to cover investment in U.S. technology by any foreigners. And they want a list of investors in our venture fund, and the investors in the transporter company."

"That's a challenge. Do we have to give it to them?"

"The law has historically been applied to mergers and joint ventures. And even there, enforcement dipped a bit under the last administration's Treasury Department, but since then has picked back up. However, the scope of its jurisdiction has always been a bit ambiguous. And I don't think you want to fight the U.S. Treasury when they ask about your investors."

"But Scott, don't we have a privacy clause protecting the identity of our investors?"

"Yes, but there is an exception for legal inquiries by authorities. I think the legal risk from your investors for complying is lower than the risk from stiff-arming Treasury."

"But they're probably just fishing around to learn more about the technology!"

"Yes, I assume so. But they have a legal pretense to do exactly that."

"Alright then, our investors are all listed as being U.S.-based."

"Spencer, I'm just your lawyer. But do you think *all* of your investors would pass a thorough background check by forensic investigators? And there's another problem." Crawford paused momentarily, and then decided to continue. "Immigration and Customers Enforcement has separately asked several of our portfolio companies for the documentation we used to establish U.S. citizenship for several of our visitors. You know that it won't hold up to real investigation."

"Crap. What's the potential consequence?"

"They charge a civil penalty of $600 for the first violation and $23,000 for the next ones. So potentially several hundred thousand dollars. The bad news is that there's a criminal sanction for a pattern of knowingly hiring undocumented workers, with up to six months in prison. The good news is that this sanction requires establishing that the employer knew the documents were forged."

"Yeah, I'm guessing that it's a bigger problem when they can't identify which country the workers are from. We're going to need you to spend time on this, and we're going to need to brief Zach on it ASAP. I did not get into teaching at Stanford to risk prison."

CHAPTER 16
On the Road Again

Man is not who he thinks he is, he is what he hides. (André
Malraux, *Les Noyers de l'Alternburg*)

"LOOK, I THINK THE time is approaching to consider revealing that the
source of all these technologies is not terrestrial in origin." Zach looked
carefully at Andrew and Beth. The three of them were in the dining room
at the visitors' rented house in the Willows. It looked like a bad 1986 Hollywood movie set most of the time. Some of the visitors had learned to
cook, but their meals tended toward high-end food delivery and takeout,
today from Jessie and Laurent's Bay Area delivery service.

Andrew put down his fork. "But Zach, you said that this would, as
you put it, 'freak people out completely.' Which I understood to be a bad
idea."

"Yes, but we never expected to keep this a secret forever. Some people
already suspect, and a few of the human CEOs we have hired are pretty
damn sure."

Beth spoke up. "How do you think your government and military
will react to a technologically superior species living among you?"

"Beth, I think there are two answers to that. First, I think that the
government may already suspect. Government agents seem to be following at least some of us. I'm sure they haven't forgotten about the White
House incident. We started getting inquiries about our investors, and
then demands for the documentation we used to confirm citizenship for
employees at our various companies. Our head of security discovered a
listening device at my office in his last scan; we don't think it was there
long, since the prior scan didn't pick it up, but it means someone is taking
an interest in my activity. Even though I hired good security to assess

whether we are being monitored, the government probably has better capabilities than the folks I hire.

Zach continued. "They may not have immediately thought that the technology was from, um, far away. But they would be intrinsically interested in the technology from a national security standpoint. As an offensive tool, for example, the transporter probably beats an aircraft carrier in terms of projecting strength. And, if other countries might have one, it's even more important to lock down defensive capabilities against others projecting their own strength. So I think they might try to dig into the origins of the technology. And you know that our cover stories for your team will not hold up to any professional level of scrutiny; you visitors don't actually have valid Social Security numbers or friends from high school.

"Second, I think that most governments on this planet, including my own, will react with suspicion and fear to the discovery that there is anyone at all on the planet that might have better technology than they have—especially any with military applications. I'm hoping that we can make the argument that since you have had both the technology and the time, if your intentions were hostile, you would have acted already. But I'm not sure how persuasive that will be. Let me ask you a question: how will you react if you and your friends are detained?"

Beth looked at Andrew, and he responded. "Mr. Randall, we do not believe in conquest or colonization, but that does not mean we would allow a less advanced species to restrict us unreasonably. We would not remain detained."

"Please unpack that statement."

"We would try not to hurt anyone, though I could not guarantee success. We would free any of our individuals with a minimum amount of force. But we would free them very soon after anyone curtailed their movement."

"Then what would you do?"

"We would reevaluate whether this world holds enough economic potential to remain. That decision would be, how do you put it, 'above my pay grade.' But I will tell you this. If we leave, we take all of our technology with us. We have been careful not to share how it's made, and we believe that reverse engineering any of it is beyond the capabilities of even your best scientists."

"So you would take your marbles and go home."

"Mr. Randall, my own colleagues back home would be disappointed to lose the return on their investment. They might quarantine the planet, so that even when you gain the ability to travel beyond your local space, you would be denied trading partners."

"That seems a little vindictive. You would punish future generations for the shortsightedness of whoever happens to run our governments today?"

"We are not typically violent, Zach. But we would never dishonor ourselves by behaving as victims. If Earth refuses us as trading partners now, we would bear that cost. After all, some startup ventures fail. But that failure would not occur without consequences for your species. If it is of consolation, it would be a very long time before anyone was even aware of these full consequences."

"Except for me, apparently."

"You are our host and our liaison. We chose you as the person with the best mix of skills and traits to represent us on your planet. We will defer to you in deciding if and when to admit our presence here. But it is also up to you to manage the reaction, and work toward an outcome of continued beneficial trade for everyone. Or we cut our losses and move on to the next project."

Zach looked away. "Right, no pressure at all."

II ⅃ : ⅂

On the short drive back to Atherton, Zach dialed Spencer and was greeted with, "Hey boss, what's shaking?"

"Hey Spencer, I have a question. What do our aliens do with their spare time?"

"What do you mean?"

"I checked. They take vacation days, they don't always work weekends. What do they do?"

"Beth tells me they like to travel around the world. And that they have their own transporter network."

"Wait, no one ever told me that. So they can go anywhere? Are you telling me they could beam into the White House or the Kremlin or wherever?"

"Yeah, but if they wanted to kidnap or kill a world leader, they wouldn't have to travel to do it. So I don't think this ability makes anyone incrementally less safe."

"I sincerely doubt that the military or Secret Service would share your casual attitude about that, Spence. Where did Beth say they go?"

"We haven't discussed it much. She once said they like adventure sports. Remember, this is like a wild and primitive vacation spot for them. I don't know if they have anything like adventure sports at their home, or if their bodies are built for it."

"We need to find out a hell of a lot more about these folks, what they like, and what their home is like. They know everything about us, and we still know nothing about them except that they have some advanced technology that makes Silicon Valley look like a kid's LEGO set, and we keep learning new things about their capabilities. We need to get out of the mode of reacting and figure out how to control where things are going."

CHAPTER 17
She's the Boss

Washington, DC is to lying what Wisconsin is to cheese.
(Dennis Miller)

ZACH STEPPED INTO THE transporter at the Palo Alto Caltrain station under 78-degree sunny skies, and stepped out a moment later at Union Station in Washington DC, where it was 60 degrees and cloudy. He found the change in weather to be the most jarring element of near-instantaneous transportation, as well as the sudden change in time of day. Moments later he and Spencer were in an Uber for the two-mile drive to their destination. Zach fidgeted in the back seat of the blue Prius as it departed the station, heading northwest on Massachusetts Avenue. "You know, it seems incongruous that we have an appointment at the center of power for the whole country if not the world, but we cover the last couple of miles the same way we would go to any other meeting."

Spencer shook his head. "No one at the White House cares how we get there, Zach. I'm still a little surprised that you were able to schedule a meeting with the acting National Security Advisor."

"I think all the publicity around our recent technology might have helped. And these government types may be as curious as the next person regarding where we're coming up with more than one groundbreaking technology in quick succession. Remember, after the incident, I had the phone number of more than one Secret Service agent."

"Seems only fair, as I'm pretty sure they're keeping track of your phone all the time as it is."

"The security guys tell me my messages are encrypted. The government may be able to tell I'm on the phone, but they can't listen in."

The Uber pulled up to the front gate of the White House, and the driver informed them that was as far as he could go. Zach wondered how he knew. How many riders in a day were going to this particular address? Enough for it to cease to be thrilling for the driver, he guessed.

He and Spencer stepped out and showed their IDs to the guards. The guards checked the names against their list of anticipated visitors for the day, and waived them to a second checkpoint where their pictures were taken and they went through an airport-style metal detector. Once through, they were greeted by a young and perky host named Dwight. Several stops later, they found themselves in a very small conference room in the unbelievably cramped West Wing, seated across from Russell Carter, the acting national security advisor. The gray-haired African American looked to be about 50 and carried himself in both demeanor and fashion as though he were an English professor rather than part of the security establishment.

Carter adjusted his plaid bow tie. "I understand that you're the golden boy tech investor who has been getting so much press. And not just for bringing the world the technology an assassin used against my boss."

"I do what I can. I don't do it to get press coverage, and I try to ensure the technology brings more good than bad. That said, there are no words to express how terrible I feel about what happened here in the White House."

"Mr. Randall, part of my job is understanding how technology can be used for bad purposes. And part of my experience is the knowledge that if can be used that way, it most definitely will be. That's not part of your own experience, which is not your fault.

"What is your fault is that you are proceeding to make critical decisions about which technologies to introduce, and how, without either having that experience or relying on those of us who do. Which is why some folks around here do not support you taking it on yourself to decide these things. But we acknowledge that you have been close to enough innovative technology to be interesting to us. You know we don't accept very many requests for meetings."

"Mr. Carter, I didn't come here to debate the track record of public versus private control of new technologies; I think one could find fault with either source over the course of history. Let me say that I think you will find this discussion worth your while. And I have a feeling that someone in your government was already paying attention to what I've been doing, even before I reached out to you."

"As to your first contention, I am counting on it being worth my while. As to your second, let's just say you attracted attention after that transporter incident." Carter looked like he might say more, but stopped.

"I got that impression."

"Regardless, Mr. Randall, you have my attention today, which is why I have allotted 20 minutes before my next meeting with my boss."

"I think you're going to want to extend the meeting. And invite your boss."

Zach told the National Security Advisor the *Reader's Digest* version of the initial encounter with the visitors and subsequent events, and Spencer provided color commentary. Spencer and Zach had previously discussed how much to share. They had decided that the government leadership deserved to know that the technology had been visitor-provided, but not that the visitors themselves remained in Menlo Park. In this way, they hoped to balance legitimate interests of government about technology with protection of their new friends. They stuck to that plan. Forty-five minutes later, Zach and Spencer found themselves in the Oval Office, flanked by Mr. Russell and Chief of Staff Thomas Stanton. President Sheryl Lynne said a brief hello and nodded to her chief of staff while remaining behind the desk.

"Are we taking this seriously?" Stanton peered over his glasses at the acting National Security Advisor. Zach's attempts to apologize to the president had been brushed away by the chief of staff, who appeared disinclined for small talk and eager to get to the heart of the matter.

Russell Carter responded. "Tom, Madam President, this guy has been associated with the development of innovations that no one else even understands, much less could duplicate. Multiple unrelated ones in rapid succession. This indicates access to revolutionary technologies, despite the fact that he himself doesn't possess a technical background nor did he know many who did before all this started. I don't have to remind you of the terrible consequences we had right here from one of those technologies, and we have been looking at Mr. Randall and his associates since then to get a better handle on the source and full capability of this tech. We already know that while these two guys have valid backgrounds, all of the technology officers at their startups have falsified their backgrounds, which incidentally makes hiring them without valid citizenship a crime for each of Mr. Randall's companies. These executives have also deployed sophisticated counter-surveillance techniques the likes of which we have never seen. So, it does appear that Mr. Randall is colluding with some kind of foreign power.

"In addition, we just ran a check of the DNA on a couple of these people to get a handle on what part of the world they came from, and it doesn't show the usual markers of ethnicity; instead, it shows a mix of markers of all ethnicities, as though they're from everywhere on the planet."

At the mention of the DNA, Zach turned to Spencer and raised his eyebrows, but remained silent. He was a bit stunned, both by the change in the security advisor's tone from friendly to hostile, and by the revelation of just how much information the government had already deduced about the visitors and Zach's involvement with them. This guy was good cop and bad cop rolled into one.

The security advisor continued. "I am not making any conclusions, but I am prepared to entertain the possibility that these men could be telling the truth about visitors. With enough probability to find it worth bringing to your attention."

Chief of Staff Stanton turned to Zach. "And, Mr. Randall, you say that you have known these, these visitors, for the better part of this year."

"That's right, sir, since January 3rd."

Stanton uncrossed his arms and leaned forward. "So let's get this straight. You're telling us that you had first contact with an advanced extraplanetary civilization, and you waited nine goddamn months to tell someone about it?"

"Well, sir, I thought it best kept to myself. I didn't want to cause any panic or overreaction. And you just said it yourself—if I had asked to speak with you at the start, as an unknown tech investor in Silicon Valley saying I had met aliens, would you have even taken the meeting?"

"Mr. Randall, after we were attacked in the White House by an armed Yemeni rebel, and *we* came to *you*, I might have listened then."

"And in the meantime, Mr. Randall, how much money have you personally made from these technologies?" interjected Russell Carter.

Spencer, who had been quiet, while vibrating enough nervous energy to power a small city, interrupted. "Look, Mr. Carter, Zach here made some money, which he shouldn't apologize for. He's working his ass off to bring life-saving and life-improving products to the world. It's also his job. Which incidentally is why he was approached in the first place—because venture investors know how to take new technologies, get them funded and produced, and guide them into products for sale in the marketplace."

Carter wheeled toward Spencer. "And that's the point, Dr. Sams. Zach here is a venture capitalist, and you're a junior faculty member at a business school. What made either of you think you're qualified to assess the national security implications of a stealthy invasion by a technologically advanced race who—by your own admission—could kill us all without breaking a sweat. You think it's better to convince us you're collaborating with aliens than have us think you're working with the Chinese or Russians? Let me lay it out for you: it's worse! You didn't just bet your lives, you bet the life of every single person in the country, and the world. The absolute goddamn arrogance. . . . What *is* it with you guys in Silicon Valley?"

"I think *you* may be missing an even larger point, Russell," a feminine voice said. The president had risen from her desk and walked around front, and was now leaning against it. "After 15 months, the primary question is not why these two guys waited. Yes, that was in fact stupid and naïve and arrogant—and there is nothing we can do about it now. My question is, what has them spooked enough to come to us now?" She peered at Zach from over her glasses, and he felt like a seventh-grader who just got caught making too much noise in the school library.

"Madam President, the bottom line is that we think that it's a secret that can't last much longer. In part because of your own government." Zach looked at the president.

"That is obvious, Mr. Randall. Ben Franklin said that three people can keep a secret so long as two of them are dead. And there are five of us in this room alone. Allow me let you in on another little secret. There are over two million people in this federal government; 99% of them were here before me and will be here after me. So even though a handful of them pretend to listen to me, it isn't *my* government. So only now that the secret is about to come out anyway, you've decided to let us in on it?"

"Um, yes ma'am. But I think we can manage the public's reaction. And, with respect, I was hoping to discuss the government's reaction, starting with yours. Ma'am."

"*You* don't get to manage shit, Zach!" The chief of staff exploded off of the couch. "It isn't up to you. We decide when and what to tell the public, we decide our own reaction, and we are the ones who work like hell to manage the public's reaction."

Spencer spoke up before Zach could. "Mr. Stanton, I know it's a lot to take in. But you have to acknowledge that the visitors deliberately chose Zach as the point of first contact. They trust him more than they trust anyone else. I don't pretend to be an expert in national security issues, but it seems to me that Zach is an important asset in managing the most important reaction of all, which is the reaction of the visitors. They already told us they wouldn't allow any of their group to be detained or harassed, and said if that happened they would, at a minimum, pack up and go home and take their ball with them. They're not threatening violence, they're threatening to leave. Given how many lives their technologies have already saved and could continue to save, that alone would cost a lot of lives. Sir."

Stanton stood up. "This is going to be a longer conversation. The important parts of which won't include you . . . amateurs. In the end, it's the president's decision and no one else's. We tolerated the piss-poor judgment you exhibited, which resulted in the deaths of two people close to me. You don't get another mulligan, and we expect you to do what you're told when it comes to the biggest national security threat any country has ever faced. Stay in touch, boys."

Zach and Spencer found themselves quickly on the other side of the White House gate, again waiting for an Uber. "Why do I feel like I just got drop kicked out of The Old Pro at closing time?" Spencer asked.

Zach was visibly smaller. "I guess it makes sense that they're pissed. They assume that they have all the most important information in the world, and they just found out that you and I know more. And they aren't wrong that maybe we aren't the most qualified people in the world to manage a first contact situation. They're right. We're amateurs. I've been in over my head from the beginning."

"Zach, the visitors approached you *because* you have a relevant skill set in bringing their technology to the world; they weren't looking for someone who picked up a master's degree in international relations at Georgetown and picked the right time and politician to attach to. And in venture capital, all the rocket-ship companies have management and investors who are in over their heads."

"Yeah, Spencer, but when someone screws up a startup, people usually don't die. Except perhaps at Theranos. And you've gotta admit, we've let the visitors set the playing field and the rules, which is never the best way to start a negotiation. We need to step away from the tactics of introducing technologies and start looking at the bigger picture. And try to keep ourselves from losing all influence over what happens. Assuming that us having influence is a good thing."

"Buddy, I grant that we may not have it all figured out. But those folks in the Oval Office aren't infallible either. I think they're just punching you because they're mad you met the extraterrestrial visitors before they did."

"I don't know, man. The president seems pretty sharp. She was thinking a couple steps ahead of everyone else."

"You usually don't get to be president without knowing how to play chess. Especially if you're the first woman to get the job. It doesn't mean she knows much more about how to deal with this than we do."

"I don't think we're setting the bar all that high, Spencer. Let's have a beer before taking the transporter back."

CHAPTER 18
Free Fallin'

The adrenaline and stress of an adventure are better than a thousand peaceful days. (Paolo Coelho, Tweet 11/10/2012)

SPENCER WAS EXCITED. HE knew that the visitors went on group outings on their days off, and this was the first time he had been invited to come along. In fact, Beth told him he was the first human they had ever asked to join. His relationship with Beth no longer seemed as exotic as it had at first. He had gotten through the strangeness of feeling attracted to someone not born on Earth—and then acting on that strangeness—pretty quickly. In fact, the main barrier was not that she was a visitor, but more her inexperience with human relationships, which had made him feel initially like he was dating a smart undergraduate. But he had discovered that he was learning as much about relationships as she was, and that it was simply easy to be with her. He couldn't imagine dating anyone else. He knew that his best friend was less sanguine about it, but Zach had his own relationship issues. In any event, they couldn't share the secret of the visitors, and the thought of spending a lot of time with anyone who wasn't aware of the visitors just seemed like a waste of time. This narrowed the dating pool quite a bit.

He met up with Beth at 2:00 p.m. at the park-and-ride lot where Woodside Road intersected Interstate 280. She had a portable transporter unit that she'd told him about but that he hadn't seen in use before. She turned it toward the two of them, and there was a brief flash.

He found himself on a very small road next to a sign that read "Alan Reids Road." Also, the sun was much lower than it had been at midday in California. He was part of a group of eight visitors, who looked, as always, like refugees from a free Cinemax weekend on DirecTV. "Where are we?"

he asked Beth.

"You're at Speargrass Flat, about 15 kilometers northeast of Queenstown," she replied with a smile.

"You mean, in New Zealand?"

"That's right. It's 9:00 a.m. tomorrow here."

"What are we doing here?"

"We are going hang gliding."

The group walked up the road to the entrance of a business. A sign over the entrance announced "Extreme Air Queenstown Paragliding and Hang Gliding."

After an hour of coaching and preparation, Spencer found himself hurtling off a cliff in a tandem hang glider. His instructor was also the owner, a friendly and knowledgeable woman named Lisa. His own harness was below the instructor's, and fear soon gave way to exhilaration as they soared. They had launched just seconds after Beth and her own instructor, and both gliders caught some of the same current to gain a small bit of altitude before gradually easing toward the ground in the valley below. For a moment, Spencer forgot all the pressure and allowed himself to feel the breeze in his hair, and the sensation of traveling very quickly in complete silence. He found himself envying the hawks and eagles that had the privilege of doing this every day.

When they landed, the instructor called to the van waiting to collect them, told her coworkers in the van where they landed, and they were soon on the drive back to where they started, so they could use their own portable transporter without being seen. As they drove back up the hill, Spencer turned to Beth. "Wow, that was genuinely fun."

"Yes, it was quite a thrill. We are amazed at the number of adventure activities that you have."

"Is that a particular interest to you and your friends?"

Beth lowered her voice to avoid being overheard by the driver. "Yes. It's not just the activities. We are not used to feeling emotions this intensely. Our own species has been evolving a bit longer, and we are a bit more analytical. We still have emotions, but our highs aren't as high and our lows aren't as low, as you might put it. It's taken us some time to adjust to the intensity of even normal human daily life. Now we're ramping it up with activities like this."

"Is that why you all have been disappearing on weekends?"

"Yes. We have recently tried whitewater rafting, rock climbing, horseback riding, and now hang gliding. Next, we plan to try skydiving."

"I didn't realize that Earth was such a great tourist destination. That's great. Hey, do you think that other visitors from your home might want to come here to try these adventure sports?"

"Spencer, they would enjoy the sports. But I don't think humans are ready for the natural form our people would take in the absence of genetically converting ourselves to human. That's okay, though, because it turns out that they don't need to come here to experience the thrill."

"How do you mean?"

"We have a technology, a form of communication, that lets us transmit not just the visuals but every aspect of an experience to someone back home. Including the emotional fear and thrill that the sender is experiencing."

"Have you, um, communicated your experiences, often?"

"Yes, I have shared several of my weekend activities with compatriots back home. They absolutely love it. Earth adventure sports are becoming a popular source of entertainment on my world."

"Wait a minute, what about other 'activities' that gets one's heart rate up?"

"No, Spencer, I haven't transmitted anything that has happened without my clothes on. Though I can tell you there would certainly be demand for that. It is often very exciting."

"Thanks. Wait, often? Well, damn. So it's just like the internet. Porn is always the first application. And now, after all my education, I finally have a chance to be a porn star. I believe that would make my television name 'Lee Quail'—taking from my middle name and the street I grew up on."

"Sometimes I find you humans to be confusing."

٦ :: ظ ·ا·

Leah Perera was on a three-way, high-resolution secure video teleconference. There were two windows open on her screen. One contained the image of acting National Security Advisor Russell Carter and the other showed the head of the FBI, a broad-shouldered, blonde-haired, and athletic 50ish woman. It was Carter who had been doing almost all the talking.

"Sir, that story is incredible." Leah was uncharacteristically uncertain about what to say. "This tech guy says there have been extraterrestrials posing as humans and living and working among us for several months, and we believe him?"

"DSAC Perera, you can form your own conclusions. Let me just say that I am willing to accept a nonzero probability that some of what they told us is accurate. And it's consistent with some earlier encounters with unexplained intruders several years ago, and with your reports of advanced technology that makes the visitor house challenging to surveil."

"Sir, let's assume for argument's sake that the story is accurate. What's the contingency plan for this type of scenario? Surely the intelligence types have war-gamed a response for this."

"Officially, there is none. Everyone always assumes there's a group in the Pentagon planning for first contact. In fact, there was a small group in DoD that tracked and investigated reports of advanced threats until 2012, but the guy who ran that group resigned in the fall of 2017 to protest the lack of resources. In March of 2018, a former Deputy Assistant Secretary of Defense wrote a piece in the *Washington Post* decrying the lack of attention. This is all public information. In 2020, the DoD released some evidence of naval aviators sighting extraordinarily advanced aircraft, and then reformed a group under the auspices of Naval Intelligence. But there is no real plan. Think about it; how do you think your reputation would develop and your career would progress if you spent your work time creating contingency plans around an invasion by little green men? How big a prioritization do you think that would get in budget allocations? I mean, we already know the Chinese and Russians and North Koreans mean us harm, so we tend to focus on those threats. Since then, the Pentagon and the rest of DC has had Covid and elections and bigger fish to fry. There is still no plan."

"Sir, you said 'officially' there is no plan. Am I to infer there is an unofficial plan?"

"Leah, this isn't the first time I have been aware of visitors. A story for another time. I have spent my career, my life, getting into a position to have some influence for this type of scenario. I haven't burned my personal capital or credibility advocating for a plan that no one wants. But I have given it some thought. And I am going to need your help. Can I count on you?"

"Yes, sir. Absolutely. What is the objective?"

"My objective is simple. The United States is the most technologically advanced power in the history of the world. If the U.S. can gain exclusive access to more advanced technology, that may be worth pursuing. But if the whole world gains access, that levels the playing field with the Chinese and the Russians and everyone else. And I find that prospect unacceptable."

"I understand, sir. We alone get the technology, or we ensure that no one does."

"That's right. Your boss here has agreed to loan your services to my direction. We will both be paying close attention to you. Stay in touch."

Leah cut the connection. She checked her inbox. She had requested a check of Bureau records from the Central Records System for any mention of strange physical security measures, like a transparent force field preventing entry into a building. There was only one record returned.

Back in 1987, two FBI agents had assisted a representative of the Defense Intelligence Agency in searching a house in Murray Hill, New Jersey, next to Bell Labs. They agents noted an inability to enter the house, which had been noted by their supervisory agent as likely reflecting insufficient competence on their part. Shortly thereafter, the persons of interest who had been in the house were found in an open field attached to nearby New Providence High School, next to some type of pod. The agents' initial use of force had no effect, and the DoD operative had rigged explosives to his own body before he moved within feet of the suspects. The engagement ended with the detonation of those explosives, killing the operative but having no apparent impact on the targets, who were able to leave in a mode of transportation that was poorly described. The name of the DoD operative was listed as Steven Carter, age 38, married with two teenage boys, Christopher and Russell. "Holy crap," she muttered to no one in particular.

CHAPTER 19
Desperado

Being risky is safe, and being safe is risky. (Seth Godin,
Purple Cow)

"YOU WANT TO GO WHERE?" Caitlyn looked pissed. She also looked
lovely, sitting on Zach's couch in black striped yoga pants and a pink
V-neck t-shirt. It was Labor Day, a rare weekday off for Zach. He had convinced Cat to join him in heading 47 miles south for dinner at the Makai
Island Kitchen tiki bar on the Santa Cruz Wharf.

Zach was pacing around his living room, and plowed forward. "I was
thinking it might be interesting to go to their planet."

"Are you listening to yourself? You know, just because you *can* travel
to a dangerous far-off place does not mean it's a good idea. When does this
stop, Zach? For two years, you moped around feeling like a failure. Now
you have some money, you have fame of a sort, and so you need a death
wish too?"

"Look, Cat. I have thought this through. We can't keep these guys a
secret much longer. And everyone is going to have a global meltdown when
it comes out. Someone has to manage that, and I think I'm the only one
who can possibly do it. And I don't think I can do that if I haven't learned
more about what their deal is, including seeing their home. Because no
one will believe they're safe if we don't know more about them. I am not
sure I will even believe it, and if I don't then I can't convince anyone else."

"What makes you think they'll let you see their world?"

"Like everybody else here in the Valley, they have cool technology
and think that makes them better than everyone else. They may not mean
us harm, but they are somewhat condescending. And they underestimate
all of us. If I tell them I need to see their planet to help with their public

118

relations, they'll humor me the way that most big tech CEOs humor the little people."

"It is your death warrant."

"I am sorry you feel that way. Especially because I was kind of hoping I wouldn't have to travel alone."

Caitlyn pulled her knees in to her chest. "No. Fucking. Way."

Zach realized that in his four years of knowing Caitlyn, it was the first time she had ever used a profanity. He guessed that everyone has a limit, and perhaps he had reached hers. He walked over to the couch to hug her, but she had already turned away.

Caitlyn continued. "Zach, first of all, I recognize that, even in the middle of this craziness with the visitors, that you're thinking about me and about us. When I suggested you could be more engaged in our relationship, I wasn't thinking that this engagement would come in the form of accompanying you to another planet—but I get that you're trying. But look, we're not in a space where we are living together and making joint decisions. Even if we were, I wouldn't want to go on some long trip that's likely to get us killed. I didn't even want to go to Africa with you. And I know the visitors look different on their home turf, but it's one thing to know and another to stare at it. Find another intergalactic safari companion. And, I am sorry to say it, but maybe you need to draft a will while you're it." Her words had heat, but he saw tears in her eyes too. "Zach, even after we took a step back—I know you believe in what you're doing and I have wanted to support you. But I didn't sign up for this carnival. I hope you don't die on this trip. But please don't include me in this project with the visitors. I care about you and always will, but I need to live my own life."

Zach found he was unable to speak. Caitlyn got up from his couch, grabbed her purse, and gave him a quick hug. She left in tears. Zach did not move for a long time.

∴ ㄴ ㅓ ㅜ

Zach and Spencer were in the office early the following day, which was unusual for Spencer but increasingly common for Zach. Zach looked into the face of acting National Security Advisor Russell Carter on his computer screen.

Zach was agitated. "You can't be serious. These people traveled across the galaxy to see us and brought technology that is revolutionizing our economy and saving lives every day. And you're talking about treating them like an enemy."

Russell Carter was unfazed. "You said it yourself. Your visitor friends have superior technology and unknown motives, and have been hiding among us for almost a year. Maybe they're friendly, maybe they're not, but we aren't willing to wait passively to find out. And if you hadn't gone native, perhaps you would have the perspective to see that."

"No, you said it yourself. They have superior technology, and they have already said they wouldn't be imprisoned. All you're going to do is treat them badly, piss them off, and make your forecast of their aggressive behavior a self-fulfilling prophecy. If they wanted to do us harm, they would have done it a long time ago, even before I met them."

"If they want to prove they're friendly, to the particular country they have chosen to live in all this time, then they could make a good faith gesture. Your transporter company could sign an exclusive contract with the Department of Defense making us the only customer that can transport multiple people without restrictions on what they carry."

"You want the visitors, and the company, to play favorites. So the U.S. military—and no others—can swoop down on anyone. Come on, Mr. Carter, you should know better. They didn't come here to prop up the existing global power structure, and pushing them to do that is just going to make them more likely to leave."

"Look, Zach. I'm told you studied history at Michigan before going into economics at Texas. You can't introduce extraterrestrials and their revolutionary technology and expect them to be divorced from politics. When Cortez brought germs with him on meeting the Native Americans in 1518, he may not have intended harm. But three million Indigenous people died from smallpox anyway."

"Yes, Mr. Carter, but Cortez brought guns and steel as well as germs. If the locals had attacked him, they would have died sooner. We are the inferior force, and we are the ones with more incentive to play nice. Let me ask another question. Who's driving this line of thinking?"

"This goes all the way to the president."

"Yeah, but I've worked in organizations before. The person who sets the agenda and frames the question for the boss is the one who drives the outcome, and lets the boss think it was her idea. Who is that here?"

"The president picks good people and listens to them. People who know a lot more about confrontation and negotiation with foreign powers than you do."

"Right, so I'm guessing that's you and maybe the chief of staff. And perhaps a couple of generals. Before you start trying to round up our visitors and force them to confront you or leave, you need to let me come back and speak to you. Whether you respect me or not, I *am* the boots on the ground and know the visitors better than anyone in the world. It wouldn't be smart to not use me as a resource. And you guys pride yourselves on being smart."

"Despite your lack of manners or grace, I will take your proposal to the chief of staff. I make no promises." Russell Carter disconnected the line before Zach realized the discussion was over.

Zach turned to Spencer, who had been eating a scone he had picked up from Café Borrone on the way to the office, observing the discussion from off-screen.

"What do you think?" asked Zach.

"I think these are powerful people who aren't in control of what happens, and they're scared. Scared people with power tend to exercise that power."

"But, come on! Even if you're strong, you don't walk into a bar and pick a fight with someone you know is a lot stronger."

"These guys run the biggest economy and biggest military in the history of the world. They can't quite grasp the concept of someone being tougher than they are. They fear it, but they may not believe it until it is proven."

"Well Spence, I really hope you're wrong."

ℾ ¡! ⁓ ⩒

On the following morning of the 4th, as Zach was walking into his office, his cell buzzed. He picked up and heard Spencer's voice: "Hey buddy, we have a problem here. Every one of the visitors has correspondence from

USCIS immigration demanding documentation and birth certificates, and their employers have also been served."

"Damn, Spencer, it looks like you were right about our government exercising its power."

"You know our friends' backgrounds won't hold up."

"Well, the White House already knows where the visitors are from. So this immigration documentation demand must mean either that parts of the government aren't in on the information, or they want a legal pretext to detain our visitor friends. Either way, I think the only way to get ahead of this is to go back to DC."

CHAPTER 20
I Fought the Law

You know what I think? I think that we're all in our private traps, clamped in them, and none of us can ever get out.
(Norman Bates, *Psycho*)

ZACH AND ANDREW FOUND the entrance to the White House West Wing much smoother than Zach and Spencer's earlier visit had been. They had again transported to Union Station (the only point in DC where anyone was allowed to transport) but had a limo waiting for them, which whisked them through the front gate and into a conference room in short order. The White House had asked Andrew how he wanted to be addressed, asking whether he should be referred to as "Ambassador." He responded that he preferred to go by his adopted name, Andrew Fox.

Instead of the perky staffer from the prior visit, Zach and Andrew found Chief of Staff Stanton himself waiting for them, along with Secretary of State Timothy Lee.

"Mr. Randall, Mr. Fox, on behalf of our government please let me welcome you." Secretary Lee reached out his hand.

Andrew was respectful, and seemed to Zach to be completely relaxed. He shook the secretary's hand, and then the chief of staff's (the secretary didn't blink, but the CoS looked visibly alarmed to touch an alien). The CoS was smooth enough to try to cover for his own reaction. "Can we get you, um, gentlemen, something to drink? I understand that you do in fact eat and drink?"

Andrew said, "I do, sir. My body is human. I would be grateful for just a coffee please, black."

Zach asked for a water, and then sat down.

"Gentlemen, we wanted to start with this small group. But in a minute, we would like to join a larger group."

Zach spoke first. "We assumed that might be the case. But just to be certain we're on the same page, Andrew here is coming as an invited guest on his own initiative, and we may leave at any time that he or I deem appropriate."

"Mr. Randall," offered Stanton. "Remember, you are the ones who declined to treat this as an official state visit. Please follow me."

The four of them went down the hall to a much larger room. There were at least twenty people seated at the conference table, half of them in military uniforms. There were also at least ten Secret Service agents standing around the room, trying and failing to look unobtrusive. Once they were seated, another door opened, and President Lynne entered. Zach noticed that everyone else at the table immediately stood. He caught Andrew's eye and they stood a second later.

The president started talking the moment she entered the room. "Mr. Randall, it is good to see you again. Mr. Fox, please let me welcome you to the White House, to our country, and to our world. Though I understand that you may have been here for some time, please know that we would have welcomed you to meet with us at any time."

"Thank you, Madam President," Andrew responded. "We wanted to start relatively unobtrusively. We selected Mr. Randall here, and he has been a gracious host for my small team."

"Mr. Fox," interjected Russell, "with your permission, we do have a few questions about the way in which you have chosen to introduce yourself to our planet, and what your plans are."

"I understand that, Mr. Carter," answered Andrew calmly. "Should I assume from your job title and the fact that you are the one asking that you collectively have concerns about my team's arrival?"

"Sir, my job is to assess potential threats to this country. And, with respect, you must agree that the arrival of a technologically advanced group that keeps itself a secret for months on end has at least the *potential* to represent a security risk."

"I understand why you might view it that way. Which is why we thought it best to establish some time locally before having this discussion. If our intent were hostile, we have had plenty of opportunity to express that. And you are correct that we would have the technological means to do so. The fact that we haven't should by itself be reassuring, should it not?"

"Yes sir, we appreciate that you haven't exhibited any aggressive intent. But we consider your secrecy to be somewhat aggressive in itself, and question why you chose, with no offense intended to Mr. Randall, a relatively less experienced junior venture executive as your point of contact between our two civilizations."

"Mr. Carter, although I understand that this is a momentous occasion for your own civilization, it is not for us. I hope you're not insulted to learn that I am not myself a senior representative of my own civilization. My colleagues and I are much like Mr. Randall."

"But surely you have the blessing of your own leaders for your exploration, don't you?"

"Technically, yes. But our leaders are more like your small-town mayors than your presidents. We did have to request permission, but it is a fairly common bureaucratic process."

Secretary Lee spoke up now. "May I ask, sir, how many civilizations have you met before?"

Andrew turned toward Lee. "A large number. Most of which have moved further into exploring beyond their own world. It is a bit unusual for us to engage with a culture that has only recently left its own gravity well."

"If it is so unusual, why did you choose this time instead of waiting?"

"Because, Mr. Secretary, we see the potential gains from trade. And because my own group would not be allowed to be part of an engagement with more mature cultures."

"And why would you be excluded from meeting with other cultures?"

"Because, Mr. Secretary, I am a student, as is the rest of my team."

"Wait, what?" Now it was Zach's turn to be confused. "What do you mean, you're a student?"

"I have not yet completed my education. I am hoping to become a trade representative to one of the more sophisticated cultures. But as part of my training, I must first start with a simpler one."

"So, you're saying that we are your training wheels?" Stanton had quickly gone from respectful to irritated. Zach guessed that was a short and frequent trip for him.

"Please understand, Mr. Stanton, we mean no offense. Doesn't your president send subordinates to manage relationships with the smallest nations on this planet?"

"Yes, but we are the most powerful nation on this planet, and our president is not in the habit of speaking to junior representatives of *any* partner, ever."

"Well, Tom, I would say that this isn't any partner, now is it?" President Lynne spoke for the first time. "Lucky for me, I had to work as a waitress to get through college, so I have some experience with not being treated as the big kahuna. Though admittedly, not recently. At least, not since the pre-election debates." The president had prevailed in a close contest against an opponent who wasn't known for his tact or diplomacy.

"So, Mr. Fox," continued the president, "you have addressed who you are, and that you come for trade. You haven't said much else about your intentions nor given any assurances that you won't take whatever you want. In short, sir, *are* you a threat to us, and why are you here?"

"Madam President," replied Andrew, "our intentions are to trade. We could in fact simply take what we want, but we are similar enough to many humans to have a working sense of ethics. We are not perfect, and do not pretend to be incapable of unethical behavior—our history is filled with tragedy, perhaps not as much as your own, but enough to be instructive. Suffice it to say, that at this place and at this time, our ethics are prevailing, which may be more than can be said for international relations around this world. In addition, it is easy enough to provide you with technology of enough value to let us buy anything we want from your world. So our intentions are benign. As to why are we here, we have an opportunity to learn, to engage, to trade. Why have humans explored any new spaces as soon as their technology allows it?"

"So Mr. Fox," injected Stanton, "I hear you saying that you have the capability to harm us."

"Mr. Stanton, we have the capability to eliminate all life on this planet, quickly, with zero risk to our own. And we have had the opportunity to do so for some time now. As I already said, the fact that we haven't should be reassuring. You could wage and win a war against any small nation on this world, say, Barbados. Should Barbados harass and question any visiting U.S. citizen because of the potential threat that the U.S. poses to that country? There is nothing I can say to reverse our technological superiority. You can believe we do not intend to exercise it, or not; that is your choice. If you threaten us, or even simply tell us to leave, we will. And we will not return. We would prefer to know now, rather than investing more time and resources into our outpost on this world."

Stanton sat back smugly in his chair. "Mr. Fox, Andrew, I don't think you have been entirely candid with us, and perhaps not with your host Zach either. This isn't the first time your people have visited us, is it?"

"No, it is not."

Zach was stupefied. "Wait, what?"

Andrew looked at Zach. "You asked us if we visitors were turned away, whether we would give humanity a second chance. I told you we would not. That is true, but not the entire truth. We came here in 1987. We assessed this country as having the most advanced technology on your planet, and approached your government directly. We were not received well. One of your officials came to see us and attempted to blow us up. He was not successful at harming us, but we were unable to prevent his attempt from ending his own life. We were horrified at the loss of life, and that team immediately returned to our planet. The team leader was penalized. This occurred before we even had a chance to explain what we could offer your people. Because of that, we made a decision to return this year and take a slower approach to the discussion. So you see, this discussion is already the second chance. Messrs. Stanton and Russell, may I ask how you know about this earlier visit?"

Russell Carter put down his glasses. He was looking not at Andrew, but rather at Zach. "Because my family has a history of government service. And the man who died in your company was my father."

Zach was incredulous. "Wait, so you're telling me—Andrew, is that true?"

"Yes, Zach. When that man attacked the contingent of my people, he posed no threat to them. But that team was unable to protect the attacker and prevent his action from ending his own life."

"This was information I needed to have. You messed up by not telling me."

The president stood up and interrupted him. "Mr. Fox, I find you credible. I would like to believe you—both that you're what you say you are, and that your intentions may be as pure as you indicate, despite the death of Mr. Carter's father. However, the United States is the most powerful nation on this world, and my responsibility to the people of this nation is to maximize their safety. If there is even a 1% chance that you're a threat, and I fail to address it, I will have failed in that responsibility. And we are 0-for-1 in past interaction. I don't have the luxury of basing the safety of our citizens on the fact that I personally find you persuasive. I want you to know that, and also that I am sorry."

With that, the president nodded to her chief of staff and abruptly left the room, flanked on all sides by Secret Service agents. Within seconds, at least twenty armed guards came in through every entrance, and immediately stood between the cabinet members at one end of the conference table, and Andrew and Zach at the opposite end, who suddenly found themselves very much on their own.

Zach found it challenging to speak or to stand. He took a couple of seconds before he could get to his feet. He didn't bother to unclench his fists, and found several agents very suddenly and quietly on the both sides of him at the fringe of his personal space. "You bastards! You planned this all before we even arrived. This was a setup."

Chief of Staff Stanton was already at the doorway, also surrounded by agents. "Mr. Randall, you're free to go, for now. Mr. Fox, with apologies, we are going to have to ask you to come with these men. You should also know that federal agents are serving a search warrant at your rental home in Menlo Park."

PART III

A Voyage to the
Land of the Houyhnhnms

CHAPTER 21
Thunder Road

A bend in the road is not the end of the road—as long as you remember to take the turn. (Joan Lunden, 1998)

"AH CRAP, SPENCER, WHAT are we going to do?" The twin blindsides of Andrew's failure to tell him about the 1987 visit and its consequences, and the White House invitation being a preconceived setup to grab Andrew, left Zach feeling as disoriented as he could remember ever being. His appearance reflected this lack of clarity, as he drove back to Atherton from the Palo Alto station.

"Zach, my question is, what else haven't the visitors told us?"

"Yeah, I'm pissed they did not trust me enough to tell me what happened back in 1987. I still think, though, that they're on the up-and-up about bringing these technologies to truly help us out."

"That may be so, Zach. But I understand better why the national security advisor and the FBI are suspicious. It seems like everyone knows more about what's going on than we do."

"I don't know how to fix it, given that I just got their leader thrown in jail."

"Zach, you did your best, and Andrew knows it. He was prepared for this eventuality, and he knowingly triggered it. He wants to know where the visitors stand on this planet before they invest more. And he already told you he doesn't have to stay detained one second longer than he chooses to."

"At least they said I could visit Andrew. I have to convince him to give me some time before he stages a jail break, and does something drastic like take all the visitors home."

"Positions seem to be getting more dug in, not less. Beth told me that

131

after I convinced them to drop the barriers on their home in the Willows, agents came and trashed the place. Andrew had told them to be ready, and the Feds didn't find anything. They also didn't detain any of the other visitors but it's clear they're prepared to do so. Even if you convince Andrew to give you time, what'll you do with it?"

"I don't exactly know just yet. But I think I know how to gather more information, which might lead to some ideas."

"How are you going to get any more information than we have now?"

"I'm going to take the mother of all road trips."

‖ ⅃ : ⅂

Zach was back at Union Station in Washington, DC for the four-mile cab ride to the naval military prison at Joint Base Anacostia-Bolling. With its location directly across the Potomac from Washington National Airport, it was the closest military prison facility to the capital (in fact, it was inside the District), and also housed the headquarters of the Defense Intelligence Agency. All of which made it a logical place for a high-value detainee. It was an unseasonably warm day in the District, the kind that always made Zach think of baseball.

The check-in process wasn't as bad as Zach would assume for entering a highly secure base holding such a VIP detainee as Andrew. If any of the personnel were wondering why a movie star was being held at a naval prison, they didn't show it.

Zach was ushered through two sets of barred gates, each with a pair of guards. However, the area he eventually reached looked more like a studio apartment—or mid-tier hotel room—than a jail cell. Zach had been briefed that about five years ago, the Navy switched its prisoners from wearing standard utilities to color-coded clothing: pre-trial uniforms were dark brown, and post-trial were tan. Of course, no one had spoken about charges or a trial, and Zach found Andrew wearing the dark brown version of the shirt and trousers, sitting at a small work table.

"Andrew, how are you?"

"About as you would expect, Zach. If you're asking if I have been physically harmed, beyond having my freedom removed and my movement restricted, and being monitored at all times, the answer is no. I have not been directly physically hurt, nor would I allow myself to be."

"What have you been told?"

"I have been told nothing. I have been questioned extensively, asked the same questions repeatedly—I assume to test the consistency of my answers."

"Have you been, um, candid?"

"Yes. I see no reason for secrecy or evasion. When I leave with my team, I think it is important that your authorities know exactly who I was and what was lost."

"Why weren't you open with me from the start about the fact that your race had been here before?"

"That was a different group, and we did not think it was relevant for you to know."

"Well, I was trying to convince some government officials to trust you. And one of them lost his father the last time your people visited. It would have helped to know I was facing that handicap."

"You're correct, Zach. I didn't think that the visit would be remembered by your government now. I am sorry I didn't share that with you."

"Andrew, you must know how sorry I am that this happened. I never would have brought you to a meeting if I had known they already had plans to, um, detain you. But if we're to have any chance at salvaging this situation, we need to be more open with each other."

"I believe that you did not expect me to be detained, Zach. You did raise the possibility, and I agreed to come. It's time to understand whether your society wants our presence and our technology, and I think I have my answer."

"Andrew, there may still be a chance, perhaps only a small one, to work this out. May I ask how long you will allow yourself to remain here?"

"Not long, Zach. I have instructed my team to remain near each other, in Menlo Park, and to make preparations to leave."

"What will happen to the technologies of the companies we've founded?"

"We will leave what is here, but you will find that after our departure, the technologies will no longer work. We cannot leave products when we're not here to ensure their safe manufacture and use. I am sorry to say that the equity valuations of our various companies will go to zero quickly, and your venture fund will have a poor rate of return."

"But I'm not the only one who would lose, am I, Andrew?"

"What do you mean?"

"Andrew, you have been generous with me, and I have gained from being the human to introduce the rest of my world to your advanced technologies. Not just because I've benefited financially, but also because it's the most rewarding work I have ever done, bringing technology to people to actually improve their lives. And because of the chance to represent humanity in meeting—and in becoming friends with—you and your team.

"However, failing to tell me about your people's prior visit isn't the only way that you have failed to be completely open about what you gain from the situation. I've respected your privacy; everything you describe sounds like a trade mission, so while I don't doubt that you have benign intentions, I do sense that your motives aren't entirely altruistic. I have seen no evidence that you buy or export any resources from my planet. I haven't seen you buy or ship oil, or water, or minerals—or anything else for that matter—with the human wealth you've generated. Whatever it is that you find valuable, it doesn't seem to be physical in nature. Now, if you're on the brink of leaving anyway, there's little to lose by telling me what you're really doing here. And perhaps it'll help me find some eleventh-hour solution to our challenge."

"Yes, Zach, you're right. Your planet has no technology of interest, much as if your own United States encountered a tribe of island natives still using rocks and fire as their primary tools. And, while your planet does have resources, it has none that cannot be acquired closer to our home planet less expensively, or synthesized."

"So, does that make you anthropology professors, just here to catalog a primitive culture?"

"We are not anthropologists and we are not teachers, Zach. But your question is still on point."

"How so?"

"We are students, Zach. Business students."

"Seriously?!? So this is a school project?"

"Of a sort."

"Please tell me you're at least graduate school students, and not elementary school children."

Andrew leaned over the table toward Zach. "We don't have a linear concept of education, Zach. Some of us are studying for an early career, some for a third or fourth career. We live much longer than you do, and our careers are chapters in our lives rather than life-long pursuits. We find it educational to pursue trade with distinctly different cultures. We gain the satisfaction of bringing better technologies to cultures like yours. But you're correct that our motives are not selfless, as we gain from seeing things through different lenses. Even if we leave now, this has been a productive project for us, Zach."

"But surely you have gained more than satisfaction and education."

"We have found, just as you have, unexpected opportunity, Zach. One that has made some of my own team reluctant to go, which is the only reason I have remained at this naval base."

"What kind of opportunity?"

〒 ： ·⊩ ⅃

After Andrew finished, Zach drew in a deep breath. "Andrew, I would like to ask if you might give me one week to try to fix this situation."

"Zach, I fail to see what will be different in a week."

"A wise pair of business professors once said, it can be more rewarding to shape the game that you play instead of playing the game you find. I think we need to break out of this dilemma—by making the benefits of continued trade and interaction of our planets more obvious to some of my countrymen."

"And how do you propose to do that?"

"I would like to visit your planet, Andrew. Soon. Can you get me a ride?"

CHAPTER 22
Eastbound and Down

Attacking or fleeing are part of the struggle, being paralyzed by fear is not. (Paolo Coelho)

LEAH PERERA FOUND HERSELF in the now-familiar situation of starting her day on East Coast time, as she listened to the acting national security advisor on her secure video link.

"DSAC Perera, you do remember that our chief objective is to avoid equal access to the visitors' advanced technologies?"

"Yes, sir."

"It's time to take action toward that objective."

"Do you want me to detain the visitors, sir?"

"No, Special Agent, I don't. Arresting them is useless; I believe them when they say they have the power to escape arrest at will. Killing them, even if it were possible, is not advisable when they have the means to retaliate in overwhelming fashion. No, the solution here is to make them stop wanting to be here, to steer things so that they voluntarily choose to withdraw."

"How do we accomplish that?"

"It starts by removing their best friend and spokesperson. We need this Zach Randall out of the picture."

"I'm sorry sir, but I need you to be specific to ensure I don't misunderstand." *And to cover my own ass,* Leah thought, and saw Russell Carter nod as though she had spoken that thought. "Also sir, I have to ask, is this related to what happened in New Jersey in 1987?"

"You've done your homework, Special Agent. You are damn right it's related. I have waited a long time, and worked very hard, to be in a position to act when these bastards returned. I am not about to recuse myself to let anyone else who does not understand what we are up against make decisions. Do you have a problem with that?"

"No sir."

"Then, to be specific, I am directing you, at a minimum, to detain Zach Randall indefinitely. And if there is even the slightest resistance, the use of lethal force against him is authorized. As far as the visitors are concerned, I am not directing you to target them, but I'm not particularly worried about collateral damage. Is that specific enough, DSAC Perera?"

"Yes, sir, it is." As he disconnected, she frowned. She had no intrinsic problem with detaining or even terminating Zach, who had certainly caused enough trouble to warrant the first solution and probably the second as well. But it was clear that Mr. Carter had some kind of personal agenda, and she had some experience with compartmentalized operations gone wrong. When they were brought to light and second-guessed, it was usually the operational person involved who took the hit. In the immediate term, she saw little wiggle room on the directive, though, and saw more upside than downside in gaining favor with someone of Carter's influence. But she was determined to keep her eyes open while capturing Zach Randall, and to keep updating her own risk-reward calculus.

$$\perp \because \, \text{\Large)} \, \dot{\boldsymbol{\exists}}$$

Zach was on his way from his office to his car when his phone rang. He saw that it was Andrew and picked up. Before he could even get a word out, he heard Andrew speaking. "Zach, you're in danger."

"What do you mean?"

"There are multiple federal agents on the way to your position right now."

"How do you know that? You know what, that's not important. So, they're going to arrest me too?"

"They're all wearing bulletproof vests and are more heavily armed than usual. Especially if they just wanted to have a discussion with you, who pose no threat."

"Well, you're right, Andrew, I'm not feeling too threatening right now. Do you have any suggestions?"

"How quickly can you get to the Willows house?"

"It's five miles, it's after rush hour, so maybe 15 minutes."

"That's too long, and the authorities are tracking your person and your car. Zach, I am going to have my team transport you."

"It's no closer to the Palo Alto train station than it is to the house, Andrew."

"No, I am going to transport you directly to the house, in ten seconds."

"I didn't know you could do that, Andrew, especially while you're in jail on the other side of the country and I am in the parking lot at the Rosewood. But if the FBI is tracking me, won't they just adjust their route to go there?"

"You won't be there long, Zach. I think perhaps you may want to move up your trip to my home planet."

It wasn't so long ago that fugitives just fled the county, but I guess we're in a whole new ball game, thought Zach. "Could you at least transport me home for two minutes before transporting to the Willows house? I need to grab a go bag, which I guess will have the side benefit of making the agents waste time driving toward Atherton."

I: ∩ ⁄ ⅃

"Okay, let's run through this again. How long does this trip take?" Zach was trying, and failing, to treat this trip like a long flight, like the time he flew from San Francisco to Dubai in sixteen hours. He had not really gotten his head around the idea of traveling to a distant star system, and accelerating that particular discussion while knowing that armed federal agents were closing in on him left him feeling more than a bit off his game. He was in the back yard of the Willows house with Beth. She had also established a direct link to his earbud so she could communicate when they were separated. Andrew could also communicate, but Beth was the one sending him off in person, and, he had to admit, she had a countenance that made it easy to trust her. "There is no objective answer to that question. At sufficiently high speeds, time can get . . . difficult, especially since our craft changes speed frequently. Some segments will involve near instantaneous transport across tens of light years, other segments will be only slightly faster than your own craft can travel. You won't experience a sensation of speed, but your sense of time may vary significantly over the

138

course of the journey."

Zach had dim flashbacks to a lecture on special relativity in his freshman-year physics course, but not enough to make him any less confused. "So when I get back to Earth, how long will it have been?"

"The round trip would be a little more than a day, plus the time you spend at the other end."

"Will I be able to sleep?"

"We don't see why not, although we don't know exactly how a human will react. Our best estimate is that, if you do sleep, your dreams may be a bit . . . unusual."

"Who would have thought that interstellar travel would treat me the same way tequila does? Who's coming with me?"

"We all have duties here."

"You don't even need a pilot? You're sending me across the galaxy to your home, and none of you are coming?"

"Zach, a pilot isn't necessary. And the expense is not trivial to add occupants for the trip. However, we have anticipated that you may have questions during the course of your journey. We have equipped an instantaneous radio system such that you can speak to me at any time."

"So you have faster-than-light communication as well as travel? Well, Beth, talking on the phone is no substitute for having a good seat-mate on a long flight, but I suppose I will make do."

"Zach, the agents are arriving here. Any other questions you have need to wait until you're en route."

Zach stood in the back yard of the Willows house at the doorway of what he could only describe as a pod, about the size of the Ford van he drove in high school, white and shaped like a football. "Pretty flimsy," he noted to no one in particular. The rational side of his brain said that, if he was traveling thousands of times the speed of light and collided with an object, the size of the vehicle probably wouldn't make a difference. But it would at least be psychologically comforting if the vehicle were a little larger, like perhaps the size of an aircraft carrier instead of a small van. These aliens seemed to pride themselves on their rationality, which struck Zach as vain.

Zach's backpack contained the essentials for any long flight: laptop, water, snacks. As he turned to retrieve it from the lawn next to the pod, he heard a shout and saw several armed men running through the wooden gate into the back yard. Their angry expressions and Sig Sauer 226 hand-guns looked completely out of place amidst the green lawns and trees of suburban Menlo Park. Zach wondered for an instant what the neighbors would think.

Beth and several of the visitors moved to stand between him and the approaching agents. "Get in now, Zach!" Beth shouted at him. He saw smoke coming off the agents' guns and sparks coming off the visitors' bodies, and it took a moment for him to put the two together.

CHAPTER 23
Truckin'

When all's said and done, all roads lead to the same end.
So it's not so much which road you take, as how you take it.
(Charles de Lint, *Greenmantle*)

ZACH'S BRAIN PARSED OUT that the bullets fired by the FBI agents were bouncing off invisible armor of some kind. As it occurred to him that he had no invisible armor of his own, shock gave way to self-preservation and he dove headfirst into the pod. As the door closed, his last image was of the visitors disappearing as they teleported out of the yard, leaving a bunch of grim-faced law enforcement types on their own.

Zach leapt to his feet from the floor of the vehicle and jumped onto a chair in the middle. He looked around and saw that there were no windows. "Shit!" Zach remembered he had an open line to Beth. "Beth! What's happening—are you alright?"

"Yes, Zach, we are fine. We transported only a few blocks away to Willows Oak Park."

"I can't believe they were shooting at you!"

"Zach, they weren't shooting at us. They were shooting at you. We just moved to stand in the way."

Zach sank deeper in the chair as he realized that, of course, she was right. His brain had struggled before that moment to accept the visual input showing that someone was deliberately firing bullets at his own self. He thought that access to advanced technologies would help his career, and also help his prospects with Caitlyn. Now his career was in the tank, he didn't even know how to describe the status of his relationship with Caitlyn, and his own government wanted him dead. It didn't seem like an auspicious foundation for a sudden journey to a distant star. *How did the*

141

incremental decisions I made end up at this point? He determined that self-pity wouldn't make for a productive journey either. His initial question was: why did someone in authority want him dead? It dawned on him that he made a less-formidable enemy than the aliens, and that taking him out of the equation could thwart the visitors' plans without constituting a direct attack. He turned back to the conversation at hand. "Thanks, Beth. That was very . . . considerate."

"We are all wearing fields, and weren't in danger."

"Am I in danger here in the pod, or do you have a field on it too?"

"We do have a field on the vehicle, Zach. But you aren't in danger anyway."

"Why not, if they're still shooting?"

"Because you're already well beyond your own solar system."

Zach managed to fish out an empty plastic bag from his backpack before he threw up. He turned his thoughts quickly to other matters. "Beth, I always assumed there would be a window, or a porthole, on this ride. Is there a way to see outside?"

"Yes, Zach, we can make your vessel entirely transparent if you want."

"Well that would make me feel a bit, ah, vulnerable. How about windows in the front and back?"

"Certainly, but for most of your journey the view won't make much sense. We can adapt your view to show you what are essentially 'snapshots' of what's outside. Would you like us to do that?"

"Yes, that sounds good. Could we start now?" Immediately, the front and back of the vehicle became windows. The view showed darkness, except for a faint point of light in the rear window. Over the course of the next several hours, he couldn't tell how much time had elapsed, or how much he slept. He felt vaguely disoriented, to a degree that varied over time without overt explanation. The windows showed pitch black most of the time. For a brief moment, however, the craft slowed down and his view was filled with light and the most beautiful collection of colors he had ever seen—deep blues and purples and oranges—for an instant before returning to the black of space. He could see stars visibly changing their orientation. He wished he had paid more attention in his one astronomy class at Michigan. Beth had given him the ability to dial up the magnification of the window, apparently without much limit, which allowed him to get a closer look at stars he couldn't identify.

"Beth, could you transmit to me some kind of travel guide with basic facts about your home planet, and about your people?"

"We don't have such a guide prepared. What did you have in mind?"

"For starters, what do you call your planet?" Zach was mildly amused as he thought, *How is it I never asked them this before?*

"There is no translation for the name; it's closest simply to the term for 'home.'"

"Okay, I'm going to call it Atlas," Zach responded, thinking of the Titan god who holds up the heavens in Earth's ancient mythology. "Next, could you go to Wikipedia and find the entry for Earth, and use that as a template for similar information about your planet? You could include size, gravity, atmospheric composition. Then provide some cultural references—perhaps you could find the entry for Russia on Wikipedia and use that as an example. Most importantly, could you provide photos of what you all look like in your natural habitat, so I can try to get used to the imagery?"

"Okay, Zach. I'll have Vonne put it together and transmit it to your phone."

"Thanks." Zach resisted the urge to bombard Beth with more questions. Instead, he turned to thinking about what to say upon arriving at the home of the first intelligent civilization that mankind had yet encountered. He'd had his public relations VP write up a speech, but decided it was too lofty and inauthentic for him. At the same time, he held a deep respect for Neil Armstrong's short-but-powerful words upon stepping onto the moon in 1969: "That's one small step for a man, one giant leap for mankind." He struggled to pull together the message he wanted to convey to his hosts that would also convey to people back home the meaning of the event. He jotted a few notes during the travel, and wished he felt more cognitively functional. Getting shot at and leaving the solar system in a couple of seconds really seemed to impact his ability to focus. Despite the length of time he had spent around Beth and Vonne, he still found it incongruous to be coached by what appeared to be two Hollywood actresses on what to expect when he landed 163,000 light years away from where every other human in history had ever been.

He felt afraid. Not of dying per se, but of the consequence of dying—that he might forever remain so inconceivably far away from everyone who had ever cared about him. He remembered a trip he had taken to Victoria Falls in Zimbabwe, where he had almost drowned while whitewater rafting with some daredevil river guides from New Zealand. In that moment, his clearest thought wasn't fear of dying, but rather the loneliness at the thought of dying so far from home. Now the concept of being in another country seemed like being across the street from his house. *Distance is all relative*, he supposed.

He was awakened from a brief doze by the sound of Beth's voice. "Zach, you have slowed down and will land in approximately 30 of your minutes. You will be met by a representative of our government."

As his craft approached the planet, Zach lacked a sense of scale but sensed that the planet was significantly larger than Earth. He checked the data that Vonne had sent to his phone screen, which indicated that the planet was 2.3 times the size of Earth and with a greater density, creating a crushing gravity of almost four times normal. (*"Normal"* . . . *what is "normal" in my life anymore?* thought Zach, distractedly.) The atmosphere did have nitrogen and oxygen, but in smaller percentages than Earth, with a higher presence of carbon dioxide, methane, and ammonia—clearly a toxic brew for an unprotected human. The planet had a lighter-blue tinge than Earth did in those "Blue Marble" photos he'd become accustomed to. Spencer had explained to Zach that the Earth's blue appearance came from oceans reflecting more of the blue part of sunlight than other parts, and that the depth of the oceans created a deeper shade of blue. Zach's best guess was that the lighter blue hue of this planet might mean the existence of water, but perhaps at less depth. The rotation of the planet was about 50 hours, which was going to make for some long days and nights. Vonne had helpfully included notes to reassure Zach that both the gravity and atmosphere would be locally managed to match Earth-normal where he was to spend his time. He also saw that there was only one continent-sized land mass, with a scattering of islands. He looked for the lights that he would see on Earth, but all of the continent was currently in very bright daylight.

As the craft descended through atmosphere, Zach's view became blocked by cloud cover. Just before landing, the clouds cleared and he had a vivid view of a landing platform. It was unmistakably a clear flat space, but it was above the ground on a base that looked vaguely reminiscent of the houses built by Antoni Gaudí in Barcelona, with a minimum of right angles. It was off, but not as far off as he would have expected, which seemed disconcerting in itself. He was reminded of the university year he had spent in England, where many referred to the culture shock with the expression "two countries separated by a common language."

After the craft settled gently to the platform, Zach stood and waited for the doors to open.

The doors opened, and Zach found himself looking at a single individual, dressed in robes. The being had six limbs, three of which were used to stand upright, much like the legs of a camera tripod. These legs bent in the middle, but it appeared that they could bend both inward and outward for increased agility. This person also had three arms coming from a cylindrical torso, roughly equally spaced around the circle, with only two of the arms visible from the direction facing Zach. The form was vaguely humanoid shaped, though the legs were too long relative to the torso and the head looked like a hybrid between a horse and an octopus. Several colors shifted and flowed rapidly across the head, including a luminescent green and purple with darker orange and black. The body itself also had shifting colors, primarily brown and purple, more muted than those on the head. The head had two eyes, also equally spaced around its circumference, almost like a bird and much further apart than Zach was used to seeing. There was a single hole that could be described as either a nose or mouth, or a combination of the two. The skin had a leathery-looking texture.

Altogether, each individual element made some sense, but they came together with a strong sense of other-ness. Zach worked to submerge his sense of wrong-ness, and did better focusing on individual parts of the alien body than trying to interpret the overall gestalt of its form. There was an undeniable beauty to the shifting colors. The individual had a necklace of thin metal that also shifted colors. The alien made no sound itself, though the colors of its face shifted more rapidly, and a speaker in the necklace said in perfect English, "Welcome to our home planet. You may refer to me as Matthew. Would you please accompany me?"

Vonne's travel guide had explained that all citizens rotated into and out of public service roles for a set percentage of their working career, and the planet had one overall manager who acted more like a CEO than a ruler. These administrators made significant decisions for the people and the planet—but without controversy, as the clear majority of citizens already agreed with the decision beforehand. Zach was not sure if this represented a stifling level of uniformity, a high level of rational decision-making, or political apathy—or perhaps a little of all three.

Zach found it unsettling to be facing just a single individual here, as though his arrival wasn't all that significant. He also was a bit befuddled on whether to assign a male or female or neutral gender to the alien. Beth's travel guide had been a bit vague on the topics of reproduction and gender. He didn't want to refer to the alien as "it," but also wasn't sure whether to use human gender-neutral pronouns like "zhe." He decided, more for convenience than accuracy, to adopt a male pronoun simply because the alien had used a human name that was typically male. He turned toward Matthew. "Thank you for your greeting. I greet you as well. Are you this planet's chief administrator?"

"No, I am not. I am sure you understand that our administrator's duties keep him fully occupied. I have just begun my first service in administration, and I was tasked with meeting you."

"Matthew, I would like to say a few words."

"That is your prerogative. I would ask only that we move indoors within ten of your minutes."

"People of Atlas—um, person of Atlas. My name is Zach Randall, and I am a human from the planet we call Earth. I come to you in the spirit of fraternity among sentient beings, as a representative of the people of Earth. Although I haven't yet notified the leaders of the governments of my home world of this trip, I am confident that they would send their own greetings to you as well. It is my personal honor to meet you. My human friends and I consider this contact with the first sentient species from a planet other than our own to be a momentous event in our human history, one that will be long remembered.

"We appreciate and understand that we are not as technologically advanced as you, and come to you wishing to be neither supplicants nor conquerors, in the hopes that we might achieve mutual respect and friendship. I look forward to getting to understand more about your species and world, so that I might share that knowledge with other humans, and in so doing serve as a bridge between our two worlds and cultures. Thank you for providing me, and humanity, with this unprecedented opportunity."

Matthew appeared unmoved. "If you are finished, please come with me. Our workday is scheduled to end shortly, and I will take you to your evening quarters."

And with that, Matthew turned and walked briskly toward the building. Zach was taken aback. He had the privilege of being the central figure in one of the most significant moments in the history of the human race, and his host was an octopus-horse-faced government intern who apparently had dinner plans that ranked higher than first contact with humanity. Perhaps they met new species literally every day. Even so, the lack of respect, while possibly unintended, reminded Zach of those 10:00 a.m. Monday meetings with his former boss. He thought he might have preferred combat; at least battle involved some level of attention and recognition. Zach recalled reading somewhere that the opposite of love is not hate, it is indifference. And he wondered how to engage with an entire planet filled with indifferent beings. At least the horse-octopus combination didn't trigger the fears of his primitive brain as much as some of the images of aliens that science fiction movies had conjured—heavy on insect and reptile analogs—which would have required significant effort to avoid some irrational revulsion.

Matthew led Zach to a building, and from there to a room. Matthew, or rather his necklace, said, "We have been briefed by our colleagues who have spent time on your world, both about the needs of your species and about you as an individual. We measured your sleep and food consumption on your trip, and we calculate that you will want rest and sustenance. We have modeled this room to approximately match the size and layout of your own dwelling. We will leave you to yourself for nine of your hours. If you wish for anything that isn't here, please simply speak out and I will ensure that it is brought to you. We will then plan to meet with you and have an orientation discussion."

After he left, Zach found a plate of a Jell-O-like substance with a note in English stating that it had all the protein and vitamins contained in one of his typical dinners. He even found a small bottle simply labeled "wine," and found it approximated at least a middling red blend, though he doubted it would make Napa worry about the competition. He barely

33333333333333333333333333333333333333333333333333 stop

made it to the platform bed before falling asleep. He didn't dream, that he could tell. It seemed like only an instant later that he heard a voice informing him of his meeting in 30 minutes.

CHAPTER 24
Back in Time

If you want to be a legend you have to fight with legends.
(Aleksei Oleinik)

EXACTLY 29 MINUTES AFTER his wakeup call, Zach stood by the door to his dwelling. A minute later it opened to Matthew standing in the hallway. "Mr. Randall, please accompany me to our meeting place."

"By all means, Matthew. Thank you for walking with me, and for my food and drink and sleep. You seem to know a lot about human physiology."

"We made the representatives to your planet genetically human before sending them, and we have stayed in contact with them. So, yes, we understand your physical needs. We have arranged for the air and gravity anywhere within one foot of your body to match that of your own home world."

"If I were to come within one foot of you or your colleagues, would it be harmful for you?"

"No. Our physiology is adaptable to a wide range of atmospheric conditions, and so it is easier for us to adjust to your narrow range of air composition than for you to adapt to the local norm." Zach wasn't sure if he had just been called a wimp, but he was impressed that it was apparently trivial to change the atmosphere around him to the mixture of 78% nitrogen and 21% oxygen that had been keeping humans alive for millennia, not to mention changing *gravity*.

Matthew continued, "My colleague that you call Beth asked me to demonstrate something that makes your species particularly interesting to those on my world." Matthew gestured toward a transparent booth containing a chair surrounded by what looked like a 360-degree screen.

"Please have a seat."

Zach sat in the booth. "What is the purpose of this? Is it some kind of video screen?"

"It has a similar purpose. It creates the impression of being somewhere else. But it goes beyond simply providing visual and audio input—instead it enables you to actually share the full experience and emotional reaction of the individual initiating the broadcast."

"I don't think I understand."

"I think a demonstration will make it clearer than a description can. Please prepare for an experience from your own homeworld, in real time. We will start with something familiar for you."

As Zach settled into his chair, he found he was instantly transported to an entirely different place. He looked around to discover that he was sitting in a roller coaster. It looked familiar, and he recognized it as the Top Thrill Dragster at Cedar Point in Ohio, where he had made the three-hour drive from Detroit on "senior skip day" in high school. He could see the park all around him, and he could also hear the sounds of others on the ride, feel a slight breeze in his hair, and smell a hint of cotton candy. It was a cool but sunny and humid fall day. He was somehow, impossibly, *there* in Ohio.

∷ ⊥ ∴ ⅃

Deputy Special Agent in Charge Leah Perera wasn't easily flustered. But all of this was outside her experience: having an unarmed suspect, trapped in a suburban backyard, manage to escape the aggressive attempts of multiple agents to kill or capture him, and to do so in a craft that lacked even the basic aerodynamic shape to operate, much less move faster than anything she had ever seen or thought possible. Not to mention the others in that backyard, with some kind of bulletproof vest—no, *field*—forming a living shield for the suspect and then just vanishing. She didn't even know how to write up her report. In the past, she'd always told the truth, and had a certain knack for telling that version of the truth that put her in the best light. Now, her interest in documenting the record for future use was tempered. She'd seen how the careers of other people in government had been stalled by their reports of unidentified aerial phenomena, and her career remained extremely important to her.

She went back to the sparse records of the 1987 incident that had cost DoD operative Steven Carter his life. Of the two other agents involved, one had retired in 2004 and passed away in 2021. The other had been pretty young at the time, and normally would have retired by now—mandatory retirement for FBI agents happened at age 57—but Israel Wenzel, according to the files, had that deadline waived; he was actually still on payroll and working in San Diego.

She called his office and introduced herself, and mentioned her interest in the 1987 incident.

"What is it with you people?!?" She had to move the phone further from her ear. "For years no one wanted to hear about it. I was told to keep quiet, and I did. And now everyone wants to revisit that day. I think you had it right the first time."

"Wait, Agent Wenzel. This is important. First, who wants to revisit that day?"

"For over 25 years, no one at all. Then DoD Intelligence wanted to hear about it in 2012, and Naval Intelligence in 2022. Then crickets again. That damn op is why I never got past GS-12 salary grade after over 35 years' service."

"If you're so forgotten, why did the brass waive your retirement age?"

"They just want to torture me some more. And keep me available in case this new group from Naval Intelligence decides to get serious. I'll be out in two years, and I have a connection to join a private group in Encinitas, and I am not doing anything in the meantime to mess with my pension."

"Look, I'm calling because I had a similar experience, watching some kind of football-shaped craft leave the ground at an impossible rate of speed, and it's possible that craft was built by the same people that you saw in New Jersey. I don't need you to say anything official. Your record says you're reliable; can you help out a fellow agent?"

"If the craft is gone, what can you do now anyway?"

"I have reason to think it's coming back, very soon. Can you tell me its habits and any vulnerabilities?"

"Ms. Perera, you ever listen to Jim Croce?"

"Can we please stay on the topic at hand?"

"Jim sang 'you don't tug on Superman's cape, you don't spit into the wind, you don't pull the mask off that old Lone Ranger.' You know what I'm saying?"

"That's not very helpful."

"Whoever these travelers are, the ones I saw didn't indicate hostile intent. I am actually helping you when I suggest you not give them reason to have any. This isn't a fight that can be won as far as I can tell. Steven Carter tried to attack them and blew his own self up. And I thank God they didn't see fit to teach us a lesson, because in their shoes, my own FBI certainly would have. And that's all I can offer you."

"Agent Wenzel, we don't get paid to walk away from threats." *Or promoted*, she added to herself. But Wenzel had already disconnected.

CHAPTER 25
Can't Find My Way Home

Coming back to where you started is not the same as never leaving. (Terry Pratchett, *A Hat Full of Sky*)

ZACH HEARD THE VOICE of the visitor Thomas (a.k.a. Andrew Thomas McCarthy circa 1985) say, "Hello Zach. Please let me assure you that you have not actually left the booth next to Matthew. I am broadcasting to you in real time from an amusement park in the American Midwest. I hope you enjoy this demonstration."

A moment later, the hydraulic launch system accelerated the roller coaster from a dead stop to 120 miles per hour in less than four seconds, and it climbed up the tower. He felt the sheer adrenaline terror, the wind in his face as the car rocketed up the tower, and then the *whoosh* and free fall 90 degrees down the other side as the impossible g-force on his body constricted his field of vision to a pinprick. His mouth was open but no sound came out. Within 30 seconds, the car had come back to a stop. His heart was still racing. He heard Thomas' voice say, "Beth asked Matthew and me to provide this demonstration. I hope you found it enjoyable. It is amazing how these human bodies react to perceived danger, even when we know intellectually that the actual danger is remote. Humans are fortunate to be capable of such experiences."

The booth turned transparent again, and the sounds and smells and touch of Ohio evaporated. Zach "returned" to his booth on a far-away planet. His heart continued to race. He turned toward Matthew, and re-experienced the shock of how utterly alien it was to be in this environment and around Matthew. He felt shaky. "That was, um, remarkable. Can you clarify what just happened?"

"You experienced what you call a roller-coaster ride. Actually,

Thomas rode the roller coaster, and he shared the experience with you. Completely. You did not have access to his thoughts, but his senses became your senses, and you saw and heard and felt exactly what he did. In real-time; this was no recording."

Matthew started walking again, and Zach fell into step with him as his heart slowly returned to a more normal state. "Can this be recorded?"

"No. And it cannot be shared with more than one individual or it becomes diluted, essentially, to a video-and-audio-only transmission like your television. These experiences are one-to-one. And quite popular among our people; the visitors to your planet have a queue of requests to share adventure activities. As part of my orientation to your people, I have tried it myself."

"What, Matthew, you rode the roller coaster?"

"No, I shared the experience of skydiving in your California. I found it . . . exciting. Also unusual and somewhat unsettling. I had never previously had my sense of reason clouded by fear or excitement." The two of them walked past the landing site and over to some chairs. Zach thought he was outside, but upon closer inspection realized that there was a transparent roof and walls that created the appearance of open air with the predictability of being indoors.

Matthew switched gears. "Are we ready to begin our discussion of more serious issues?"

I guess we're done with small talk, thought Zach, but responded, "Yes, thank you. Matthew, are you caught up on recent events with your representatives on Earth?"

"Yes, I am. I understand that your people have detained our team coordinator. And that he has permitted his movement to be restricted. And that he has already explained to you that his willingness to remain on your planet under those conditions is limited. Do you have the authority to release him?"

"Unfortunately, no. Those who do have that authority are fearful. Human motivation, particularly around political leadership, is more slanted toward avoiding risk than pursuing opportunity. I hope to show our political leaders that the risk is lower and the opportunity greater than they currently realize. I am hoping for your help to do that. You certainly don't owe it to me, but I traveled here in the hopes that you might be willing to discuss it."

"What is the benefit of more discussion? Your leaders can make their decision."

"First, because it's the initial opportunity that anyone from my planet has ever had to visit another planet. I am awed and honored to have this chance to learn more about you, since you already know so much about my people. And second and more to your point, because I'm hoping that we might find a solution that avoids your team leaving Earth. Earth has already benefited from the technologies that your colleagues have provided, and has much more to benefit from engagement with you."

"We gave you humans a chance to partner with us four of your decades ago. You declined. This was already your second chance."

"Why? Andrew said you don't give more than one chance. Why did you make an exception for us?"

"It took some time for us to agree to this exception. We are accustomed to consensus, and each decision we have made regarding your planet has challenged our ability to achieve such consensus. In this case, we learned that we may have inadvertently contributed to a new danger to your people, and so decided that an exception was warranted."

"What danger?"

"Do you think that your species and mine are the only two in the universe?"

Zach's mind reeled. "Matthew, I am still trying to wrap my brain around contact with one new species outside of my own. But to answer your question, yes, I understand that you have visited other worlds."

"We have made contact with many civilizations, and are aware of many more who have not yet developed sufficiently to warrant contact. Several of my colleagues believe that you're in that category, and that it was too early."

"We would like to meet others, and learn from them. Will you introduce any of them to Earth?"

"Your people and leaders have not been up to the task of accepting or welcoming one new species. You clearly are not ready for others. And we would not presume to speak for other species; it is up to them, and to you, whether to meet."

"Yeah, in my line of work we call that dual opt-in. You don't introduce two people unless both agree ahead of time, so that you don't introduce unwelcome new people to your own contacts. Never thought of it in galactic terms before, though. If you aren't going to introduce us, then why are you telling me this?"

"Because some of these other races are not as noninterventionist as we are. And some pay attention to where we go. It appears that a particularly hostile race observed our first trip to Earth."

Zach's hair stood up on end, and he lost his breath. "So are you saying that humans' next interaction will be with a hostile species?"

"Yes, that is likely. And they're almost as advanced technologically as we are. Your planet's chance of surviving the interaction is . . . low."

Zach barely pushed down the urge to vomit. He drew in a long breath as he felt a cold fury build. "Your first trip was four decades ago. And you're just now telling us?!?"

Matthew was either unaware or unimpressed by Zach's change in tone. "We did not want your leaders to welcome us only so we could fend off another threat. Andrew did not withhold this information from you; we did not share this information with Andrew. We wanted to determine your genuine response to engagement with an advanced but non-threatening race like ours."

"Wait, so you're just going to leave us to this hostile race?"

"We already intervened to help, by giving you a second opportunity to embrace a relationship with us."

"A trade relationship is a lot different than getting us killed!"

"Yes, it is regrettable that we caused the other race to be aware of yours. We gave you a second chance. We are not aggressive, but also we do not do what you humans would call 'pro bono work.' It would be expensive for us to protect your world, and there is little upside to us for doing so. We do regret the situation."

Zach's mind reeled. He had considered the visitors to be benign. But now he saw that their lack of explicit hostility didn't preclude a callous indifference to the fate of humanity. He was angry at this bureaucrat—who spoke of the extinction of the human race as some kind of bad day at the office—and also at himself for anthropomorphizing the visitors. Just because the Atlas natives who visited Earth took human form didn't mean they thought like humans; their celebrity faces made it so easy to forget that. Or perhaps the visitors were in fact behaving like humans, he realized with a start, thinking about the various times that superpower nations brought unintended consequences to weaker countries and simply walked away if there was no overriding strategic interest in helping them out.

He tamped down his anger, realizing that it was getting in the way of finding a solution; screaming seemed unlikely to convince Matthew to be helpful. He bizarrely thought of a phone call with an airline back in the time of Covid when he tried to convince an underpaid ticket agent to refund the charges for flights he could no longer take; that had not gone well, either. The stakes here, as well as his anger levels, were considerably higher. He knew he had to regain control over his emotions. This was no longer about his career or his life, but about the life of every single person on Earth. He didn't let himself think about the weight of responsibility, as he was sure it would crush him. Instead, he tried to adopt the attitude from his high school debate competitions, which involved persuading a judge of a point of view.

"Matthew, you say you have the capability to protect Earth from a hostile invasion, which you admit you triggered through your own carelessness, but that you find it too expensive? Is that accurate?"

"What you say is perhaps oversimplified, but the gist is not inaccurate."

"You feel no moral obligation to fix the vulnerability that your first trip created?"

"We do not threaten you. We regret that another race may do so. We took the unusual action of providing your leaders with a second opportunity to invite us to start a relationship."

"Without telling us the implications of saying no!"

"It is not a genuine relationship if it starts merely to avoid a threat."

"In my experience, that's how a lot of relationships start. So, you don't feel a moral obligation to help us; if we could pay you, would you consider shielding us from the consequences of your carelessness?"

"How is it that you could pay us?"

┊ ⅃ ⅀ ⅂

Only four hours later, Zach got in the vehicle for the return trip to Earth. He found it a lot less nerve-wracking than the outbound trip, though still not exactly a normal commute. They had given him the instantaneous phone connection back to Earth, where Beth and Spencer were on the line.

"Spencer, I think we need to publicize my arrival."

"Zach, while I'm sure our PR department can get some reporters to return our calls, most of our contacts are business reporters on the Silicon Valley beat. And none of them will believe that a venture capitalist is about to land after a short vacation to a galaxy in the Large Magellanic Cloud."

"First, smartass, it was a business trip, not a vacation. Second, Beth can control this vehicle. I want to ask her to remove its stealth so that it can be seen coming, and slow it down substantially when it enters our solar system. And tell both our friends at NSA and amateur astronomers exactly where to look. So the whole world can see me coming."

"You want to blow the visitors' cover?"

"It's all but blown already, plus we have nothing to lose. If they're going to leave anyway, we can take control of events out of the government's hands. It's time that we do less reacting and more directing."

"Okay, Zach. But they may simply start shooting when you arrive."

"Oh, I think I can probably assume the vehicle isn't easily harmed. Beth?"

"That is correct."

Spencer cut back in. "What about when you exit the vehicle? Are you forgetting that they shot at you when you left for your little trip?"

"No Spence, but I'm hoping that when I reveal the visitors' presence, there will no longer be a reason to keep me quiet."

"Zach, you're giving our federal agents a lot of credit there. And you're also giving the public a lot of credit. Have you thought about just how much people are going to freak out when we tell them that we have been hosting extraterrestrials for almost a year?"

"Yes, in fact I'm counting on it. But Spencer, I suggest you not tell them that you're dating one."

Spencer ignored the jibe. *He must be stressed, Zach thought. Hell, I must be stressed too.* Instead Spencer asked, "Where do you want to land?"

"I was thinking of making it easy for the media. First, when I enter the solar system tomorrow and slow down, I plan to start streaming video through this portal—and I'm going to send you footage from my stay on Atlas—and you can share that with the media. Then, why don't you ask Beth to land this thing on the front lawn of CNN's headquarters in Atlanta? And, as a courtesy, let's first ask our friend and lawyer Mr. Yakoboski at Hermes Air to let the Air Force and the FAA know that I'm coming before they learn it from the news outlets."

Zach continued, "There is another thing you need to know: with no offense intended to Beth, just because the Atlasians aren't our enemies doesn't mean they're our friends."

Beth responded first. "I take no offense, Zach, and I don't disagree."

Spencer added, "I consider it progress that you recognize that. You've had a tendency from the beginning to assume good intentions. Just because they didn't come in shooting doesn't mean they're always looking out for our best interests."

"I get it, and I think you were trying to say that at the very beginning of all of this. But now I know that we aren't just playing for the lives of those with curable diseases, but rather with the lives of everyone on Earth." Zach explained what he had learned about a second alien race and their hostile intentions. Zach had labeled this second race the Gozerians (although Atlas was from Greek mythology, he thought it best to spread the mythology around, so he followed the lead of *Ghostbusters* in this label for the bad guys, drawing on Mesopotamian mythology circa 6000 BCE).

Beth spoke first. "Zach, I want you to know that, while I am aware of this unpleasant race that you refer to, I was unaware that they were made aware of the existence and location of Earth. I am sorry to learn this."

Spencer was less circumspect. "Holy shit, Zach. I don't even know what to say. How did we get from pheromone perfume to . . . here? Are we going to tell everyone about that?"

"I think we should start just with telling people about the friendly aliens, before we mention the unfriendly ones. There's only so much people can absorb at once."

"Yeah, no doubt, Zach. I am one of those people."

$$\text{⅃ ⁻ ‖ ⅈ}$$

Because of Zach's request to slow down upon entering the solar system, his return trip took longer. He made it the first 99% of the way in the same

11 hours that the outbound trip had taken, but then found himself outside the orbit of Uranus moving at a much slower speed, one that would take about 12 hours to cover the last two billion miles to Earth. Still, he figured that traveling at over 160 million miles per hour was bound to attract some attention; he asked Beth to it slow down even more so that it'd take him a full hour to go the final 239,000 miles from the moon's orbit to Atlanta.

He found himself wishing he had packed more formal clothes for the trip, but realized that he looked like exactly what he was: a businessman on a redeye flight who was wearing clothes he could comfortably sleep in. He was, however, apparently not upscale enough to warrant a shower and a hot meal before his first meeting at the destination.

Spencer and Beth were able to pipe some news feeds to him through their portal, and he was able to watch them on his standard smartphone. For the first few hours, there was nothing unusual; evidently it was taking Spencer a while to convince any media outlet that a venture capitalist was inbound from outer space. So Spencer had settled for announcing a news conference from the investor who had brought the world several revolutionary products. And Spencer also spread the word to governments, universities and amateur astronomers exactly where to look for the intergalactic Acela version of a spacecraft. When multiple observers found what appeared to be a small comet streaking directly toward Earth at an unusually high speed, disbelief turned to alarm, and those same media outlets turned to Spencer after all.

Spencer worked very hard to convince the media, and then Russell Carter, that the fast-approaching object contained Zach, and that Zach had no plans to slam into the Earth at his current speed. Although the asteroid that killed the dinosaurs had been larger than Zach's vehicle, that asteroid had been traveling at a leisurely 45,000 miles per hour. Zach's speed, even slowed down to make his trajectory easy to track, would make that asteroid seem like a pebble softly tossed into a pond. It would also have made Zach distinctly the first casualty, followed very soon thereafter by all other living things on Earth.

After some discussion, Spencer and Zach agreed to wait on releasing the footage from his stay on the visitors' home planet in order to space out the doses of shock they were asking people to absorb. They did tell the media that Zach was returning to Earth from a trip to space in a fast vehicle. Several stories focused on whether Zach was planning to outcompete Richard Branson's Virgin Galactic and those trips to space provided by Elon Musk and Jeff Bezos. Zach wasn't a fan of Musk, but thought that at least Musk's spaceship wasn't as phallic-looking as Bezos's, which bordered on the uncomfortable.

As he entered the atmosphere, Zach found it unsettling that he didn't slow down. His intuition was based on chemical rockets producing thrust, which require as much time to decelerate as they take to accelerate. While Zach intellectually understood that the physics had to be different for this particular vehicle, his lizard brain still expected to go splat. Zach started to relax when the vehicle finally did slow down at about 40,000 feet, until he saw a rather large collection of fighter jets circling over his intended landing zone. Spencer had told him there were at least three Air Force bases in Georgia (Moody, Robins, and Dobbins), and he suspected the Air Force may have been willing to bring in planes from other states as well.

He reminded himself of the arguments for why the Air Force planes would probably not fire on him. He also reminded himself that if they did, the visitor technology would *probably* protect him, but *probably* didn't seem like enough right now. He was unused to taking on any military folks as a potential opposing force, much less at least ten U.S. F-22 fighter jets. He had always wanted to fly in one, and realized with a jolt that getting encircled by many in a decidedly unfriendly dynamic was arguably an even more unique flight story, though he harbored serious doubts regarding whether he had "the right stuff" of the other pioneers in flight.

As Zach peered at the space between himself and the ground, he noticed that two of the fighter jets were climbing toward him, closing the distance rapidly. He saw a bright flash emanate from each jet. Before he could even interpret that visual information, he saw a visual display appear in front of him with two dots quickly approaching his own craft. His craft abruptly lost all downward velocity and moved horizontally—at almost a right angle—very quickly. He had already learned that he was insulated from gravitational force, so wasn't quite as surprised that sudden changes in vector didn't flatten him into goo against one side of his comfortable form-fitting chair, as he would have previously expected. The display showed that the narrowing distance between his craft and the missiles slowed, and then began to increase. After a few seconds, the missiles appeared to stop accelerating, and then became bright flashes as they self-destructed.

"Holy shit—they're shooting at me!" Zach shouted. Again . . . and now with way bigger bullets, he added silently to himself.

CHAPTER 26
Danger Zone

The media is the most powerful entity on earth . . . they
control the minds of the masses. (The Autobiography of
Malcolm X, 1965)

LEAH WASN'T A FAN of video conferences. She preferred to just hear the
brass in DC without having to make herself presentable and maintain
eye contact while speaking. She did believe there were times when video
might be useful, but right now her presentability was the last thing on her
and everyone else's mind. Russell Carter was unhappy about Zach's public
return.

She looked directly at the camera to create the impression of eye contact. "Sir, we know where he's landing, and we know it's a foreign aircraft
violating our airspace. Can't the Air Force eliminate the threat?"

"That is Plan A, Ms. Perera, which I just discussed with General
Heathfield in Colorado Springs. But we need to prepare for contingencies.
If he makes it out of the craft, I need you to take him out."

"Sir, he is likely to be on worldwide live TV before his craft even
lands. Do you want us to take aggressive action during a televised event?"

The national security advisor took off his horn-rimmed glasses and
peered directly into the camera on his computer. "I want you to find a way
to get it done, Leah. I don't want him telling stories about these visitors
and trying to make anyone sympathetic toward them."

"I understand, sir."

¡! ȧ :: ꓘ

Lieutenant Peggy Nelson had almost managed to put the inbound meteor
incident from January out of her mind when she found herself once again

facing the general in charge of NORAD. General Heathfield had just completed a discussion with Space Operations Command, which was relatively easy to do since both were at Peterson AFB in Colorado Springs. He had directed her to reach out to the HQ for the Continental NORAD Region at Tyndall Air Force Base in Florida, as there was—again—an object coming very fast toward Earth, which this time might or might not contain a U.S. civilian. She was to scramble jets out of Tyndall to intercept this object and to keep the general updated.

Peggy had friends from the Academy who had ended up in overseas postings, and a few who had had tense moments going up against Russian or Chinese aircraft incursions into the airspace of U.S. allies. She had thought her posting in Colorado would be relatively tame, but she didn't know anyone else who had twice in one year faced incredibly fast objects coming in from space, and she still wasn't sure if her repeated exposure to the general would be a good or bad thing for her and her career in the long run.

⸱⸱ ¡! ⸻ ⅃

Zach heard Beth's voice speaking calmly. "Well yes, Zach, they're shooting at you. Those were two of what your government calls AIM-120C medium-range air-to-air missiles. Your craft neutralized that threat automatically by outrunning them. Your defenses should be fine."

"If my own government is launching missiles at me, I am definitely going to worry, Beth. That is really not cool."

Spencer's voice came on the line. "Zach, they had to guess you could deflect that attack. Maybe it was a test."

"How do we know when the test is over?" *Especially since there is no proctor to call time.*

Zach looked at the display showing the locations of the various F-22s in the area. He saw that they were no longer near each other, but had moved to form an approximate sphere with him at the center. At that point, there was an explosion of flashes in the sky. Zach's display helpfully summarized that there were now 58 additional missiles launched from 10 aircraft, and that these missiles were again AIM-120C AMRAAM, with a range of at least 50 nautical miles. Zach's craft went horizontally straight at the nearest missile for a second, then turned straight upward. Both the right-angle of the turn and the speed of the ascent shouldn't have been possible. The missiles, however, weren't fooled: although they lacked the ability to ignore inertia, they were still more maneuverable than any aircraft (other than Zach's alien ride) that carried fragile humans. All 58 missiles turned toward his new trajectory. Several were already coming at him from above, and those did not have to deviate as much to line up with his new vertical path.

The display in front of Zach showed a significant amount of information, though Zach had a hard time looking away from the text saying simply "Distance to Object" with a number of miles counting down at—again—a seemingly impossible rate. *I may have to come up with a new word to replace "impossible,"* Zach thought briefly. When that number dropped below 10, he saw beams of light erupt from his own craft, and three blindingly bright suns simultaneously appeared close by. His vehicle accelerated directly through these explosions, like a running back behind solid blocks, and outran the other 55 missiles until they too fired their self-destruct mechanisms. Zach's craft then resumed a more leisurely downward descent. "Do you think they're still testing me?"

"Yeah, brother. I think we all just learned a lot about what your aircraft can do. Forget the missiles, I can't believe you survived those evasive maneuvers alone! I think you demonstrated that they can't shoot you down, at least not while you're moving."

"What about when I stop moving, Spence?"

"You said it before: I think it would be best to get you on camera. It would look bad to shoot at you when you're sitting there looking defenseless. Then you need to say your piece, and quickly. They want to stop you from talking, but once you've talked, there should be no point in killing you—it wouldn't prevent anything and would make them look, you know, aggressive."

"Those are a couple of really big assumptions, Spence. . . . But ones I think I'm committed to making."

And then his trip ended rather suddenly. The CNN Center adjoined the Omni Atlanta Hotel, and his craft landed directly across Marietta Street NW on the grass in front of the Centennial Olympic Park concert stage. The authorities (presumably different ones than had just fired missiles at his ride) had thoughtfully roped off a section of the lawn next to the stage, far more than his small craft required.

"Zach, are you okay?" He heard the voice of Spencer through his earbud.

"Yeah, I'm fine."

"If you're trying to make an entrance, then wait a couple minutes to disembark. They're letting a couple of cameramen get set up right next to your vehicle. Though I have never seen reporters or camera guys look this nervous."

"Yeah, I was thinking of coming out dressed in a lizard suit, or like the robot Gort from *The Day the Earth Stood Still*, but I'm not sure everyone here has a highly developed sense of humor."

"Yeah, brother, my suggestion is to make yourself as nonthreatening as possible, like you're a Rottweiler approaching a sensitive toddler. Some of the welcoming committee are armed. And, even though we think they won't harm you in public view, I am doubting the protections that the visitors gave your spaceship are extended to your body."

"Got it, not bulletproof. Thanks."

Zach waited three minutes while practicing breathing exercises, and verified that the media had set up near his small vehicle. He stepped outside. There were enough flashes that he found it hard to see clearly, but he could tell there were several microphones close enough to pick up anything he might say. He also saw both police and national guard, all armed. An uncomfortably high percentage of them were facing him rather than the crowd.

"Hello everyone, and thanks for coming to my press conference. I'm Zach Randall."

"Where are you landing from, Zach?" a voice shouted.

"Well, let me get to that. Some of you already know my background. I do have a prepared statement.

"Ladies and gentlemen, I am not sure there is a graceful way to ease into what I want to share with you, so I'm simply going to lay out the facts, which many of you may find hard to believe. I have just returned from a three-day visit to another planet. That planet is in the Large Magellanic Cloud, a satellite galaxy to our own Milky Way, approximately 163,000 light years away. I call the planet Atlas. I know this sounds incredible—I mean literally *not credible*—but the fact that hundreds of astronomers just tracked the tail end of my journey from the outside of the solar system to Atlanta in a handful of hours should lend some credence to my statement.

"I am not from that planet. I was born and grew up in Michigan, and I live and work now in California. Before this week, I had never traveled further than Dubai. Some of these news organizations have business and technology reporters who know me. I am not particularly famous outside the business press, but I have been an investor in some successful Silicon Valley tech startups that many people are now familiar with.

"To address some of the most immediate questions: I didn't build this vehicle; I borrowed it. I borrowed it to visit the home of those who *did* build it, on that far-away planet. I am here to tell you, definitively, that there is other intelligent life in this universe. I have met some of them, and am proud to call them friends."

Zach paused there. He heard a couple of screams from a block or two away, and even some laughter, but mostly the people he could see were standing in a sort of stunned silence. Even the reporters looked to be at a loss for words. The cameramen, ever professional, kept their cameras and microphones trained on him. He tried not to think of how many people were watching and listening to him at this moment. He remembered state debate quarterfinals from his senior year in high school, when he competed in an auditorium instead of a classroom; that had seemed like a lot of people at the time. He decided to speak simply to the people here at Centennial Olympic Park. Suitably, the park was built to bring together people from all over the world for the camaraderie of sports in those 1996 Olympic games, and Zach hoped that he could channel that spirit of generosity to those from different lands. In any event, he thought, *in for a penny, in for a pound*, and decided to bulldoze his way forward.

"You see, this isn't this vehicle's first trip to Earth. I met our visitors in January, when they first landed in California. I was the first person they met. They deliberately made themselves look like us, not to deceive us but rather to avoid scaring us. They brought us advanced technology that helped us improve our lives, including fragrances, transporters, and the promise of cures for some of our most terrible diseases. They have done nothing aggressive, and have made no demands. In short, they're not a threat. Instead, we now face a significantly larger threat: the danger that they will leave.

"I have made our U.S. government aware of this small group of 20 visitors. These visitors have assumed a human appearance, and even look like younger versions of celebrities. Last week, the leader of this small team of visitors, who goes by the name of Andrew Fox, was detained and is currently in a naval prison. He has the means to leave when he chooses, but while here he has agreed to respect the wishes of our authorities. However, this clearly isn't in anyone's interest, and unless we act very soon, our visitors will leave and take their technology with them. They won't be back. I am here to ask our government, our president, and all of you people—not just in Atlanta or the United States, but all over the world—to welcome these visitors, and to welcome the technology they have already brought and can continue to bring. That is why I am telling this story now.

"We have a decision to make, and I trust you collectively to make the right decision. I no longer wish to carry this burden myself, and no longer wish to hide the truth from anyone. You may not believe me, and you may be shocked by all this. But we don't have the luxury of slowly processing this information. Either we choose to embrace our visitors, or they leave. If they leave, our lives will be poorer for it. And, without their medical advances, more human lives will end sooner than they have to.

"Not so long ago, we faced a global pandemic. Some of our leaders in government and business rose to the challenge early on, some faced the challenge after a delay, and others simply didn't get it together to make any constructive difference. But the majority of everyday citizens did what they needed to, pulled together, supported those with the skills and the training to help us get through it. And we pulled through, based on the heroism of everyday people.

"Major inflection points in human history are sometimes not recognized at the time they occur. The discovery of fire, the invention of the wheel are distant memories. More recently, Gutenberg invented the printing press in Germany in 1440. Fleming discovered penicillin in London in 1928. We had the first nuclear reaction in December 1942 under the bleachers at the University of Chicago. Yuri Gagarin circled the Earth in April 1961, and then Neil Armstrong stepped out onto the lunar surface in July 1969. And today, this day, we have learned that we aren't alone in the universe. We, all of us, have the privilege of being alive and being here, at this time, in this place, in human history. Are we equal to the moment?

Are *you* equal to this moment?

"I won't be taking questions. I implore President Lynne to release Andrew Fox, today, and I will ask Andrew to consider giving his own press conference. Thank you for listening."

Zach stopped talking. And then the world erupted in an explosion of sound. People were yelling everywhere. Spencer had arranged to have a group of larger-than-average security guards surround Zach. As they moved toward a nearby armored police van, parked just southeast of the stage on Walton Street NW, the reporters rushed him like defensemen attacking a running back. They shouted many questions, but the only one that Zach comprehended was "what are you going to do now?"

Zach responded, "I need a shower and a meal and a good night's sleep." The guards got him into the armored van and took him directly to the nearest transporter at the Peachtree Center Transit Station. Zach emerged from the transporter into the humid air of the Kahului Airport in Maui, which was not supposed to be possible, as Maui was not one of the 14 official transporter stations. He realized that the visitors were enhancing his use of the transporter network. He was not too surprised to see Spencer standing in front of him. Spencer handed him a baseball hat and sunglasses and whisked him quickly into a waiting Suburban. An hour later, he was sitting in a suite at the Four Seasons Wailea. He put on a pair of the Scaeva headphones that came with the suite, set the music to a Spotify mix of chill tunes, and got halfway through a room service hamburger and a bottle of Heineken before he fell asleep in his chair.

Zach awoke six hours later in the bed, with no memory of having shifted from the chair. He picked up his phone. There were too many texts and emails to digest, so he dialed Spencer. "I just woke up, I don't know anything—what's going on?"

Spencer sounded tired. "Hey, my friend, we have well and truly stepped in it now. The reaction to your press conference has been, let's just say, animated."

"Can you just give me the highlights?"

"Yeah. You're getting news coverage, but it's inconsistent. At least half of the media think it is more likely that this is a publicity stunt than real. They don't believe that you traveled to Atlanta from space, or if from space, then not from very far or very fast. At least one of the cable news channels is going with that. Other media are reporting that you yourself are an alien. The *Detroit Free Press* already got your mom and one of your middle school teachers to vouch that you actually were a child and have a history, but the conspiracy theorists just shifted to saying that you arrived on Earth at a young age. They got some woman who was an 8th grade classmate to say you were kind of strange, and another who said you were cute."

"If nothing else, at least this is a way to get feedback on who liked me in middle school."

"Unfortunately, they also figured out your connection to Caitlyn. There's a photo of her on the cover of the *New York Post* next to the caption 'I Dated an Alien.'"

"Shit. It's probably the first time they've thought that statement could actually be true. Is she pissed?"

"It's safe to say that she isn't happy. She says it's not about the tabloid per se but more about being known more for her link to you than for anything she's done herself. She said if the media coverage were a movie, it would all fail the Bechdel test of seeing her as her own person.

"Separately, Zach, at least one network is exploring the possibility that what you said is true, noting that too many people documented your fast trip in, and that it's consistent with the technologies you've helped bring to market this year."

"Okay, that's the media. What about the public at large?"

"It's too early to say. There are no survey results yet. There's a lot of action on Twitter, running about two-thirds in support, and there's already a new religion springing up in East Texas where you play a prominent role. I think most people are waiting for someone in authority to confirm or refute what you're saying."

"Any statement from the president?"

"Well, she gave a vague statement about how your story is interesting, it needs to be looked into, and she's going to find out if there is an Andrew Fox in federal detention. So publicly she's hedged her bets. But I think we can assume that she's also pissed at you."

"Great, she and Caitlyn can have a girls-night-out and bond over drinks. Why do you assume she is any more pissed off than usual?"

"Because there's a warrant out for your arrest."

"For god's sake, you've got to be kidding me! Now I'm a fugitive? On what charge?"

"For starters, flying an aircraft without a license. If you want the specifics, it is 49 U.S. Code § 46317, which has a maximum sentence of three years and fine of up to $250K. They're also talking about a charge for inciting a riot but that's not official just yet. We have the lawyers on it. At least they're not still shooting at you. But obviously it means that someone wants to know where you are and have an in-person chat with you. You don't need to worry about your phone though, Beth has made it untraceable. And your hotel room is in another name. But you may want to keep your head down and your sunglasses on."

"Any word from Andrew?"

"Yes, Andrew says that this has been a tremendous opportunity to learn more about humans. He said to tell you he will tolerate detention another three days as a result. He said that absent an invitation to remain, he will take the team with him in three days, but until then he's content to follow your lead. As am I. Which leads me to ask, um, do we have a plan, Zach?"

"I'm working on it. Give me some time."

ㄴ ㅓ ㅜ ㅣ

Zach stepped out of the transporter at the San Francisco Caltrain station at 4th and King. This was not an official transporter station either, but rather another use of the visitors' ability to transport anywhere. The visitors still liked to use other transport hubs where people were arriving and leaving, so that users would not be seen materializing in front of houses or random locations. Eight minutes later, his Uber dropped him off three doors down from Caitlyn's recent rental in the city, a narrow blue house with soaring ceilings in the Mission District. Three reporters were standing out front on the sidewalk, so Zach cut into the alleyway behind her row of houses and knocked on her back door. Through the curtain, he saw movement and stage-whispered through the door, "Hey Cat, it's me. Can you talk?"

Caitlyn opened the door, gasped, and hugged him tightly enough to cause pain. Then she pushed him back and punched him, hard, in the chest. He stumbled back. "Cat, I am so sorry. I am trying to juggle it all, and I didn't think through how my press conference would make you a prisoner in your own house. I know you want to remain anonymous."

"Yeah Zach, apparently no one told the media I haven't seen much of you lately." Her face softened. "I am pissed off about the damn media pestering me, but I don't blame you for that. I blame you for risking your life. You could have died out there!"

"I had to go, Cat. How could I say no to that kind of opportunity? And our government was not encouraging me to stay. Why don't you get out of here? I can get you a transporter to a nice place without media."

"Zach, I don't want to run off to a damn resort! I live here, I work here. I don't want my life to be dictated by, by all this." She gestured vaguely toward the media in front of the house.

"I know, Cat. And I want nothing more than for you to have whatever life you choose, quiet and normal. Even if it's without me, I want that for you because that's what you want. I am sick that I got you into this mess. That's why I'm here."

"Zach, you never should have come here. They're looking for you everywhere, and they know you would want to come here."

"She's right, Mr. Randall." Zach whirled to see Leah Perera standing next to him on the back porch, wearing a windbreaker that said simply "FBI." He recognized her now as one of the people who'd been standing in front of the house; he'd assumed they were all paparazzi. He looked up and saw a small Nightingale drone about 100 feet above them, with a clear view of both the front and back yards. She continued, "You're coming with me. Now. This time you're definitely under arrest."

"Cat, call Spencer!" Zach said, panicking. Caitlyn nodded through her tears and fished out her phone.

CHAPTER 27
Lawyers, Guns, and Money

I'm stuck in Folsom Prison and time keeps draggin' on.
(Johnny Cash, "Folsom Prison Blues")

LEAH BROUGHT HIM AROUND front. One of the actual reporters shouted, "Is that Zach Randall?" while her cameraman filmed him being put in the back seat of yet another Chevy Suburban. This particular group of agents was not as talkative as the last bunch, and Zach sat in silence as they drove off. He noted that they weren't headed to the FBI field office on the east side of the 101, but instead right back to the Palo Alto transporter station. The queue had been cleared, and they marched him out of the car and directly through the transporter. He emerged in a familiar setting, recognizing (yet again) the arched ceiling of DC's Union Station. He wondered if he could introduce frequent flyer miles to transporter travel, though it occurred to him that at least this trip was already free. It was less than a mile in another Suburban to the J. Edgar Hoover building on Pennsylvania Avenue. He was taken into a conference room. Other than telling him to stand or sit or move, no one had said a word to him.

Ten minutes after entering the room, he remained handcuffed and seated. The door opened and Russell Carter walked in.

"Mr. Randall, you're in a world of hurt."

Despite his real fear, Zach had to laugh. "Why, because I don't have a pilot's license?"

"That's the charge. Personally, I think that the fact you went on national television to embarrass the president might have had something to do with it. Why in the world did you think that would achieve your goals?"

"Because all you people see in the visitors is a threat. I see a lot of lives saved. And now I've been to their home planet. I am not in charge of this first contact, and neither are you. The visitors chose me, and now they have hosted me. I am the first person to set foot on any other planet, much less one with intelligent life, and you respond by putting me in fucking handcuffs?"

"You might want to tone down your outrage, Mr. Randall, if you want to get any help. Because I am not the one you have to convince."

The door opened again, and President Sheryl Lynne walked in, trailed by Chief of Staff Thomas Stanton.

"Hello Mr. Randall. I hope my friends here at the FBI building have been treating you well."

"If you wanted to see me, you could have simply called." Zach did not stand this time; he was becoming less impressed by finding himself in the presence of the leader of the free world.

"We did call, Zach. You didn't answer. That doesn't happen to me often. It turns out you were out of town. You made the most important trip in human history, and didn't think it might have warranted a mention in advance?"

"Madam President, Andrew offered humanity the biggest gift ever, and you responded by putting him in jail and trying more than once to kill me. You rejected working with me. I traveled to his home world to try to salvage the situation."

"First of all, I didn't approve anyone shooting at you, and it should be clear from the fact that you're currently alive that this particular order has been canceled—at least unless you're found talking to the Chinese or the Russians. Second, you call it 'salvaging the situation' to go on television telling the world there are aliens living among us, all on your own? People are freaked out. Many of them want to do a lot more to your friend Andrew than restrict his movement. People need to see that someone is in control."

"And how do we achieve that?"

"Zach, one of your many mistakes is assuming that people make decisions based on facts and data. They don't. People make decisions based on emotions and *then* find the facts and data to support their decisions. Right now people are afraid, and you're the source of that fear. So one way to calm the situation in the short term is to show that you're under control.

As in handcuffs. It's not personal. Your detention will be comfortable."

"So, why are you detaining Andrew? You haven't publicized that you're doing that, so it isn't to manage the public's fear."

"I detained Andrew to manage my own concerns, Zach. It's literally my goddamn job to protect our citizens from anyone who enters the country illegally, particularly those with advanced weaponry and technology—technology that got my own husband killed. The fact that a 30-year-old tech bro decided to be beer buddies with the aliens doesn't change that. Nor does their threat that they might leave. One might see that as *solving* a problem rather than creating one. If they leave, they remove two risks from my perspective: one, that the planet has a more technologically advanced power than the United States, and two, that every country becomes as technologically advanced as the United States."

"Do you believe Andrew is who he says he is?"

"Yes, I think it is probable, Zach. But that was never the issue."

"Then you know that he can leave detention, and the planet, any time. The fact that he hasn't is itself an indication that he wishes to follow our rules."

"He seems to pick and choose which rules he follows, Zach. But I grant that your publicity stunt has made keeping him hidden a moot point. And it helps that he looks inoffensive. Which makes you more of an irritant and a wild card than he is."

"Madam President, we have an even larger problem. You know that the visitors were here once before and were turned away. They don't usually offer a second chance. Have you wondered why they're making an exception?"

"No, Zach, I don't see the point in speculating on their motivations. They say they're friendly. They have the technology to represent a threat, and I want to stay focused on what we know."

"They're making an exception because there are other alien races out there, Madam President. Some are as hostile as you fear they might be, looking to enslave or kill other species before they can become a threat. And our visitors, despite being friendly, have inadvertently revealed our presence to some of these uglier aliens during their first visit. We can't survive without their protection or a relationship with them."

The president's look of astonishment faded quickly. This woman was nothing if not quick on her feet. "Do you have independent proof of this other race of aliens, Zach, or did our visitors tell you?"

"They told me, and it is credible."

"It's also convenient that, after we said no to engaging with them, they've come up with a new bogeyman to justify that engagement. I have no reason to believe this is true."

"Didn't you say that even a small probability of harm warrants rejecting our visitors? So wouldn't a small probability that what they're saying about a second set of aliens is true mean we should embrace the only real means of defense against a hostile group?"

"Zach, what you're describing is hypothetical and unproven and in the future; the aliens we have here are real and a threat today. And I feel safer if we have no aliens on Earth. We can deal with new ones if and when they arrive."

"I get the sense the new ones aren't going to start by offering us technologies and offering to trade with us. By the time they're arriving, it will be too late."

"Now that we know there are any aliens out there, Zach, we will amp up our defense capability. Which I like better than relying on the kindness of strangers."

"Madam President, in that case would you consider at least releasing Andrew?"

"I already have. Turns out I need the space for another prisoner."

The president stood up and left with her advisors in tow so abruptly that Zach had no time to respond.

II ⅃ : ⅄

"Spencer, can you hear me?"

"Loud and clear. How are you calling me from jail?" Zach was in the same apartment-style detention room that Andrew had occupied shortly before.

"The visitors gave me an embedded communication technology, nanites inside my head that let me direct my voice to your cell phone without needing my own. It's convenient."

"You're more willing than most to take things on trust, Zach. But I hear you just fine. Andrew is back here in California. Not sure how this hostage exchange helps us, though."

"Spence, I am trying to keep Andrew from pulling the plug on this project too soon. It wasn't helping that the authorities here wanted him detained, even if he could choose whether to go along."

"Okay, boss, so what are you thinking we do now?"

"The president reminded me that we need better public relations. One element of that is not to simply describe how lives are improved by visitor technologies, but to make it real. First, I want you to get some former Alzheimer's patients and their families on the media to tell their stories. Second—do you have the video footage I took from their planet?"

"We have it, but haven't shared it. I didn't want to add fuel to the fire without checking with you."

"I think it is time to release it. I have footage of my arrival, their city, and the speech I gave. Let's not include any footage of what the aliens look like just yet; that takes some, um, adjustment. Next, I think we need some prominent people to start vouching for us. People who are known and trusted."

"You mean like, celebrity endorsements?"

"Exactly like that. And I have a pretty good idea which celebrities to start with."

＞ :: ᴅ́ ·l·

"Thank you all for coming."

Spencer looked out at the conference room of the Beverly Hills Hilton. He stood next to Caitlyn. She had surprised him when she insisted on coming; she was not as easily impressed by celebrity as Zach was, and he thought she wanted nothing to do with Zach. She had explained to him that if Zach was going to risk his life and now his freedom to help bring visitor technology to the people, she could step up and do more herself to support the effort. She also suggested that celebrities might respond better to a co-ed team, and she had dressed more fashionably than her usual straightforward style. Even though he was up on much of the latest academic research on marketing, he concluded that Cat may have understood the practice at a more fundamental level.

Eddie Murphy—the actual Edward Regan Murphy who was born in 1961 in New York—stood up. "Hey, y'all asked us to help, but you need to explain exactly how we can do that."

"Yes, Mr. Murphy." Spencer turned to an area behind the stage and said, "Regan, can you come out front, please?" The visitor version of Eddie Murphy at age 23 walked forward and joined Spencer.

"Are you fucking kidding me!?" Eddie Murphy yelled. "You brought an impersonator?"

"Not exactly. Could the rest of you come out now also?"

The youthful visitor versions of Sigourney Weaver, Harrison Ford, Elizabeth Shue, Charlie Sheen, Sharon Stone, Mel Gibson, Julia Roberts, Andrew McCarthy, and several other celebrities came out from backstage. Their real-life counterparts, most of them in their 60s, stared.

Caitlyn broke the silence. "You all heard Zach Randall's press conference. And I think you already know these aren't Vegas-style celebrity impersonators. These are visitors, they're friendly, and we could really use your help."

Spencer chimed in. "You've all acted in movies about supporting newcomers against forces that oppose them. Mr. Murphy, when you developed the story for *Coming to America*, you showed us a visitor from another culture overcoming hardship and hostility to win over the locals. Mr. Ford, in *Raiders of the Lost Ark* your character, Indiana Jones, worked to keep advanced technology out of the hands of Nazis who would use it for their own advantage to enslave other nations. Ms. Weaver?"

The real Sigourney Weaver replied, "Please tell me you aren't going to remind us what happened in *Alien*?"

"Um, no, that doesn't really fit the narrative I'm going for."

Sigourney smiled. "There are a lot of movies besides my own where the aliens kill everyone: *Independence Day*, *Mars Attacks*, and *Starship Troopers* come to mind."

"Well, I think our visitors got stuck a bit in the 1980s, so I was going to avoid the 1990s—though I must tell you how completely awesome you were in *Galaxy Quest*." Spencer smiled like a teenager, and Sigourney rolled her eyes. It was clearly not the first time that someone had picked that particular role to compliment her for. Spencer continued, "But if we are going later, how about the story in your movie *Avatar*, where you showed how people from different planets can learn and love?

"My point is, you're all incredible performers, and you're popular because you have brought to life the victories of the human spirit. People look up to you. And now people have a chance to choose between fear and opportunity, to welcome visitors who have already offered us so much. You can influence that choice, in the real world. These visitors have made you the face that they show the whole world. That goes beyond even the huge accomplishments that you've already had."

Julia Roberts spoke up. "I don't know, Dr. Sams. What many of us are seeing is how much better we looked when we were younger. That's not really a nice thing to do, you know." She paused, while Spencer looked horrified. "I am kidding you know. Well, mostly anyway. I can't speak for the rest of these relics, but I'm in."

One hour later, Spencer called Zach. "Okay, the celebrities will help. Mostly because they want to help get people over the xenophobia to get access to amazing technologies. But Caitlyn and I did end up promising board seats to several of them. And photo shoots with their counterparts. And, if you make a documentary about this, they want to portray the visitors that resemble them."

CHAPTER 28
Go Your Own Way

If our children can live safely for one more day, it would
be worth the one more day that we defend this island.
(Ken Watanabe, *Letters from Iwo Jima*)

"ANDREW, A LOT HAS happened since we last spoke." Zach was speaking from his studio-like detention area. He could see a projection of Andrew like a hologram in front of him, kind of an on-demand 3D version of Zoom. He was sure that his minders could hear his side of the conversation, but wasn't sure it mattered much.

"Yes, Zach, you have been quite busy." Andrew was back in his Menlo Park compound, with a blur of activity behind and around him.

"I asked you to give me some time to try to manage the situation. You want a clear-cut invitation from our leaders to stay. As you can see, opinions can form rapidly; not everyone in this country has the same view, and we are just one of many countries."

"I admit that I still don't fully understand why it takes humans so long to arrive at a decision. I have provided all the relevant facts, but there is still no clear consensus among your public or your leaders."

"I think I have a partial understanding of our cultural differences. Your society is very analytical and data-driven in making decisions, correct?"

"Yes. Once our people have a shared understanding of the facts, they tend to arrive at a decision quickly, and to arrive at a similar conclusion."

"Andrew, why do your team members engage in thrill-seeking activities in their off time?"

"Because their human construction means they experience the same intense emotions that your people do: fear, excitement, adrenaline. In our

180

native bodies, our people have emotions but they're more muted. We seek satisfaction more than excitement."

"Right, but you find our emotional highs and lows to be thrilling, right? So much so that I understand some of your team members transmit the visceral experience to individuals back on your home world, so that they can have the thrill of adventure-seeking activities."

"Yes, and it has made your planet more interesting than many of the others that we have reached out to."

"Here's the thing. You can't get the benefits of feeling strong emotions without the drawbacks, which is something that our president reminded me of. Most humans are *not* data-driven. It's not that we're impervious to data and facts; our own evolution and survival as a civilization depends on understanding and adapting to reality. But most people have a strong emotional component to the decisions they make, and then they seek the data that supports the decision they already want to reach.

"People may be approximately rational and understand their self-interest when the situation is one they have some experience with. They develop rules of thumb. But in a new situation those rules will not apply. People were only just told of your existence. Some believe it, some don't. It'll take time for people to understand and accept the facts that you and I know, and more time for them to process those facts. If I am to help them understand and develop an opinion, I need time, and I need to appeal to their emotions as well as to their sense of core cost-benefit tradeoffs."

"Zach, I have learned some of this just by observing you. You risked your career and your relationships to build a stronger connection with us visitors. We thought this all stemmed from a logical desire to bring technology to your people. But now you have risked your very life. We're not used to this level of passion. You've made a big impression on us, on me. I have learned from you."

Andrew continued. "Having said that, my team has been here for ten months of your time. Even by our own standards, this is a long field trip. Our presence is now known; some of our initial technologies are understood and used. We see little reason to wait."

"What about the fact that your colleagues' earlier visit tipped off the Gozerians to our existence and galactic address? Don't you feel responsible for protecting us?"

"Matthew told you, Zach, that exposure was part of why my team was sent here—to give your people a second chance to engage with us. You decided that sharing this with your people would create panic. Plus, your leaders don't believe it."

"Couldn't you show them proof?"

"Anything we could show them could be faked. And we don't view it as our job to demonstrate that we are truthful. We gave your planet a second chance to engage in a relationship that benefits you even without our protection from hostile species. And we also now told you about the threat you face. My team is ready to leave. I know you're doing your best, but the fact that you have to work so hard to convince your fellow humans to invite us to stay is itself a sign that your people are not ready, regardless of the threat. I am sorry, but my timeline remains until the end of this week."

∴ ⌐ ꓒ ╤

"Hey buddy, how're you holding up?" Spencer asked when Zach came on the line.

"Well, Spencer my friend, it's still strange to hear your voice inside my head with no phone. And the tally isn't so good. I am in jail. Half the world thinks I'm a liar, the other half thinks I am an extraterrestrial myself. Trading has been suspended on all our portfolio companies that are already public. Safe to say our market valuations are all approximately zero. My mom is in hiding. Caitlyn thinks I have wrecked her life, and she isn't wrong. And the visitors are about to pack up their marbles and head home.

"You didn't mention the other, more nasty aliens who will eventually show up. But it's been a hell of an adventure, hasn't it? We made history, man. You and me, first contact. We helped millions of people. We made a boatload of money, even if we subsequently lost it. We met the president, even if she put handcuffs on you. You went to another planet! We are *players*, Zach. You always said you wanted to make an impression, to matter. I think we achieved that."

"You sound chipper for someone whose girlfriend is about to go back home. I don't get the impression our visitors are big on long-distance relationships."

"Yeah, Zach, about that. If it comes to that, I am thinking of going with her."

Zach stopped short, and neither spoke for a long moment. "Wow. We all thought you had a fear of commitment, and now you're going to commit to someone who lives 163,000 light years away. Good for you, man."

"She makes me happy, man. And let me tell you, everything you said about the situation is accurate. But you know what you do have?"

"What's that?"

"You have me. And almost nothing left to lose. There is nothing more dangerous than someone with nothing to lose. People with wealth and comfort don't often take chances. You've had it, you've lost it. But you're a fighter, Zach. And the facts are on our side. Why don't we play it out and see what happens?"

"Yeah. I have a couple of ideas left. Gonna need you to make stuff happen. I can talk from here but that's about all I can do."

"So talk."

ᒋ ¡! ⹝ ᓀ

"Thank you all for coming. We'll start the press conference now." Spencer looked out at the rows of journalists, sitting in the same Beverly Hills Hilton conference room where he had met with the celebrities. The power of Hollywood could still attract more journalists than discussions about life-saving technologies or extraterrestrial visitors could on their own.

"My name is Spencer Sams. I am a professor in the Stanford Graduate School of Business, where I took a leave of absence earlier this year to join my friend Zach Randall in forming one of the most successful venture capital firms in Silicon Valley, Regio Li. Our firm brought several businesses with amazing products to the world, including pheromone-based scents, a cure for Alzheimer's, and transporter transportation. We have several other businesses with even more exciting products in development. I would like to welcome to the stage the actor from television and movies that we all know and love, Michael J. Fox." The actual Michael Andrew Fox, known professionally as Michael J. Fox, born in Canada in 1961, joined Spencer on stage, his late-stage Parkinson's (and medication-related dyskinesia) clear in his walk but with a steady look in his eyes.

Michael J. Fox spoke slowly but clearly. "Thank you, Spencer; I would not be here if it weren't important. In turn, I would like to invite someone else to join me on stage. Andrew, could you please join us?" Andrew walked out, dressed identically to his human counterpart but clearly 35 years younger and in perfect health. Seeing the duo side by side made for a vivid visual contrast.

"Thank you, Mr. Fox. I want to say hello to the media present, and to all the people watching. I go by the name of Andrew Fox, and I am the coordinator of a small team of visitors who brought these technologies to market with the help of Professor Sams and Mr. Randall. Almost forty of your years ago we started making plans to visit your planet. Since we wanted to fit in when we arrived, we referenced some of your movies to determine what humans looked like. We didn't update those plans, and so we look like humans who were well known from that time. These same humans have been gracious hosts to us today. I would like to invite my colleagues, and our hosts, to join us on stage now."

Each celebrity and their youthful visitor equivalent, came out one pair at a time: Harrison Ford, Andrew McCarthy, Eddie Murphy, Sigourney Weaver, Elizabeth Shue, and Sharon Stone. The visitors were dressed identically to their elder hosts. The younger versions of Charlie Sheen, Mel Gibson, and Julia Roberts came out on their own; Sheen and Gibson had refused to participate and Roberts had other plans. Two other celebrities, Bono and Ashton Kutcher, were also present despite not having a visitor counterpart, attending in their capacity as venture investors themselves.

The older and real Harrison Ford came to Andrew's microphone. "Hi everyone. Look, three days ago I was as surprised as you when I saw Zach Randall's press conference in Atlanta. And I was skeptical too. Then I met this fellow here." Harrison pointed to his counterpart. "I call him Jay. A couple of interesting things about Jay. For one, yes, he is almost as good looking as I am. Second, he's a better pilot." Ford paused for a moment and gave his trademark grin, to which the assembled crowd responded with a collective guffaw. "Third, and this kind of got my attention, we have identical fingerprints. And blood types. And shoe size. You get the idea. Over the past three days, I've spent time with him and his friends. I have looked at the data about Mr. Randall's flight in on Sunday. I have no doubt that these visitors are exactly who they say they are."

Beth took the stage next. "Hello. All of us came on this trip based on a desire to help another civilization. Getting ready to fit in on your world involved some physical discomfort for us. We came for friendship, and for trade. And . . ." she trailed off, looking over at Spencer, "we found so much more. We aren't accustomed to individuals who think so differently from one another as you all do. We were ready for a positive or negative reception, and weren't ready to find both at the same time. Your weakness, and your strength, is your passion and capacity to live and to love. We came to learn, and we have learned much about how to live a fuller life ourselves. We aren't a threat to you, and we won't stay if we aren't welcome."

Beth passed the microphone to the real Sharon Stone, who (like her counterpart) was wearing an emerald green dress. Stone briefly flashed her radiant smile. "I also spent some time with Vonne here, and gave her a bit of advice about being new to California while looking like a 25-year-old me—advice I wish someone had given to me. Since the arrival of these visitors in January, we have seen an unbelievable renaissance of new technologies from Silicon Valley, and we now know the source of these technologies. To take just one example, many of us have lost someone close to us to Alzheimer's, and some of us see the prospect of soon liberating loved ones from that disease. Think of what other diseases could be eradicated with the technology that they're offering. It would be a tragedy if humanity acted like poor hosts and told our guests to leave. For us and for them. Please, do not let that happen."

Spencer came back to the stage. "I was the second person to meet these visitors. The first was my friend Zach Randall, who you heard from on Monday. Zach would like to be here with us, but he has been arrested, which tells you everything you need to know about our government's initial reaction to the generosity of our visitors. We don't have much time left to convince them to remain. Please make up your own minds about what's going on and let our government—and each other—know what you think. If anyone has a call to be upset with the visitors, it would be the people whose DNA they copied in order to fit in. And you now know what they think, and what I think. Thanks for coming today. Now, who would like pictures with celebrities from two very different places?" The room erupted in noise and flash bulbs. Spencer wondered if he could start yet another career as a film agent.

❗ ⁊ � ⠛

The next day, Spencer reached out to Zach, who skipped the pleasantries and answered with "So what was the impact of the celebrity endorsements?"

"Okay, before the celebrities weighed in, the average of recent surveys was running about 40% pro, 30% against, and 30% undecided. Our press conference was one of the most watched ever, and it seems to have made some difference. Things are still in flux, but the best guess is about 53% pro, 28% against, and 19% undecided. In this country. Some different percentages in other countries. I think the president being against helps other countries report being pro-alien on the theory that anything the U.S. government is against must be good for them."

"Spence, you worked your butt off, and I couldn't be more grateful to you for winning this battle. But I don't think it's going to win us the war. It was always a little ambiguous what level of support the aliens need to see in order to stay. Andrew told me that they didn't envision anything close to the 50-50 lack of agreement that we seem to have; he said that most societies, including his own, gravitate to a consensus. Which is why they don't get very carried away with who is in charge over there, because the decisions made tend to be similar regardless. So, even if we get like 50 to 60% of government leaders and citizens in the world, I don't get the sense it'll persuade them to stay."

"So what's the threshold? Majority of world leaders and 80% of citizens, or what?"

"I don't know. That sounds like as good an estimate as any, and there's no way we're going to get 80% of the global population to embrace an advanced alien race in a week. I spoke to Andrew today. He and the visitor team appreciate our work, and they don't expect unanimity among the populace, but they're looking for more agreement than I think is possible for a world that couldn't even agree on how to long to stay home when Covid hit in 2020. They're confused, Spence. They brought cool technologies, saved a bunch of lives. They understand why a society would be cautious in the face of technological superiority, but they don't really grasp the concept of xenophobia, or of giving up known benefits just on the chance that friendly behavior is some kind of ruse. And anyway, this group of visitors isn't some kind of grand best-of-the-best from their culture. They're students on a field trip. Andrew is a good guy, but he's less of an ambassador than a teaching assistant, and I get the sense they miss home just as much as we would. They don't think they should have to work so damn hard just to be believed when they've done nothing but follow our norms and rules all along. They think they've earned better treatment. And I damn well agree with them."

CHAPTER 29
Into the Mystic

Travel isn't always pretty. It isn't always comfortable. Sometimes it hurts, it even breaks your heart. But that's okay. The journey changes you; it should change you. It leaves marks on your memory, on your consciousness, on your heart, and on your body. You take something with you. Hopefully, you leave something good behind. (Anthony Bourdain, *No Reservations*)

THE FOLLOWING DAY, THE aliens announced they would leave in just three days time, and asked the authorities (in the form of NASA) where they wanted the visitors to depart from. In what might be described as a failure of imagination, and despite knowing they could leave from almost any random driveway in the world, NASA told them that space launches were designated to occur in only a couple of spots, and suggested Cape Canaveral in Florida. Zach was able to convince Andrew that any entity reporting to the U.S. president shouldn't be the final word in their departure. After fending off some serious lobbying by both the Russians for using the Baikonur Cosmodrome location in Kazakhstan, and Elon Musk offering the South Texas launch center for SpaceX near Brownsville, Spencer got the U.S. government to reluctantly agree to take Richard Branson up on the offer to launch from his Spaceport America, 180 miles south of Albuquerque. This had the advantage of being near no population center, so it was easier to secure.

On Friday, while Zach was eating breakfast at the naval prison, a guard knocked on the door and told him to expect a visitor in an hour. Two hours later, there was another knock, and President Lynne came in with her chief of staff. The president wasted no time. "Zach, I'm guessing you're upset with me."

"Madam President, you have had agents try to kill me, and now have me in prison. I would not describe our relationship as constructive."

"Zach, I did not give the order to shoot at you in Menlo Park, or at your craft over Georgia. In fact, I only just learned about those incidents. You and I already knew about the death of Mr. Carter's father the last time the visitors were here. In his lust for revenge, I assessed that he had lost track of the national interest, and today I accepted his resignation. I grant that firing him may not seem like a large consequence from your point of view, but I can't afford the scandal of publicizing his rogue activities, and I think he valued his career more than his freedom or life anyway."

"Ma'am, I take little comfort in hearing that trying to kill me multiple times turned out to be a bad career move for a bureaucrat. But this is about larger issues than my feelings. We, and with respect I mean you, ma'am, are certainly walking away from the greatest gift of technology ever. And I believe the visitors when they tell me we will all get exterminated soon without their help."

"Yes, Zach, I am rejecting the invitation. And you may not believe this, but I will even admit that this decision may haunt me later. But this was too big a choice to leave to you—or my—interpretation of their intentions. A vastly superior and more advanced race wanted to make a home here, leaving us in a position where we would have to trust in their continuing goodwill, every year, for all the years to come. Look at history, Zach. What happened to the inhabitants of Africa when the British arrived, or to the Native Americans when the Europeans showed up? What happened to every colonized people in history after immigrants with better weapons arrived, regardless of the initial intentions of those immigrants?"

"Madam President, those are all *human* examples. What if these visitors aren't just more evolved technologically, but also behaviorally? What if they're actually trustworthy? What will we have sacrificed?"

"A hell of a lot, Zach. But since we have a choice to avoid taking that risk, I choose to avoid it. That wasn't your oath, but it is mine. As to the nastier group of aliens your visitor friends claim may know where we live, well, we will deal with that if and when the time comes. I came here to tell you this in person. I owe that to you. And to tell you that you're free to go. I wouldn't want you to miss your friends' departure Sunday."

"Are you going?"

"I would actually like to, but don't want to send a mixed message. Besides, that kind of thing is what vice presidents are for. Monk will be there, and you're welcome to sit with him."

〒 ⋮ ⋅⊩ 凵

Sunday was a hot day, even by the standards of New Mexico in October. Eighty-five degrees by 10:00 a.m. and not a drop of moisture in the air. Branson's people had set up rows of chairs outside, and the seating area looked tiny compared to the vast size of the facility. There was a similarly small and unassuming-looking vehicle parked on the tarmac. Zach didn't see how twenty visitors would fit, but Andrew had told him they didn't have the need to move very much.

Zach and Spencer had seats in the front, which wasn't to be assumed, as several countries had sent their UN ambassadors from New York for the event. Some of those ambassadors were elbowing their way into speaking to Andrew, who looked as calm as if he were having tea.

On his way toward the front, Zach passed a familiar face. "You here to kill me, Agent Perera?"

"Not today, Mr. Randall. But I try to stay ready for any contingency."

"Always a real pleasure to see you."

"Mr. Randall, if I meant to do you harm, you wouldn't see it coming. So it should in fact be a pleasure to see me."

Zach moved past the agent, taking what small measure of satisfaction he could from the fact that his seat was several rows closer to the front than her own. He stepped past a tall woman with a serious expression and the single blue bar indicating the rank of Air Force lieutenant, who seemed to be studying him intently. He nodded to her, and then took Spencer aside and put his arm around his oldest friend. "Are you sure about this, man?"

"As sure as I've ever been, Zach. I love Beth, and I'll be the first person to ever actually live on another world."

"Will they let you come back here?"

"She can't come with me, but they said I can make the trip on my own like you did."

"Dammit Spencer, I'm really worried that you're going so far away.

Not just for my sake—you were already my best friend even before we went through the last year—but also for yours. Going to a planet where you'll only know one individual at first, and no one with a shared human context. Are you sure you want to do that?"

"I am, Zach. I love you, man, but this is my chance to explore in a way no one has done before. And I can't let Beth leave without me."

"Well then, brother, I have an additional bit of news for you. Vice President LeClerc said I could tell you myself. You have been officially designated as the representative to Atlas, not just from the United States but from the United Nations. They passed a resolution last night. You're officially representing all of humanity. I think there might even be a pension included."

"Wow, Zach, that's unbelievable!"

"Yeah well, before you get all self-important, I also discussed this with Andrew. He says you'll have a position in their eyes too. But remember how these visitors are essentially on a school field trip?"

"Yeah."

"You have a posting at their school, which I think makes you some kind of adjunct professor. It's kind of a step down, given that you'd be a shoo-in for tenure at Stanford GSB next year if you stayed."

"That's okay, Zach. I'm not getting hung up on titles, at this point. You know I spent some time as a lecturer at Texas before I started the Stanford gig. It didn't pay well, but it wasn't all bad."

Zach wasn't sure what else to say. He embraced his friend, and they continued toward their seats wordlessly, where Caitlyn was waiting. She had been standing with the group of actual Hollywood celebrities, who had chartered a plane and turned the event into some kind of cross between Burning Man and the Oscars. They hadn't been allowed to land their charter at the Spaceport, but it turned out the local airport in Truth or Consequences had a 7,200-foot runway that could handle it. Caitlyn had developed a bond with the real Michael J. Fox, and Zach had a feeling he would be seeing more of the guy who had played Marty McFly, which was about as close to a movie version of Zach's past year as any he could think of.

Vice President Monk LeClerc said a few words about the bond that had been established between the two worlds in the past year. Zach tuned him out; it was so opposite of the reality of what the administration had done that he couldn't bear to listen. He supposed that the more aggressive the action, the more happy-talk was needed to make it palatable. He decided he would make a poor politician.

Then the VP invited Andrew to speak, and he took the podium.

"I would like to thank the vice president for his kind words, and to thank the people of New Mexico, the United States, and your world. We came here ten months ago as explorers to learn, to teach, and to trade. We formed businesses that gave your world better transportation, better medicine, and it appears most importantly, better cologne." Zach exchanged a look with Caitlyn, conveying with his eyes *hey, did the alien just try to make a joke?*

Andrew continued. "If I may be candid, we are disappointed that a higher percentage of your leaders and your citizens did not find our actions sufficient to ask us to stay. That their fear of us for being technologically advanced outweighed their interest in continued access to our life-enhancing and life-saving products. That they became friendly only when we announced our departure." Zach was a bit surprised at the level of candor coming from Andrew, and glanced at the vice president, who had a fixed and somewhat tight-looking smile. Andrew plowed forward. "I find it interesting that the least developed nations on your world had the highest percentage of citizens asking us to stay—I suspect it is because they're used to living in a condition where they have to trust the good intentions of other cultures with superior weaponry.

"Despite that disappointment, we are grateful to the majority of people who have treated us with generosity and kindness. Most thought we were human. Some thought we were celebrities. Several knew exactly who we were. Our mission might not have been possible, and certainly would not have been enjoyable, without their work and their friendship—starting with my good friend Zach Randall.

"We find your greatest weakness, and your greatest strength, to be your passion. We have not met a race that has advanced as far as yours and has ventured into space while still making decisions based so much on emotion. This, in fact, is the greatest asset that humans have to offer. There are no natural resources on your planet that cannot be obtained elsewhere, and your intelligence and technological advances are praiseworthy but no more advanced than those of other star-faring species. However, your ability to experience joy and sorrow, fear and exhilaration, is astonishingly unique.

"You also retain an inclination for making irrational decisions, which seems inconsistent with your progress but is similarly unique. You combine the progress that all species make in science and engineering and medicine with a joy to be alive, and a willingness to change your views and adapt, and this has earned our deepest respect. You have shown my people that we may have evolved further than is optimal toward more reason and less emotion; we have learned from you, and for that we are grateful.

"We told your leaders that we will not be back, and that remains true. We have other worlds to explore, and we rely on the initial reaction of those civilizations we reach out to. However, that does not mean we will cut off all contact and trade. We have granted the request of one of your citizens, Professor Spencer Sams, to accompany us back to our home world and continue to teach us about your ways of business and living. In addition, we will sustain a long-distance business arrangement with Zach as our local trade representative. I will let him tell you about that. However, in order to buy what we want, we must offer something to sell. So, although we will close almost all of the businesses and terminate all of the technologies that we have brought so far, we will leave one of our businesses open on your world. This is the business that has provided medical advances, beginning with a cure for Alzheimer's. We will continue to sell that product at a low cost, and may consider a cure for a second type of disease later. We could have done more.

"And now, we will return home."

The rest of the visitors quickly filed into the small vehicle. Andrew gestured for Spencer to precede him, and the two of them boarded last. Within seconds, the craft rose in the air. Zach knew it was going much more slowly than its typical departure, which had actually been his suggestion, as the aliens didn't have much flair for showmanship. Even at the slower speed, within seconds the craft was barely visible, and then it just disappeared. The news crews later said it moved so fast that it was out of the solar system within seconds.

The crowd was subdued. Caitlyn was crying softly. Even Vice President LeClerc looked unsure of what to do next, and he started walking toward his waiting limousine. Zach gave Caitlyn a bittersweet smile, and put his arm around her.

Caitlyn looked up. "Well Zach, in Atlanta you asked everyone on the planet if we would be equal to the moment. And we most certainly weren't."

"Thanks, Cat. I am heartbroken that we couldn't keep access to more technologies. Some of them were life-changing and others were life-saving. And we let the visitors just walk away out of our own fear. I know it was a lot to ask of people, but damn, what a cost."

"Zach, isn't the fact that we still won't be able to cure several fatal diseases the least of it? Didn't you say that the Gozerians are going to come wipe out humanity anyway?"

"Yes, they are. But we don't know when. Maybe it takes them a couple of millennia to get ready. More importantly, I haven't given up on our Atlasian friends."

"Zach, they just left! And it doesn't look like they're coming back."

"I know, Cat. But I was able to strike a deal."

"And you're just now telling me!? What kind of deal?"

"I couldn't convince the visitors to stay, but I was able to persuade them not to cut off contact entirely. Like Andrew said, I'm going to shut down my venture firm and most of the businesses I helped get started this year. But I will continue to sit on the board of the pharma company. Plus, I have a new job as a broker of sorts. You know how the visitors liked adventure sports? It turns out they were transmitting those back home, as sort of a visceral reality show. They have a device that communicates not just the video and audio, but the actual emotions of the person experiencing an event. It turns out they've become addicted to experiencing intense human emotion."

"Are you saying that, of all the things they could experience on our planet, the Atlasians got hooked on reality television?"

"Yes. But each experience can only be transmitted to one other person, or else it gets diluted. So the whole alien world can't share the same vicarious experience. Which means they all want their own personal connection to a human. The aliens are going to pay humans to transmit their experiences to them. And I have the exclusive franchise. I am using the working name 'Vicarious Brokerage.'"

"And you get a cut."

"That's what a broker does."

"How much are they willing to pay?"

"Enough that they needed to let us have the medical cures to generate the local currency to pay."

"Wait a minute here. You control the cure for Alzheimer's, and you're the sole broker for entertainment for an entire planet addicted to reality shows? You're a con artist, Zach Randall! And not so poor after all. But what does it matter when the Gozerians invade?"

"Well, I wouldn't describe their interest as reality shows. They love the visceral thrill of adventure, which brings them closer to what it means to be human. As far as the other aliens invading, I think we may have that covered. You see, I convinced Matthew that the cost of defending us from the Gozerians is justified to protect their interest in the vicarious experiences. Kind of like NATO protecting a third-world country with natural resources."

"So we are protected from the Gozerians."

"Yes, or at least we have a start. I'm hoping that just the existence of our relationship with Atlas will be a deterrent to the Gozerians. We need to build on that foundation."

"Wow, Zach, so there may be a future to plan for after all."

"Yes, but I am heartbroken that, at least in the immediate term, we lost the opportunity to address diseases that could have been cured by welcoming the visitors to stay. I failed—and our leadership failed—all those present and future sick people. And, closer to home, none of that changes the fact that my valuations are shot, my investors are disappointed—to put it mildly—while the tabloids and most of Twitter think I'm an alien, and my oldest friend just left us for a girl from outer space. At least I may have some more time on my hands. I'm hoping that one of the ways I might spend that time is with you. And I promise to *never again* complain about my career being boring."

Caitlyn sniffed softly and raised her chin. "I may have to check my schedule and get back to you, Zach." But her eyes told a different story than her words, and Zach's heart leapt. "What's the second way you want to spend your time?"

"Cat, when I told you that most of the companies are now worthless, that was true. And in terms of getting access to most of the visitor technologies, it breaks my heart that we told them to go away and lost all that potential to help people. And it's still true that I won't ever again let my work get in the way of what's most important.

"But it turns out I will get paid again. I believed Andrew when he said that their interest in an altruistic project would wane if it wasn't invited or appreciated. But I've seen before that projects based on self-interest often last longer, and I was able to find that self-interest element to get the visitors to give us access to at least some small fraction of their technology. They're starting by leaving us the Alzheimer's cure, but if the Vicarious Brokerage business takes off, I'm hoping to expand the pharmaceutical business into a cancer cure. Even for just the Alzheimer's, this country alone spent over $300 billion last year on care; the amount spent on cancer is astronomical. Spencer estimates this could make me worth more than Jeff Bezos, while I get paid from people on both planets. So, even though I don't wish to define myself by work, I will have a job. I'm hoping that's okay with you, particularly since I would like us to work together at least part-time."

"So now you think I want to work with you? In what job?"

"The medical company is going to need to expand its board of directors. They need someone with a medical background and pharmaceutical sales experience. And I told them where they could find such a person."

"Okay. This isn't what I expected when I graduated nursing school, but it's a chance to get back to helping sick people on a bigger scale." She smiled. "But I'll do it, only since you won't be my boss. You drove several businesses into the ground, you know."

Zach smiled. "I'm aware. I also want to invest in another startup."

"I don't know, Zach, since your pheromone business, most of your startups seem to have flamed out. What does this company do?"

"There are a couple of billionaires out there already getting a lot of press for privatizing local space travel just around here. I've been looking into how we can help with privatizing a more effective response to contact from other civilizations. If the government won't make time for it, perhaps we should. I have even identified a group in Encinitas that has already made a start at doing just that."

"Sounds like a business that you're uniquely qualified to help, Zach.

But that leads to another question. The visitors said they were in touch with other civilizations, right?"

"Yes, Cat, hundreds."

"Well, now that we are on the galactic triple-A travel guide, what makes you think that every one of the hostile civilizations are less advanced than our Atlasian friends?

"That's a really good point, Cat. I knew we'd do better with you on the team. I think we have a lot of work to do."

— *THE END* —

APPENDIX

Characters

LEADS

Zach Randall	Associate, Trancos Venture Capital
Caitlyn Gordon	Pharmaceutical sales representative
Spencer Sams	Associate Professor, Stanford Graduate School of Business

HUMAN CHARACTERS

Margaret "Peggy" Nelson	Lieutenant, U.S. Air Force
Jenna Sams	Spencer's mother, retired and living in Atherton
Bill Abrams	General Partner, Trancos Ventures
Leslie Gould	CEO, Irresistible Fragrances
Scott Crawford	Partner, Wilson Sonsini (law firm)
Nick Yakoboski	General Counsel, Hermes Air
Charlie Mendelevitch	CEO, Beam Technologies
Eola Jean "EJ" Beeber	Administrative Assistant, Regio Li Ventures

FBI AGENTS

Leah Perera	Deputy Special Agent in Charge (DSAC), FBI
Kyle McGee	Special Agent, FBI
Israel Wenzel	Assistant Special Agent in Charge (ASAC), FBI

WHITE HOUSE STAFF

Sheryl Lynne	President of United States
Maxwell "Monk" LeClerc	Vice President of the United States
Russell Carter	Acting National Security Advisor
Thomas Stanton	White House Chief of Staff
Timothy Lee	Secretary of State

VISITORS AND HUMAN CELEBRITIES

Andrew Fox	Michael J. Fox
Regan Murphy	Eddie Murphy
Jay Ford	Harrison Ford
Alexandra Weaver	Sigourney Weaver
Vonne Stone	Sharon Stone
Judson "Beth" Shue	Elizabeth Shue
Irwin Sheen	Charlie Sheen
Gerard Gibson	Mel Gibson
Thomas McCarthy	Andrew McCarthy
Fiona Roberts	Julia Roberts
Nicoletta Scacchi	Greta Scacchi
	Richard Branson

ALIEN

Matthew	Liaison, Planet of Atlas

References

In several chapters of this book, Spencer describes lessons for management that have been established by actual academic research in the real world. Much of this is summarized in the author's nonfiction book *Unlocking the Ivory Tower: How Management Research Can Transform Your Business* (coauthored with Joe LiPuma, published in 2012 by Kauffman Fellows Press in the U.S., and the Japanese language version published by Keio University in 2016). For those who would like to learn more about the sources for Spencer's talks, a list of relevant publications is below.

CHAPTER 3: STARTUPS

Thiel, Peter and Blake Masters. 2014. *Zero to One: Notes on Startups, or How to Build the Future*. New York, Currency Books.

CHAPTER 7: STRATEGY

PRIMARY REFERENCES

Agrawal, Anup and Jeffrey Jaffe. 2000. "**The Post Merger Performance Puzzle**." In C. Cooper and A. Gregory (editors), *Advances in Mergers and Acquisitions*. Stamford, JAI Press. pp. 119–156. https://doi.org/10.2139/ssrn.199671.

Brandenberger, Adam and Barry Nalebuff. 1995. "**The Right Game: Using Game Theory to Shape Strategy**." *Harvard Business Review* 73(July–August), 57–71. https://hbr.org/1995/07/the-right-game-use-game-theory-to-shape-strategy.

Cording, Margaret, Petra Christmann, and L. J. Bourgeois. 2002. "**A Focus on Resources in M&A Success: A Literature Review and Research Agenda to Resolve Two Paradoxes**." *Academy of Management Meetings*, Denver, August. https://citeseerx.ist.psu.edu/viewdoc/download?doi=10.1.1.201.7773&rep=rep1&type=pdf.

D'Aveni, Richard. 1994. *Hypercompetition*. New York, Free Press.

Davis-Floyd, Robbie. 1998. "**Storying Corporate Futures: The Shell Scenarios**." In G. Marcus (editor), *Corporate Futures*. Chicago, University of Chicago Press. pp. 141–176.

Hamel, Gary and C. K. Prahalad. 1989. "**Strategic Intent**." *Harvard Business Review* 67(May–June), 63–76.

Luehrman, Timothy. 1998. "**Strategy as a Portfolio of Real Options**." *Harvard Business Review* 76(September–October), 89–99. https://hbr.org/1998/09/strategy-as-a-portfolio-of-real-options.

Mintzberg, Henry, Richard Pascale, Michael Goold, and Richard Rumelt. 1996. "**The Honda Effect Revisited**." *California Management Review* 38(4), 78–117. https://doi.org/10.2307/41165855.

Nahapiet, Janine and Sumantra Ghoshal. 1998. "**Social Capital, Intellectual Capital, and the Organizational Advantage**." *Academy of Management Review* 23(2), 242–266. https://doi.org/10.2307/259373.

Neilson, Gary, Karla Martin, and Elizabeth Powers. 2008. "**The Secrets to Successful Strategy Execution**." *Harvard Business Review* 86(May–June), 61–70. https://hbr.org/2008/06/the-secrets-to-successful-strategy-execution.

Porter, Michael. 1980. *Competitive Strategy*. New York, Free Press.

Porter, Michael. 1985. *Competitive Advantage*. New York, Free Press.

Porter, Michael. 1987. "**From Competitive Advantage to Corporate Strategy**." *Harvard Business Review* 65(May–June), 43–59. https://hbr.org/1987/05/from-competitive-advantage-to-corporate-strategy.

Prahalad, C. K. and Gary Hamel. 1990. "**The Core Competence of the Corporation**." *Harvard Business Review* 68(May–June), 79–91. https://hbr.org/1990/05/the-core-competence-of-the-corporation.

Wernerfelt, Birger. 1984. "**The Resource-Based Theory of the Firm**." *Strategic Management Journal* 5(12), 171–180. https://doi.org/10.1002/smj.4250050207.

Williamson, Oliver and William Ouchi. 1981. "**The Markets and Hierarchies Program of Research: Origins, Implications, and Prospects**." In A. H. Van de Ven and W. F. Joyce (editors), *Perspectives on Organizational Design and Behavior*. New York, Wiley. pp. 347–406.

Supplemental Readings

Ahuja, Gautam. 2000. "**Collaboration Networks, Structural Holes, and Innovation: A Longitudinal Study.**" *Administrative Science Quarterly* 45(3), 425–455. https://doi.org/10.2307/2667105.

Amit, Raffi and Paul Shoemaker. 1993. "**Strategic Assets and Organizational Rents.**" *Strategic Management Journal* 14(1), 33–46. https://doi.org/10.1002/smj.4250140105.

Amram, Marth and Nalim Kulatilaka. 1999. *Real Options: Managing Strategic Investment in an Uncertain World.* Cambridge, Harvard Business School Press.

Ansoff, Igor. 1965. *Corporate Strategy: An Analytic Approach to Business Policy for Growth and Expansion.* New York, McGraw-Hill.

Banerji, Shameet, Paul Leinwand, and Cesare Mainardi. 2009. *Cut Costs + Grow Stronger.* Cambridge, Harvard Business School Press.

Barney, Jay. 1991. "**Firm Resources and Sustained Competitive Advantage.**" *Journal of Management* 17(1), 99–120. https://doi.org/10.1177/014920639101700108.

Borison, Adam. 2003. "**Real Options Analysis: Where Are the Emperor's Clothes?**" presentation to Real Options Conference, Washington, DC, July. https://www.realoptions.org/abstracts/abstracts03.html.

Brandenberger, Adam and Barry Nalebuff. 1997. *Co-Opetition.* New York, Doubleday.

Buono, Anthony and James Bowditch. 1989. *The Human Side of Mergers and Acquisitions: Managing Collisions Between People and Organizations.* San Francisco, Jossey-Bass.

Buono, Anthony, James Bowditch, and John Lewis. 1985. "**When Cultures Collide: The Anatomy of a Merger.**" In P. Buckley and P. Ghauri (editors), *International Mergers and Acquisitions: A Reader* [2002]. London, Cengage Learning EMEA. pp. 307–323.

Burt, Ronald. 2000. "**The Network Structure of Social Capital.**" *Research in Organizational Behavior* 22, 345–423. https://doi.org/10.1016/S0191-3085(00)22009-1.

Camerer, Colin. 1985. "**Thinking Economically About Strategy.**" In J. Pennings and Associates (editors), *Organizational Strategy and Change.* San Francisco, Jossey Bass. Ch. 2.

Chandler, Alfred. 1962. *Strategy and Structure: Chapters in the History of the American Industrial Enterprise.* Cambridge, MIT Press.

Chatterjee, Sayan, Michael Lubatkin, and Yaakov Weber. 1992. "**Cultural Differences and Shareholder Value in Related Mergers: Linking Equity and Human Capital.**" *Strategic Management Journal* 13(5), 319–334. https://doi.org/10.1002/smj.4250130502.

Chi, Tailan. 1994. "**Trading in Strategic Resources: Necessary Conditions, Transaction Cost Problems, and Choice of Exchange Structure.**" *Strategic Management Journal* 15(4), 271–290. https://doi.org/10.1002/smj.4250150403.

Collis, David and Cynthia Montgomery. 1995. "**Competing on Resources, Strategy in the 1990s**." *Harvard Business Review* 73(July–August), 118–128. https://hbr.org/1995/07/competing-on-resources-strategy-in-the-1990s.

Collis, David and Cynthia Montgomery. 2005. *Corporate Strategy: A Resource-Based Approach*, 2nd edition. New York, McGraw-Hill.

Connor, Kathleen. 1994. "**A Historical Comparison of Resource-Based Theory and Five Schools of Thought within Industrial Organization Economics: Do We Have a New Theory of the Firm?**" *Journal of Management* 17(1), 121–154. https://doi.org/10.1177/014920639101700109.

Copeland, Thomas and Vladmir Antikarov. 2001. *Real Options: A Practitioners Guide*. New York, Texere.

Dierckx, Ingemar and Karel Cool. 1989. "**Asset Stock Accumulation and Sustainability of Competitive Advantage**." *Management Science* 35(12), 1504–1511. https://doi.org/10.1287/mnsc.35.12.1504.

Duke, Annie. 2018. *Thinking in Bets: Making Smarter Decisions When You Don't Have All the Facts*. New York, Portfolio/Penguin.

Eisenhardt, Kathleen and Jeffrey Martin. 2000. "**Dynamic Capabilities: What Are They?**" *Strategic Management Journal* 21(10/11), 1105–1121. https://doi.org/10.1002/1097-0266(200010/11)21:10/11<1105::AID-SMJ133>3.0.CO;2-E.

Fink, Ronald. 2001. "**Reality Check for Real Options**." *CFO Magazine*, 13 September. https://www.cfo.com/accounting-tax/2001/09/reality-check-for-real-options/.

Fowell, Walter. 1990. "**Neither Market Nor Hierarchy: Network Forms of Organization**." In B. Staw and L. Cummings (editors), *Research in Organizational Behavior*, vol. 12. Greenwich, JAI Press. pp. 295–336.

Ghemawat, Pankaj. 1991. **Commitment: The Dynamic of Strategy**. New York, Free Press.

Godfrey, Paul and Charles Hill. 1995. "**The Problem of Unobservables in Strategic Management Research**." *Strategic Management Journal* 16(7), 519–533. https://doi.org/10.1002/smj.4250160703.

Goshal, Sumantra and Peter Moran. 1996. "**Bad for Practice: A Critique of the Transaction Cost Theory**." *Academy of Management Review* 21(1), 13–47. https://doi.org/10.2307/258627.

Grantham, Charles, James Ware, and Cory Williamson. 2007. *Corporate Agility: A Revolutionary New Model for Competing in a Flat World*. New York, AMACOM.

Hagel, John. 2005. *Microsoft Business Summit presentation*. September 7, 2005. Redmond, Washington.

Haleblian, Jerayr and Sydney Finkelstein. 1999. "**The Influence of Organizational Acquisition Experience on Acquisition Performance: A Behavioral Learning Perspective**." *Administrative Science Quarterly* 44(1), 19–56. https://doi.org/10.2307/2667030.

Hall, Richard. 1993. "**A Framework Linking Intangible Resources and Capabilities to Sustainable Competitive Advantage**." *Strategic Management Journal* 14(8), 33–46. https://doi.org/10.1002/smj.4250140804.

Hamel, Gary. 1991. "**Competition for Competence and Inter-Partner Learning within International Strategic Alliances.**" *Strategic Management Journal* 12(S1), 83–103. https://doi.org/10.1002/smj.4250120908.

Hamel, Gary. 1996. "**Strategy as Revolution.**" *Harvard Business Review* 74(July–August). https://hbr.org/1996/07/strategy-as-revolution.

Haspeslaugh, Philippe and David Jemison. 1991. *Managing Acquisitions: Creating Value through Corporate Renewal.* New York, Free Press.

Hayward, Matthew and Donald Hambrick. 1997. "**Explaining the Premium Paid for Large Acquisitions: Evidence of CEO Hubris.**" *Administrative Science Quarterly* 42(1), 103–127. https://doi.org/10.2307/2393810.

Henderson, Bruce. 1968. *Perspectives on Experience.* Boston, Boston Consulting Group.

Henderson, Bruce. 1970. "**The Product Portfolio.**" In C. Stern and M. Deimler (editors), *The Boston Consulting Group on Strategy*, 2nd edition [2006]. New York, Wiley. pp. 35–38.

Huang, Christine and Brian Kleiner. 2004. "**New Developments Concerning Managing Mergers and Acquisitions.**" *Management Research News* 27(4/5), 54–62. https://doi.org/10.1108/01409170410784473.

Isaacson, Walter. 2011. *Steve Jobs.* New York, Simon & Schuster.

Jemison, David and Sim Sitkin. 1986. "**Corporate Acquisitions: A Process Perspective.**" *Academy of Management Review* 11(1), 145–154. https://doi.org/10.2307/258337.

Jensen, Michael and William Meckling. 1976. "**Theory of the Firm: Managerial Behavior, Agency Costs and Ownership Structure.**" *Journal of Financial Economics* 3(4), 303–360. https://doi.org/10.1016/0304-405X(76)90026-X.

Kesner, Idalene, Debra Shapiro, and Anurag Sharma. 1994. "**Brokering Mergers: An Agency Theory Perspective on the Role of Representatives.**" *Academy of Management Journal* 37(3), 703–721. https://doi.org/10.5465/256707.

King, David, Dan Dalton, Catherine Daily, and Jeffrey Covin. 2004. "**Meta-analyses of Post-Acquisition Performance Indications of Unidentified Moderators.**" *Strategic Management Journal* 25(2), 187–200. https://doi.org/10.1002/smj.371.

KPMG. 2000. "**White Paper on Post-Merger Integration.**" KPMG Insights Series.

Krishnan, Hema, Alex Miller, and William Judge. 1997. "**Diversification and Top Management Team Complementarity: Is Performance Improved by Merging Similar or Dissimilar Teams?**" *Strategic Management Journal* 18(5), 361–374. https://doi.org/10.1002/(SICI)1097-0266(199705)18:5<361::AID-SMJ866>3.0.CO;2-L.

Kroll, Mark, Peter Wright, Lesley Toombs, and Hadley Leavell. 1997. "**Form of Control: A Critical Determinant of Acquisition Performance and CEO Rewards.**" *Strategic Management Journal* 18(2), 85–96. https://doi.org/10.1002/(SICI)1097-0266(199702)18:2<85::AID-SMJ833>3.0.CO;2-H.

Lado, Augustine and Mary Wilson. 1995. "**Human Resource Systems and Sustained Competitive Advantage: A Competency-Based Perspective**." *Academy of Management Review* 19(4), 699–727. https://doi.org/10.5465/amr.1994.9412190216.

Learned, Edmund, Carl Christensen, Kenneth Andrews, and William Guth. 1965. *Business Policy: Text and Cases*. New York, Richard D. Irwin Publisher.

Marks, Mitchell. 1997. "*Consulting in Mergers and Acquisitions: Interventions Spawned by Recent Trends*." *Journal of Organizational Change Management* 10(3), 267–279. https://doi.org/10.1108/09534819710171112.

McArthur, John and Bruce Scott. 1969. *Industrial Planning in France*. Boston, Harvard University Press.

Myers, Stewart C. 1977. "**Determinants of Corporate Borrowing**." *Journal of Financial Economics* 5(2), 147–175. https://doi.org/10.1016/0304-405X(77)90015-0.

Osterwalder, Alexander and Yves Pigneur. 2010. *Business Model Generation: A Handbook for Visionaries, Game Changers, and Challengers*. Hoboken, John Wiley & Sons.

Page, Larry. 2009. **University of Michigan commencement address**. Transcript retrieved from https://googlepress.blogspot.com/2009/05/larry-pages-university-of-michigan.html.

Pascale, Richard 1984. "**Perspectives on Strategy: The Real Story Behind Honda's Success**." *California Management Review* 26(3), 47–72. https://doi.org/10.2307/41165080.

Penrose, Edith. 1959. *The Theory of Growth of the Firm*. London, Basil Blackwell.

Perrow, Charles. 1981. "**Markets, Hierarchies, and Hegemony**." In A. Van de Ven and W. Joyce (editors), *Perspectives on Organizational Design and Behavior*. New York, Wiley. pp. 347–406.

Peteraf, Margaret. 1993. "**The Cornerstones of Competitive Advantage: A Resource-Based View**." *Strategic Management Journal* 14(3), 179–191. https://doi.org/10.1002/smj.4250140303.

Porter, Michael. 1990. *The Competitive Advantage of Nations*. New York, Free Press.

Porter, Michael. 1991. "**Towards a Dynamic Theory of Strategy**." *Strategic Management Journal* 12(S2), 95–117. https://doi.org/10.1002/smj.4250121008.

Porter, Michael. 2008. *On Competition*. Cambridge, Harvard Business Press.

Rogers, Paul and Marcia Blenko. 2006. "**Who Has the D? How Clear Decision Roles Enhance Organizational Performance**." *Harvard Business Review* 84(January–February), 53–61. https://hbr.org/2006/01/who-has-the-d-how-clear-decision-roles-enhance-organizational-performance.

Schoenberg, Richard. 2000. "**The Influence of Cultural Compatibility within Cross-Border Acquisitions: A Review**." *Advances in Mergers and Acquisitions* 1, 43–59. https://doi.org/10.1016/S1479-361X(00)01003-6.

Selznick, Philip. 1957. *Leadership in Administration*. New York, Harper & Row.

Shanley, Mark and Mary Correa. 1992. *"Agreement between Top Management Teams and Expectations for Post Acquisition Performance."* Strategic Management Journal 13(4), 245–267. https://doi.org/10.1002/smj.4250130402.

Simon, Herbert. 1947. *Administrative Behavior*. New York, Free Press.

Sirower, Mark. 1997. *The Synergy Trap: How Companies Lose the Acquisition Game*. New York, Free Press.

Smith, James and Robert Nau. 1995. **"Valuing Risky Projects, Option Pricing Theory and Decision Analysis."** Management Science 41(5), 795–816. https://doi.org/10.1287/mnsc.41.5.795.

Teece, David, Gary Pisano, and Amy Shuen. 1997. **"Dynamic Capabilities and Strategic Management."** Strategic Management Journal 18(7), 509–533. https://doi.org/10.1002/(SICI)1097-0266(199708)18:7<509::AID-SMJ882>3.0.CO;2-Z.

Trigeorgis, Lenos. 1998. *Real Options: Managerial Flexibility and Strategy in Resource Allocation*. Cambridge, MIT Press.

Tversky, Amos and Daniel Kahneman. 1983. **"Extensional Versus Intuitive Reasoning: The Conjunction Fallacy in Probability Judgment."** Psychological Review 90(4), 293–315. https://doi.org/10.1037/0033-295X.90.4.293.

Tzu, S. 2008. *The Art of War*. Translated by Lionel Giles. North Clarendon, Charles E. Tuttle Co.

Williamson, Oliver. 1996. **"Economic Organization: The Case for Candor."** Academy of Management Review 21(1), 13–47. https://doi.org/10.5465/amr.1996.9602161564.

Zajac, Edward and Cyrus Olsen. 1993. **"From Transaction Cost to Transaction Value Analysis: Implications for the Study of Interorganizational Strategies."** Journal of Management Studies 30(1), 131–145. https://doi.org/10.1111/j.1467-6486.1993.tb00298.x.

CHAPTER 10: LEADERSHIP

PRIMARY READINGS

Barnard, Chester. 1938. *The Functions of the Executive*. Cambridge, Harvard University Press.

Bennis, Warren. 1989. *Why Leaders Can't Lead*. New York, Jossey-Bass.

Kets de Vries, Manfred. 1989. **"Leaders Who Self-Destruct: The Causes and Cures."** In R. Vecchio (editor), *Leadership*, 2nd edition [2007]. Notre Dame, University of Notre Dame Press. pp. 216–227.

Kotter, John. 1990. "**What Leaders Really Do.**" In R. Vecchio (editor), *Leadership*, 2nd edition [2007]. Notre Dame, University of Notre Dame Press. pp. 23–32.

Lipman-Blumen, Jean. 1996. *The Connective Edge*. New York, Oxford University Press.

Machiavelli, Niccolo. 1513. *The Prince*. Translated by Robert Adams [1992]. New York, Norton.

Mintzberg, Henry. 1975. "**The Manager's Job: Folklore and Fact.**" In R. Vecchio (editor), *Leadership*, 2nd edition [2007]. Notre Dame, University of Notre Dame Press. pp. 33–50.

Riggio, Ronald and Jay Conger. 2006. "**Getting It Right: The Practice of Leadership.**" In J. Conger and R. Riggio (editors), *The Practice of Leadership*. San Francisco, Jossey-Bass. pp. 331–344.

Schein, Edgar. 1992. *Organizational Culture and Leadership*. San Francisco, Jossey-Bass.

Tourish, Dennis and Naheed Vatcha. 2005. "**Charismatic Leadership and Corporate Cultism at Enron: The Elimination of Dissent, the Promotion of Conformity, and Organizational Collapse.**" *Leadership* 1(4), 1–26. https://doi.org/10.1177/1742715005057671.

Supplemental Readings

Bandiera, Oriana, Andrea Prat, Raffaella Sadun, and Julie Wulf. 2012. *Span of Control and Span of Activity*. Harvard Business School Working Paper 12–053. https://www.hbs.edu/ris/Publication%20Files/12-053_5de59810-1c7a-4101-a58b-309376366347.pdf.

Chandran, Jay. 1998. "**The Relevance of Chester Barnard for Today's Manager.**" Unpublished paper, Devos Graduate School of Management, Northwood University. https://citeseerx.ist.psu.edu/viewdoc/download?doi=10.1.1.554.7612&rep=rep1&type=pdf.

Chen, Carolyn, 2022. *Work Pray Code: When Works Becomes Religion in Silicon Valley*. Princeton, Princeton University Press.

Conger, Jay. 1990. "**The Dark Side of Leadership.**" In R. Vecchio (editor), *Leadership*, 2nd edition [2007]. Notre Dame, University of Notre Dame Press. pp. 199–215.

Conger, Jay. 2006. "**Best Practices in Corporate Boardroom Leadership.**" In J. Conger and R. Riggio (editors), *The Practice of Leadership*. San Francisco, Jossey-Bass. pp. 244–260.

Howard, A. 2006. "**Best Practices in Leader Selection.**" In J. Conger and R. Riggio (editors), *The Practice of Leadership*. San Francisco, Jossey-Bass. pp. 11–40.

Johnson, Craig. 2006. "**Best Practices in Ethical Leadership**." In J. Conger and R. Riggio (editors), *The Practice of Leadership*. San Francisco, Jossey-Bass. pp. 150–171.

Kaplan, David. 2006. "**Intrigue in High Places**." *Newsweek*, 4 September. https://www.newsweek.com/phone-records-scandal-hp-109411.

Kets de Vries, Manfred and Danny Miller. 1985. "**Narcissism and Leadership: An Object Relations Perspective**." In R. Vecchio (editor), *Leadership*, 2ⁿᵈ edition [2007]. Notre Dame, University of Notre Dame Press. pp. 194–214.

Kotterman, James. 2006. "**Leadership versus Management: What's the Difference?**" *Journal for Quality and Participation* 29(2), 13–17.

Larcker, David, Charles O'Reilly, Brian Tayan, and Anastasia Zakolyukina. 2021. "**Are Narcissistic CEOs All That Bad?**" *Stanford Closer Look Series*, 7 October. https://www.gsb.stanford.edu/sites/default/files/publication/pdfs/cgri-closer-look-93-are-narcissistic-ceos-all-that-bad.pdf.

London, Manuel, James Smither, and Thomas Diamante. 2006. "**Best Practices in Leadership Assessment**." In J. Conger and R. Riggio (editors), *The Practice of Leadership*. San Francisco, Jossey-Bass. pp. 41–63.

Marks, Mitchell. 2006. "**Best Practices in Leading Organizational Change: Workplace Recovery Following Major Organizational Transitions**." In J. Conger and R. Riggio (editors), *The Practice of Leadership*. San Francisco, Jossey-Bass. pp. 201–223.

McCall, Morgan and George Hollenbeck. 2006. "**Getting Leader Development Right: Competence Not Competencies**." In J. Conger and R. Riggio (editors), *The Practice of Leadership*. San Francisco, Jossey-Bass. pp. 87–106.

Mitroff, Ian. 2006. "**Best Practices in Leading Under Crisis: Bottom-Up Leadership, or How to be a Crisis Champion**." In J. Conger and R. Riggio (editors), *The Practice of Leadership*. San Francisco, Jossey-Bass. pp. 263–276.

Mumford, Michael, Dawn Eubanks, and Stephen Murphy. 2006. "**Creating the Conditions for Success: Best Practices in Leading for Innovation**." In J. Conger and R. Riggio (editors), *The Practice of Leadership*. San Francisco, Jossey-Bass. pp. 129–149.

O'Connor, Patricia and David Day. 2006. "**Shifting the Emphasis of Leadership Development From 'Me' to 'All of Us'**." In J. Conger and R. Riggio (editors), *The Practice of Leadership*. San Francisco, Jossey-Bass. pp. 64–86.

Offermann, Lynn and Kenneth Matos. 2006. "**Best Practices in Leading Diverse Organizations**." In J. Conger and R. Riggio (editors), *The Practice of Leadership*. San Francisco, Jossey-Bass. pp. 277–299.

Senge, Peter. 1990. "**The Leader's New Work: Building Learning Organizations**." *Strategic Management Review* 32(1), 7–23. https://sloanreview.mit.edu/article/the-leaders-new-work-building-learning-organizations/.

Senge, Peter. 2006. *The Fifth Discipline: The Art and Practice of the Learning Organization*. New York, Crown Business.

Stagl, Kevin, Eduardo Salas, and C. Shawn Burke. 2006. "**Best Practices in Team Leadership: What Team Leaders Do to Facilitate Team Effectiveness.**" In J. Conger and R. Riggio (editors), *The Practice of Leadership*. San Francisco, Jossey-Bass. pp. 172–198.

Teagarden, Mary. 2006. "**Best Practices in Cross-Cultural Leadership.**" In J. Conger and R. Riggio (editors), *The Practice of Leadership*. San Francisco, Jossey-Bass. pp. 300–330.

Waldman, David. 2006. "**Best Practices in Leading at Strategic Levels: A Social Responsibility Perspective.**" In J. Conger and R. Riggio (editors), *The Practice of Leadership*. San Francisco, Jossey-Bass. pp. 224–243.

Yukl, Gary. 2006. "**Best Practices in the Use of Proactive Influence Tactics by Leaders.**" In J. Conger and R. Riggio (editors), *The Practice of Leadership*. San Francisco, Jossey-Bass. pp. 109–128.

Zaleznik, Abraham. 1977. "**Managers and Leaders: Are They Different?**" *Harvard Business Review* 82(January) [2004]. https://hbr.org/2004/01/managers-and-leaders-are-they-different.

CHAPTER 12: ORGANIZATIONAL BEHAVIOR

PRIMARY READINGS

Csikszentmihalyi, Mihaly. 2008. *Flow: The Psychology of Optimal Experience*. New York, Harper Perennial Modern Classics.

Kanter, Rosabeth Moss. 1979. "**Power Failures in Management Circuits.**" *Harvard Business Review* 57(July–August), 65–75. https://hbr.org/1979/07/power-failure-in-management-circuits.

Kerr, Steven. 1975. "**On the Folly of Rewarding A while Hoping for B.**" *Academy of Management Executive* 9(1), 7–14 [1995]. https://www.jstor.org/stable/4165235.

Latham, Gary and Craig Pinder. 2005. "**Work Motivation Theory and Research at the Dawn of the Twenty-First Century.**" *Annual Review of Psychology* 56, 485–516. https://doi.org/10.1146/annurev.psych.55.090902.142105.

Page, Scott. 2008. *The Difference: How the Power of Diversity Creates Better Groups, Firms, Schools, and Societies*. Princeton, Princeton University Press.

Pfeffer, Jeffrey. 2010. *Power: Why Some People Have It and Others Don't*. New York, Harper Business.

Pfeffer, Jeffrey. 2015. *Leadership BS: Fixing Workplaces and Careers One Truth at a Time*. New York, Harper Business.

Schein, Edgar. 2010. *Organizational Culture and Leadership*. San Francisco, Jossey-Bass.

Seligman, Martin. 2012. *Flourish: A Visionary Understanding of Happiness and Well-Being*. New York, Atria Books.

Sitkin, Sim. 1992. "**Learning through Failure: The Strategy of Small Losses.**" In B. Staw and L. Cummings (editors), *Research in Organizational Behavior*. New York, Elsevier Science. pp. 231–266.

Trice, Harrison and Janice Beyer. 1993. "**Changing Organizational Cultures.**" In J. M. Shafritz, J. S. Ott, and Y. S. Jang (editors), *Classics of Organization Theory*, 6th edition [2005]. Belmont, Wadsworth. pp. 383–392.

Zimbardo, Philip. 1972, "**Pathology of Imprisonment.**" *Society* 9(6), 4–8.

Supplemental Readings

Adolph, Gerald, Karla Elrod, and J. Neely. 2006. "**Nine Steps to Prevent Merger Failure.**" *Harvard Business School Working Knowledge for Business Leaders*, 27 March. https://hbswk.hbs.edu/archive/nine-steps-to-prevent-merger-failure.

Arango, Tim. 2010. "**How the AOL-Time Warner Merger Went So Wrong.**" *The New York Times*, 10 January. https://www.nytimes.com/2010/01/11/business/media/11merger.html.

Argyris, Chris and Donald Schon. 1996. *Organizational Learning II*. Reading, MA, Addison-Wesley.

Ashford, Susan and J. Stewart Black. 1996. "**Proactivity During Organizational Entry: The Role of Desire for Control.**" *Journal of Applied Psychology* 81(2), 199–214. https://doi.org/10.1037/0021-9010.81.2.199.

Axline, Sheryl. 2001. "**Proactive Adaptation in ERP Teams: Mechanisms of Team Learning.**" Unpublished doctoral dissertation, Claremont Graduate University. ProQuest Dissertations & Theses Global, Dissertation No. 3015939.

Bargh, John and Melissa Ferguson. 2000. "**Beyond Behaviorism: On the Automaticity of Higher Mental Processes.**" *Psychology Bulletin* 126(6), 925–945. https://doi.org/10.1037/0033-2909.126.6.925.

Brynjolfsson, Erik and Lorin Hitt. 1996. "**Paradox Lost? Firm-level Evidence on the Returns to Information Systems Spending.**" *Management Science* 42(4), 541–558. https://doi.org/10.1287/mnsc.42.4.541.

Cable, Daniel and D. Scott DeRue. 2002. "**The Convergent and Discriminant Validity of Subjective Fit Perceptions.**" *Journal of Applied Psychology* 87(5), 875–884. https://doi.org/10.1037/0021-9010.87.5.875.

Cotter, John. 1995. *The 20% Solution: Using Rapid Redesign to Create Tomorrow's Organization Today*. New York, Wiley.

Culbert, James. 2008. "**Get Rid of the Performance Review!**" *The Wall Street Journal*, 20 October. https://www.wsj.com/articles/SB122426318874844933.

Davenport, Thomas, Jeanne Harris, and Robert Morrison. 2010. *Analytics at Work: Smarter Decisions, Better Results*. Cambridge, Harvard Business Press.

Earley, Chris. 2002. "**Redefining Interactions across Cultures and Organizations: Moving Forward with Cultural Intelligence.**" In B. M. Staw and R. M. Kramer (editors), *Research in Organizational Behavior: An Annual Series of Analytical Essays and Critical Reviews*. Kidlington, UK, Elsevier. pp. 271–299.

Erez, Amir and Alice Isen. 2002. "**The Influence of Positive Affect on Components of Expectancy Motivation.**" *Journal of Applied Psychology* 87(6), 1055–1067. https://doi.org/10.1037/0021-9010.87.6.1055.

Francalanci, Chiara and Hossam Galal. 1998. "**Information Technology and Worker Composition: Determinants of Productivity in the Life Insurance Industry.**" *MIS Quarterly* 22(2), 227–241. https://doi.org/10.2307/249396.

George, Jennifer and Jing Zhou. 2002. "**Understanding When Bad Moods Foster Creativity and Good Ones Don't: The Role of Context and Clarity of Feelings.**" *Journal of Applied Psychology* 87(4), 687–697. https://doi.org/10.1037/0021-9010.87.4.687.

Golliwitzer, Peter. 1999. "**Implementation Intentions: Strong Effects of Simple Plans.**" *American Psychologist* 54(7), 493–503. https://doi.org/10.1037/0003-066X.54.7.493.

Haslam, Alexander, Clare Powell, and John Turner. 2000. "**Social Identity, Self-categorization, and Work Motivation: Rethinking the Contribution of the Group to Positive and Sustainable Organizational Outcomes.**" *Applied Psychology: An International Review* 49(3), 319–339. https://doi.org/10.1111/1464-0597.00018.

Hitt, Lorin, D. J. Wu, and Xiaoge Zhou. 2002. "**Investment in Enterprise Resource Planning: Business Impact and Productivity Measures.**" *Journal of Management Information Systems* 19(1), 71–98. https://doi.org/10.1080/07421222.2002.11045716.

Hwang, Victor and Greg Horowitt. 2012. *The Rain Forest: The Secret to Building the Next Silicon Valley*. Los Altos Hills, Regenwald.

Keichel, Walter. 1979. "**Playing the Rules of the Corporate Strategy Game.**" *Fortune*, 25 September, 110–115.

Kohli, Rajiv and Sarv Devaraj. 2003. "**Measuring Information Technology Payoff: A Meta-analysis of Structural Variables in Firm-level Empirical Research.**" *Information Systems Research* 14(2), 127–145. https://doi.org/10.1287/isre.14.2.127.16019.

Latham, Gary, Edwin Locke, and Neil Fassina. 2002. "**The High Performance Cycle: Standing the Test of Time.**" In S. Sonnentag (editor), *The Psychological Management of Individual Performance: A Handbook in the Psychology of Management in Organizations*. Chichester, Wiley. pp. 201–208.

Lewis, Michael. 1989. *Liar's Poker*. New York, W.W. Norton & Company.

Lewis, Michael. 2004. *Moneyball*. New York, W.W. Norton & Company.

Locke, Edwin. 1996. "**Motivation through Conscious Goal Setting**." *Applied & Preventative Psychology* 5(2), 117–124. https://doi.org/10.1016/S0962-1849(96)80005-9.

Locke, Edwin. 2000. "**Motivation by Goal Setting**." In R. Golembiewski (editor), *Handbook of Organizational Behavior*. New York, Marcel Dekker. pp. 43–56.

Locke, Edwin and Douglas Henne. 1986. "**Work Motivation Theories**." In C. L. Cooper and I. T. Robertson (editors), *International Review of Industrial and Organizational Psychology*, vol. 1. New York, John Wiley. pp. 1–35.

Malka, Ariel and Jennifer Chatman. 2003. "**Intrinsic and Extrinsic Orientations as Moderators of the Effect of Annual Income on Subjective Well-being: A Longitudinal Study**." *Personal Social Psychology Bulletin* 29(6), 737–746. https://doi.org/10.1177/0146167203029006006.

Markus, M. Lynne. 1998. "**Lessons from the Field of Organizational Change**." *Journal of Strategic Performance Measurement* 2(2), 36-45.

Mata, Francisco, William Fuerst, and Jay Barney. 1995. "**Information Technology and Sustained Competitive Advantage: A Resource-based Analysis**." *MIS Quarterly* 19(4), 487–505. https://doi.org/10.2307/249630.

Mayo, Elton. 1945. *The Social Problems of an Industrial Civilization*. London, Routledge [2007].

Melville, Nigel, Kenneth Kraemer, and Vijay Gurbaxani. 2004. "**Information Technology and Organizational Performance: An Integrative Model of IT Business Value**." *MIS Quarterly* 28(2), 283–322. https://doi.org/10.2307/25148636.

Naylor, James, Robert Pritchard, and Daniel Ilgen. 1980. *A Theory of Behavior in Organizations*. New York, Academic Press.

Nelson, Bob. 1994. *1001 Ways to Reward Employees*. New York, Workman.

Oliver, Dean. 2004. *Basketball on Paper: Rules and Tools for Performance Analysis*. Dulles, Potomac Books.

Parsons, Henry. 1975. "**What Happened at Hawthorne?**" *Science* 183(4128), 922–932. https://doi.org/10.1126/science.183.4128.922.

Pfeffer, Jeffrey. 1981. "**Understanding the Role of Power in Decision Making**." In J. M. Shafritz, J. S. Ott, and Y. S. Jang (editors), *Classics of Organization Theory*, 7th edition [2011]. Boston, Wadsworth. pp. 277–290.

Pritchard, Robert and Stephanie Payne. 2003. "**Motivation and Performance Management Practices**." In D. Holman, T. D. Wall, C. W. Clegg, and P. Sparrow (editors), *The New Workplace: People, Technology and Organization: A Handbook and Guide to the Human Impact of Modern Working Practices*. New York, Wiley. pp. 219–244.

Salancik, Richard and Jeffrey Pfeffer. 1977. "**Who Gets Power—and How They Hold on to It: A Strategic Contingency Model of Power**." *Organizational Dynamics* 5(3), 3–21. https://doi.org/10.1016/0090-2616(77)90028-6.

Schneider, Benjamin, D. Brent Smith, and M. C. Paul. 2001. "**P-E Fit and the Attraction-Selection-Attrition Model of Organizational Functioning: Introduction and Overview**." In M. Erez, U. Kleinbechk, and H. Thierry (editors), *Work Motivation in the Context of a Globalizing Economy*. Mahwah, Erlbaum. pp. 231–246.

Seijts, Gerard and Gary Latham. 2000. **"The Effects of Goal Setting and Group Size on Performance in a Social Dilemma."** *Canadian Journal of Behavioral Science* 32(2), 104–116. https://doi.org/10.1037/h0087105.

Shafritz, Jay and Steven Ott. 1996. ***Classics of Organizational Theory***, 4th edition. Boston, Wadsworth.

Steers, Richard and Carlos Sanchez-Runde. 2002. **"Culture, Motivation, and Work Behavior."** In M. J. Gannon and K. L. Newman (editors), *The Blackwell Handbook of Principles of Cross-cultural Management*. Bodmin, MPG Books. pp. 190–216.

Winters, Dawn and Gary Latham. 1996. **"The Effect of Learning versus Outcome Goals on a Simple versus a Complex Task."** *Group Organizational Management* 21(2), 236–250. https://doi.org/10.1177/1059601196212007.

CHAPTER 14: DECISION-MAKING

PRIMARY READINGS

Ball, Eric, Stephen Rice, Debra Summers, Prosper U. Amie, Aislin Q. Liu, Cjache (Jake) Kang, and Carol Mimura, **"The Relationship of CEO Gender and Age to Performance of Venture-Backed Startups."** Berkeley Office of Intellectual Property & Industry Research Alliances working paper, July 17, 2020. https://ipira.berkeley.edu/sites/default/files/shared/docs/Gender-Age-ROI-Study-January-2021.pdf.

Bazerman, Max and Don Moore. 2008. ***Judgment in Managerial Decision Making***. New York, Wiley.

Gawande, Atul. 2009. ***The Checklist Manifesto: How to Get Things Right***. New York. Metropolitan Books.

Kahneman, Daniel. 2011. ***Thinking, Fast and Slow***. New York, Farrar, Straus, and Geroux.

Kahneman, Daniel and Gary Klein. 2009. **"Conditions for Intuitive Expertise: A Failure to Disagree."** *American Psychologist* 64(6), 515–526. https://doi.org/10.1037/a0016755.

Kahneman, Daniel, Oliver Sibony, and Cass R. Sunstein. 2021. ***Noise: A Flaw in Human Judgment***. New York, Little, Brown Spark.

Page, Scott. 2018. ***The Model Thinker: What You Need to Know to Make Data Work for You***. New York, Basic Books.

Tetlock, Philip and Dan Gardner. 2016. *Superforecasting: The Art and Science of Prediction*. New York, Crown Publishing.

Thaler, Richard and Cass Sunstein. 2021. *Nudge: The Final Edition*. New York, Penguin Books.

Supplemental Readings

Camerer, Colin, George Loewenstein, and Drazen Prelec. 2005. "**Neuroeconomics: How Neuroscience Can Inform Economics**." *Journal of Economic Literature* 43(1), 9–64. https://doi.org/10.1257/0022051053737843.

Glimcher, Paul, Colin Camerer, Page Poldrack, and Ernst Fehr. 2008. *Neuroeconomics: Decision Making and the Brain*. New York, Academic Press.

Kagel, John and Alvin Roth. 1997. *Handbook of Experimental Economics*. Princeton, Princeton University Press.

Kahneman, David and Amos Tversky. 1982. "**The Simulation Heuristic**." In D. Kahneman, P. Slovic, and A. Tversky (editors), *Judgment Under Uncertainty: Heuristics and Biases*. Cambridge, UK, Cambridge University Press. pp. 201–208.

Kauffman Foundation. 2016. "**Kauffman Compilation: Research on Gender and Entrepreneurship**." https://www.kauffman.org/wp-content/uploads/2019/12/gender_compilation_83016.pdf.

Mishkin, Shaina. 2020. "**How Artificial Intelligence Could Lead to Better Investment Decisions**." *Barron's*, 6 July. https://www.barrons.com/articles/how-artificial-intelligence-could-lead-to-better-investment-decisions-51594048894.

Piatelli-Palmarini, Massimo. 1994. *Inevitable Illusions: How Mistakes of Reason Rule Our Minds*. New York, Wiley.

Raina, Sahil. 2016. "**Research: The Gender Gap in Startup Success Disappears When Women Fund Women**." *Harvard Business Review*, 19 July. https://hbr.org/2016/07/research-the-gender-gap-in-startup-success-disappears-when-women-fund-women.

Thaler, Richard. 1985. "**Mental Accounting and Consumer Choice**." *Marketing Science* 27(1), 15–25. https://doi.org/10.1287/mksc.4.3.199.

Tversky, Amos. 1995. "**The Psychology of Decision Making**." *AIMR Conference Proceedings: Behavioral Finance and Decision Theory in Investment Management* 7, 2–6. https://doi.org/10.2469/cp.v1995.n7.2.

Wadhwa, Vivek. 2012. "**Innovation Without Age Limits**." *MIT Technology Review*, 1 February. https://www.technologyreview.com/2012/02/01/187568/innovation-without-age-limits/.

Top-Grossing Movies of the 1980s

		Worldwide Revenue
10.	*Indiana Jones and the Temple of Doom*	$333 million
9.	*Rain Man*	$355 million
8.	*Top Gun*	$357 million
7.	*Back to the Future*	$382 million
6.	*Raiders of the Lost Ark*	$390 million
5.	*Tim Burton's Batman*	$412 million
4.	*Indiana Jones and the Last Crusade*	$474 million
3.	*Star Wars: Return of the Jedi*	$475 million
2.	*Star Wars: The Empire Strikes Back*	$538 million
1.	*E.T. the Extra-Terrestrial*	$793 million

Other top-grossing movies: *Beverly Hills Cop, Ghostbusters, Crocodile Dundee.*

IMDB Box Office Mojo. 2022. "Top Lifetime Grosses." 28 January.
https://www.boxofficemojo.com/chart/top_lifetime_gross/?area=XWW.

Acknowledgments

I want to thank—without implicating—several people who made this book possible. I benefited greatly from helpful comments from Honor Doherty and Leslie Peters at Together Editing, and from those who read early drafts (Spencer Ball, Tim Sams, Sheryl Axline, and Kevin Miller).

Much of the academic research in management mentioned in this book was garnered from my doctoral program at Claremont's Drucker-Ito School, and from my coauthor Joe LiPuma for our nonfiction book *Unlocking the Ivory Tower: How Management Research Can Transform Your Business*.

My many colleagues at Oracle and elsewhere helped me learn practical lessons for managing in a tech company, and I have learned much about entrepreneurship and venture investing from Don Lucas Sr. (may he rest in peace). I have also learned from the staff and fellows of the Kauffman Fellows Program, and from the small-but-mighty teams at Impact Venture Capital (Jack Crawford and colleagues) and its portfolio companies, including CapConnect+ (Suresh Perera, Richard Lautch, and colleagues). I should also acknowledge the pandemic's role in creating enough time in my evenings to develop this story. Hopefully a sequel will not require another global health crisis.

About the Author

Dr. Eric Ball is a technology finance professional and investor. He is Co-Founder and General Partner at Impact Venture Capital, which makes early-stage investments in technology companies.

He also serves on multiple boards at public companies (including SoundHound), startups, and nonprofits. In 2015-16, Eric was CFO at C3 AI, and from 2005-15 was Senior VP & Treasurer at Oracle. He has worked in finance roles at Flex, Cisco Systems, Avery Dennison, and AT&T.

Eric holds a PhD in management from Claremont's Drucker-Ito Graduate School of Management. He is coauthor of the management book *Unlocking the Ivory Tower: How Management Research Can Transform Your Business*. Originally from Michigan, Eric lives and works in Menlo Park, California. This is his debut novel.

Also by Eric Ball: *Unlocking the Ivory Tower*

Unlocking the Ivory Tower: How Management Research Can Transform Your Business

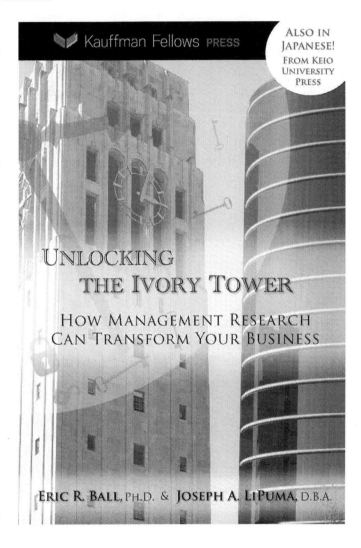

REVIEWS FOR *UNLOCKING THE IVORY TOWER*

Too often, academic research lacks relevance to real-world business problems, or its most relevant lessons do not come to the attention of the people who can apply them. ***Unlocking the Ivory Tower* is a valuable bridge between academic findings and the people who can most benefit from them.** It delves into a variety of classical and recent works from major academic fields and critically evaluates their relevance. (The annotated table of contents is an unexpected treat, too, providing an overview of a variety of important concepts.) Along the way, Ball and LiPuma also educate the reader about the evolution of each field, providing a rare—and fun—does of intellectual history.

> Noam Wasserman, Dean Sy Sims School of Business at Yeshiva University, Director of Founder Central Initiative at USC, longtime Harvard Business School professor, author of *The Founder's Dilemmas: Anticipating and Avoiding the Pitfalls that Can Sink a Startup and Life is a Startup*

Imagine the greatest business thinkers in the world, all combined in a single classroom. Eric Ball and Joe LiPuma have written a monumental work that surveys the world of cutting-edge management thinking and makes it easy to grasp. **This is no ordinary business book: it is both a useful tool for practitioners and a powerful exploration of the workings of organizations, entrepreneurship, innovation, and finance.**

> Victor Hwang, Cofounder (T2 Venture Capital, Victor & Company, Right to Start), former VP Entrepreneurship at the Kauffman Foundation, coauthor *The Rainforest: The Secret to Building the Next Silicon Valley*

Business leaders need to be able to ground their decision-making with state-of-the-art insights. Eric Ball and Joe LiPuma make this eminently possible through **their wide-ranging and thoughtful compendium of leading management research** on topics such as finance, strategy, entrepreneurship, leadership, and innovation. Their work **allows a business** leader to harness the best the ivory tower has to offer to create real-world professional success.

> Mark Zupan, President Alfred University, former Dean of the William E. Simon Graduate School of Business at the University of Rochester

When academic management research and operational business management look at each other, there is often a sizeable gap. **Based on their own practice and variety of experience**, Eric Ball and Joe LiPuma bring us a powerful and insightful view on essential themes. *Unlocking the Ivory Tower* **demonstrates how the academic and business worlds can efficiently get together to generate added value.**

> Dominique Carouge, serves on boards, retired Executive Vice President Business Transformation at Sanofi

Ball and LiPuma do an **impressive job of collecting and illuminating important business research in a wide range of areas. Even better, they translate that research into practical takeaways for managers.**

> Steven N. Kaplan, Neubauer Family Distinguished Service Professor of Entrepreneurship and Finance at the University of Chicago Booth School of Business

This book offers practical guidelines for clear thinking and informed decision-making distilled from the best business research. **Eric and Joe masterfully remove the academic clutter, bringing into focus simple yet powerful frameworks for thinking clearly and making informed business decisions.**

> Clint Korver, Cofounder Ulu Ventures

Peter Drucker taught us that in today's rapidly changing world, people "have to be prepared to live and work simultaneously in two culture – that of "the intellectual," who focuses on words and ideas, and that of "the manager," who focuses on people and work. *Unlocking the Ivory Tower*

bridges those often alien cultures beautifully, and in doing so it stands as a major contribution.

Rick Wartzman, Director of the Drucker Institute

Unlocking the Ivory Tower is an excellent resource for business managers looking to make critical decisions based on best practices. The book represents a valuable summary of management research in key fields. Not only do Ball and LiPuma survey the literature past and present, but they inform what kind of research agendas can have the biggest real-world impact outside of the university environment. **Their book should be required reading for both students and faculty in business schools globally.**

Audrey MacLean, Venture Investor, Consulting Professor, Stanford University and Chairman, Coraid

Appealing to both academics and business leaders, **Eric Ball and Joe LiPuma not only provide the reader with grounded insight into a selection of themes that are critical to business success, but offer a valuable resource in bridging the worlds of academia and business.** *Unlocking the Ivory Tower* demonstrates how management research is relevant, and can be accessible to firms, in a very straightforward and concise manner.

Rickie A. Moore, Past Chair of the Management Consulting Division, Academy of Management

Unlocking the Ivory Tower
Table of Contents and
Thesis Summaries by Section

Chapter 1: Strategy

Strategy is the long-term direction and scope of an organization as that organization pursues advantage through its configuration of resources, to meet the needs of markets and to fulfill stakeholder expectations (Johnson and Scholes 2006). Corporate strategy addresses which business a corporation will participate in, and business strategy focuses on how a particular business competes within its industry.

1. Michael Porter's Competitive Forces

There are five competitive forces whose collective strength determines the ultimate profit potential in an industry: threat of new entrants, bargaining power of suppliers, bargaining power of buyers, threat of substitutes, and rivalry among existing firms. Managers can use these frameworks to determine the fit of their firm to the industry.

2. The Institutional Economics Approach

A transaction cost is a cost of coordination incurred in making an economic exchange, including search and information costs, bargaining costs, and enforcement costs. Costs associated with market transactions sometimes favor in-house production (i.e., hierarchies) and sometimes favor contracts (i.e., markets).

3. The Resource-Based View of the Firm

Strategies that are not based on resources are unlikely to succeed. Firms have different resource endowments, and it takes time and money to change these endowments. In addition, competitive market dynamics ensure that a firm will always be up against the best in whatever market it chooses to compete.

4. Strategic Capabilities

Executives are now judged on their ability to identify, cultivate, and exploit the core competencies that make growth possible. It is not resources but rather resourcefulness that drives success, and the resourcefulness of a company can be stimulated by choosing ambitious goals that are clearly beyond a firm's existing capabilities.

5. Game Theory

It is more rewarding and profitable to shape the game you play rather than to play the game you find. Maximizing payoffs requires evaluating both win-win as well as win-lose opportunities versus other players in your space. Having a unique product is optional, but creating the right game is essential to building the best long-term position.

6. Learning versus Planning

There is evidence suggesting that competitive advantage is not arrived at through a systematic implementation of a carefully developed plan, but rather through an often disjointed series of reactions to external events (learning).

7. Sustainable Competitive Advantage and Social Capital

Strong competitive positions are temporary, and competition is defined as the process of building a series of new temporary advantages over time. Networks of relationships represent a valuable resource; the interaction of relationship capital and intellectual capital underpins organizational advantage.

8. Mergers and Acquisitions

Studies show that 50-80% of acquisitions fail, and acquirers experience a negative average impact to their stock price. Acquisitions remain popular despite the high failure rate, and most of the explanations proposed by academics are not flattering to the executives of acquiring firms. For those committed to pursuing mergers, we give advice on how to beat the odds.

9. Real Options

Specifically identifying the real options created by projects or strategies can improve decisions about the sequence and timing of strategic investments.

10. Scenario Analysis

Financial projections are an incomplete form of planning for the future. Scenarios in the form of stories are a valuable tool for evaluating different possible futures.

11. Strategy Execution

Making it clear who owns decisions and ensuring that information flows to where it's needed are the key levers for the successful execution of strategic initiatives.

Chapter 2: Entrepreneurship

Shane and Venkataraman (2000, p. 218) define the academic field of *entrepreneurship* as the "scholarly examination of how, by whom, and with what effects opportunities to create future goods and services are discovered, evaluated, and exploited." Why do some people, and not others, discover and exploit the opportunities that are the heart of entrepreneurship?

1. Entrepreneurship and Why We Should Study It

The historical context for entrepreneurship provides insight into the field's economic and behavioral roots, grounding managerial decisions. In particular, entrepreneurial thought in the first half of the 20th century gave rise to the term "creative destruction" that has found its way into standard business jargon.

2. Opportunities and Opportunity Recognition

Much of the entrepreneurship literature focuses on opportunities and whether they exist independent of individuals, or whether entrepreneurs have specialized traits or abilities to identify or develop opportunities. The "individual–opportunity nexus" is a basis for entrepreneurship research and teaching. Mistakes by one entrepreneur can provide opportunities for another.

3. Entrepreneurial Entry and Organizational Emergence

Where do entrepreneurs come from and why do they become entrepreneurs? Is the number of entrepreneurs in a context bounded? How can we understand the motivations and mindset of the individual entrepreneur along with the broader macroeconomic context that may facilitate (or impede) entrepreneurship?

4. Entrepreneurial Finance and Economic Impact

For entrepreneurs, the source of funds is a critical element related to opportunity enactment, as access to various forms of capital (financial, social, and human) affects entrepreneurs in a number of ways. Resource availability is impacted by the value that entrepreneurship creates.

5. International Entrepreneurship

Research on international entrepreneurship has two main components: the study of differences in entrepreneurship across countries, and the study of ventures that enter foreign markets at an early age.

Chapter 3: Leadership

Leadership is a process whereby an individual influences a group of individuals to achieve a common goal. We look at competing views of what leaders should do, what they actually do, how leaders establish organizational culture, and what are the elements of constructive leadership.

1. Leadership Classics

Machiavelli provides a description of how leaders achieve their own ends by manipulating their followers. Barnard argues instead that the primary responsibility of an executive is to define the organization's purpose. The executive must inspire loyalty so that managers put aside their personal interests and cooperate, which requires executives to satisfy their employees rather than view them as production inputs.

2. What Leaders Actually Do

Rather than systematically organize their activities, managers tend to take on many projects, encourage interruption, and respond quickly to any stimulus. They avoid abstract thinking, and make decisions incrementally. Routine work will displace strategic thinking, unless leaders empower employees to make decisions. Management is about coping with complexity, while leadership is about coping with change.

3. Leadership and Organizational Culture

Culture is the deeper level of assumptions shared by members of the organization, and is critical to the organization's success. The first task of a leader is to create and sustain the organization's culture.

4. Constructive and Destructive Leadership

Leadership in an organization is isolating, employees tend to have high expectations, and some leaders create their own failure from guilt or fear. Organizations today have shorter timeframes. Leaders must use a broad set of implementation styles matched to a particular context. Research shows differences between how upper- and mid-level managers lead, and between how men and women lead.

5. Leadership Research Findings

Leaders need to engage their followers. They need to monitor, measure, and adapt. Leaders need to model the way forward and proactively address challenges before they become crises. Effective leadership is a long-term developmental process.

Chapter 4: Organization and Processes

Organizational design is the alignment of structure, process, rewards, metrics, and talent with the strategy of the business. In this chapter, we describe what has (and has not) been established to promote organizational effectiveness.

1. Organizational Culture

Identifying the pattern of shared basic assumptions within a group is a powerful tool to understand organizational behavior. With cultural change, losses are more certain than gains; therefore, managing change entails convincing people that the likely gains outweigh the losses.

2. The Impact of Structure and Situation

In determining the behavior of individuals in groups, situations can have a larger impact than inherent personalities. Poor organizational structure can predetermine destructive outcomes.

3. Organizational Learning

Failure is an essential prerequisite for learning—organizations must allow people to fail in order to grow. Success fosters reliability, while failure fosters resilience.

4. Aligning Organizational Incentives

Organizations repeatedly reward behaviors that are inconsistent with the desired behavior. This misalignment of incentives can be confronted and reversed.

5. Motivation

Job satisfaction does not actually drive job performance. Setting goals, particularly specific and challenging goals, does lead to higher job performance. Context is the key to job motivation, particularly that provided by culture, job characteristics, and job fit; in addition, workers are motivated by subconscious as well as conscious sources.

6. Power

Power accrues to those who cope with the organization's problems, and is therefore the secret of success. Powerlessness (not power) breeds bossiness. Power can mean efficacy and capacity. To expand power, share it.

7. Information Technology and Productivity

Modern information technology can enable organizations to eliminate non value-added activities instead of merely automating them to make them more efficient. Studies employing better methodologies tend to find a positive connection between IT and organizational productivity.

Chapter 5: International Business

All companies—even new companies in new industries—must consider the global environment in which they operate. Key international business literature addresses dimensions such as theories of multinational enterprises, international political economy, multinational management, and culture. These dimensions provide managers with tools and concepts needed for growing beyond national borders.

1. Theories of the Multinational Enterprise

Understanding the reasons, processes, and outcomes associated with multinational business has been aided by recent development of theories of the multinational enterprise (MNE). Such theories address international operations and the control-based forms of multinationals, product lifecycles, stage theories of inter**national**ization, and the eclectic theory based on ownership, location, and **internal**ization advantages.

2. Internationalization Advantages and Approaches

Internationalization is intended to provide companies with competitive advantages, and companies take various approaches to their foreign market entry and expansion in the context of broader economic, political, and business activities. Knowledge acquisition and internalization are key to multinational corporate evolution.

3. International Political Economy

The environment in which MNEs operate affects—and is affected by—the MNEs. As economic actors, MNEs affect other companies, the labor force, technological and overall economic growth in their host countries. As political actors, MNEs may influence the political environment in these countries in ways that can be inconsistent with the political aims of the corporate headquarters.

4. Multinational Management

MNEs, as HQ and subsidiary units, affect the environments in which they operate (both politically and economically). In this context, MNE managers must determine how to structure the activities between headquarters and subsidiary. How should the structure map to the firm's strategy and learning, and the market needs of the industry globally and locally?

5. Culture

In the international context, corporate culture mixes with national culture and becomes even more central to organizational performance. Culture affects foreign market entry mode, multinational management, and international negotiations.

Chapter 6: Innovation

Contexts for innovation vary based on location, industry, and country. We look here at how innovation diffuses or spreads and thus how current technology such as the web and social media might affect the adoption of innovative outputs. It is essential that managers understand the contexts for innovation at the firm, industry, and country levels in creating and managing innovation strategies.

1. Issues in Technology and Strategy

Ideas, information, invention, and innovation are related, and require the innovator's investment to extract returns. The economics related to perfect markets and the market for information may lead to under-investment in innovative activities, thwarting invention and subsequent economic growth. Managers must develop strategies and policies to promote innovative company cultures and practices.

2. Patterns of Technological Innovation, Technology Trajectories, and Industry Lifecycles

Economic theory may not be the best for explaining the birth, growth, and death of firms. Innovation associated with venture emergence and growth is path-dependent: the history of the entrepreneur and of the company matter. Despite societal variance in creative individuals and economic growth, innovation and industry lifecycles follow standard patterns, the knowledge of which can aid strategic decision-making.

3. Technology Competition

Innovation and innovative competition may vary based on the size and position of the firm and the nature of the industry. Innovation may be driven by industry incumbents, entrants, or by users. Protecting proprietary information is key for innovators, as getting the value from innovation motivates innovative activities.

4. Institutions and Innovation: The Role of the Government in Innovation, and University/Industry Interactions

Governments can play a role in the creation of environments conducive to innovation, entrepreneurship, and economic growth. Governmental actions can facilitate the development of systems of innovation, but may be less important than the actions of entrepreneurs.

Chapter 7: Finance

Finance is the study of how investors allocate their assets over time under conditions of certainty and uncertainty, and typically examines the relationship between money, time, and risk.

1. Capital Structure

The value of a company is unaffected by how that firm is financed (in an efficient market absent taxes or bankruptcy costs). Those who argue that capital structure impacts valuation should start by showing how relaxing assumptions leads to a different result.

2. Capital Asset Pricing

Investor diversification can eliminate stock-specific risk so that only non-diversifiable market risk remains. Investment choice then becomes a combination of a single riskless asset and one combination of risky assets. The capital asset pricing model provides a price for any security, given a riskless rate and the expected return for the market, based solely how sensitive that security's return is to the market return.

3. Market Efficiency

Asset prices reflect all information contained in the history of past prices, and also reflect all publicly available information. Prices may even reflect much non-public information (except that detailed information held by stock exchange specialists and corporate insiders).

4. Agency Theory

When one group (managers) performs on behalf of another group (owners), the interests of the two groups can diverge. Contracts can minimize the differing incentives, and it can be in the best interest of managers to contractually restrict their own behavior.

5. Imperfect Information

When entrepreneurs have inside information about their project quality, the value of the firm will increase with the share held by that entrepreneur. Financing does matter. Knowing that management has inside information, investors will interpret any issuance of equity as evidence it is overvalued. This will cause firms with limited debt capacity to pass up good investments.

6. Business Measurement

You can only manage what you measure. The financial statements prepared for investors are an inadequate source of information for managers. Companies need to identify performance metrics, and link this scorecard to ongoing executive action. Companies can achieve higher shareholder value if they use an economic measure of value added rather than an accounting measure.

7. Behavioral Finance

Agents are not rational, and markets are not efficient. People exhibit persistent and significant cognitive biases in how they process information, assess risk, and make investment decisions. These risks are consistent enough across people to be predictable.

Chapter 8: Emerging Topics in Management

1. Managing Non-Profits (and Businesses)

Ensure everyone lives the mission. Be action-oriented and driven by results. Know who your customers are. Define performance concretely and keep score on yourself. Allocate your own life, make yourself a leader by focusing on what you want to be remembered for. Develop your strengths, not your weaknesses.

2. Decision Making

People are bounded in: the time they take to make decisions, their rationality, their awareness, and their ethicality. Individuals tend to take cognitive shortcuts which result in misestimating risk and probability and making suboptimal or inconsistent decisions, even when the stakes are high. Understanding these tendencies can enable us to make better decisions, and to better evaluate decisions made by others.

3. Marketing

Marketing is inseparable from strategy. The market orientation of a business determines its performance. Such orientation is facilitated by management's response to customer needs, higher interdepartmental connectedness, and decentralized decision-making. Consumers' cognitively biased tendency to engage in mental accounting has implications for marketers seeking to influence consumer behavior.

4. Complex Systems

A complex adaptive social system consists of interdependent, interacting agents whose micro behavior responds to macro patterns they produce, resulting in a system which evolves. Computational modeling tools are well-suited to such systems. A variety of social phenomena (e.g., political, financial, economic, and natural behaviors) appear to be better understood using this perspective.

Made in the USA
Monee, IL
10 August 2022

10472948R10141